PRAISE FOR

Die Buying

"One hell of a great novel! This novel will crack you up with
DiSilverio's humor and razor's-edge wit. A great book to
curl up with over the weekend. You won't be able to put it
down."   —*Suspense Magazine*

"This is a wonderful start to a new series with likable characters, lots of humor, and a swift-moving story that will grab
anyone who has ever stepped foot in a mall . . . I'm adding
Die Buying to my cozy favorites for the year—even though
I hate to shop."   —*AnnArbor.com*

"Charming, fun, and refreshing."
                                    —*Seattle Post-Intelligencer*

"Laura DiSilverio has come up with a unique hook whereby
she reels in her readers . . . I'm eager to read the next install-
ment in this offbeat series."   —*Mystery Scene*

All Sales Fatal

Laura DiSilverio

BERKLEY PRIME CRIME, NEW YORK

THE BERKLEY PUBLISHING GROUP
Published by the Penguin Group
Penguin Group (USA) Inc.
375 Hudson Street, New York, New York 10014, USA

Penguin Group (Canada), 90 Eglinton Avenue East, Suite 700, Toronto, Ontario M4P 2Y3, Canada
(a division of Pearson Penguin Canada Inc.) • Penguin Books Ltd., 80 Strand, London WC2R 0RL,
England • Penguin Group Ireland, 25 St. Stephen's Green, Dublin 2, Ireland (a division of Penguin
Books Ltd.) • Penguin Group (Australia), 250 Camberwell Road, Camberwell, Victoria 3124, Australia
(a division of Pearson Australia Group Pty. Ltd.) • Penguin Books India Pvt. Ltd., 11 Community
Centre, Panchsheel Park, New Delhi—110 017, India • Penguin Group (NZ), 67 Apollo Drive,
Rosedale, Auckland 0632, New Zealand (a division of Pearson New Zealand Ltd.) • Penguin Books
(South Africa) (Pty.) Ltd., 24 Sturdee Avenue, Rosebank, Johannesburg 2196, South Africa

Penguin Books Ltd., Registered Offices: 80 Strand, London WC2R 0RL, England

This is a work of fiction. Names, characters, places, and incidents either are the product of the author's
imagination or are used fictitiously, and any resemblance to actual persons, living or dead, business
establishments, events, or locales is entirely coincidental. The publisher does not have any control over
and does not assume any responsibility for author or third-party websites or their content.

ALL SALES FATAL

A Berkley Prime Crime Book / published by arrangement with the author

PUBLISHING HISTORY
Berkley Prime Crime mass-market edition / May 2012

Copyright © 2012 by Laura DiSilverio.
Cover illustration by Ben Perini.
Cover design by Rita Frangie.
Interior text design by Laura K. Corless.

ISBN: 978-0-425-24803-4

BERKLEY® PRIME CRIME
Berkley Prime Crime Books are published by The Berkley Publishing Group,
a division of Penguin Group (USA) Inc.,
375 Hudson Street, New York, New York 10014.
BERKLEY® PRIME CRIME and the PRIME CRIME logo are trademarks of
Penguin Group (USA) Inc.

PRINTED IN THE UNITED STATES OF AMERICA

10 9 8 7 6 5 4 3 2 1

ALWAYS LEARNING   **PEARSON**

*In gratitude for the friendship of women
who made and make my life richer:
Dawn Taylor, Linda Petrone, Sally Logan,
Cindy Stauffer, Katie Larsh,
and Jill Gaebler*

Acknowledgments

As always, I want to thank Michelle Vega and all the Berkley Prime Crime crew for their insight and attention to detail that make my books so much stronger. Thanks also to my agent and friend, Paige Wheeler, and her folks at Folio Literary Management. Finally, thank you to the mystery writing community that encourages me and motivates me by believing that stories are important and by writing excellent books that illuminate my world, move me, and show me what it's possible to achieve with words. They inspire me to work harder at my craft. They include Elaine Viets, Hank Phillippi Ryan, Reed Farrel Coleman, Marcia Talley, Brad Parks, Sophie Littlefield, Hallie Ephron, Tracy Kiely, Margaret Maron, and many, many others.

One

. . .

In my more profound moments, I think of malls as cathedrals to capitalism, airy sanctuaries filled with sunshine and optimism, embracing all comers with warmth and light, and offering cookies and Orange Julius in place of the wafer and the wine.

This was not one of those moments.

Hands balled on my uniformed hips, I regarded the middle-aged man in front of me gripping the handle of a kid's red wagon, upon which rested a large leather ottoman. With the complexion and girth of someone who thinks a Quarter Pounder is a light appetizer, he gave me an affronted look when I asked if he had a receipt for his purchases.

"Are you implying I stole this, miss?" he asked, patting the ottoman with a beefy hand. "I have the receipt right here." He fumbled in his suit pocket and thrust a crumpled slip of paper toward me.

"Not the ottoman, sir, the wagon. The manager at Jen's Toy Store notified mall security that you had forgotten to

pay for it." In the year plus that I'd been working as a security officer at Fernglen Galleria, "forgot to pay" had become
my favorite euphemism for "shoplifted."

He snorted. "How else was I supposed to get this to my
car?" He thumped the ottoman again. "It's damn heavy."

"I'm sure the furniture store could arrange for delivery, or—"

"Yeah, for fifty bucks. I'm not paying—"

"The point is, sir, that if you want to use the wagon as a
cargo dolly, you have to pay for it first."

He goggled at me as though I'd suggested he do the hokey
pokey. Nude. In the parking lot. "Fine, just fine!" He bent
and wrapped his arms around the ottoman, lifting it off the
wagon. His red face grew redder with the effort. "If I get a
hernia, I'm going to sue the mall and you personally for
every penny you've got." He nodded his head firmly, thunking his chin against the ottoman so hard his teeth snapped
together. "Ow!"

"I'll get the door for you," I said politely, zipping to the
exit on my two-wheeled electric Segway and dismounting
to push the heavy glass door wide. A slight breeze riffled
my bangs. Without so much as a thank-you, the man stomped
past me, breathing hard. Giving him a cheery wave and a
"Thanks for shopping at Fernglen!" in my best chipper,
flight-attendant-like voice, I let the door close.

The radio clipped at my left shoulder crackled as I
returned to the Segway. "EJ, Captain Woskowicz needs to
see you on the double." The southern-accented voice
belonged to Joel Rooney, the youngest officer on the mall's
security team. As low man on the totem pole, he frequently
got stuck with dispatch duty.

"I'll be there in five," I said, retrieving the wagon and
heading toward Jen's Toy Store with it trundling behind me.
My brother Clint and I had had a wagon just like it when

we were kids. I still had a half-moon-shaped scar under my chin from when he'd lost control of the wagon with me in it and I'd careened down our steep driveway before crashing into a neighbor's Lamborghini parked at the curb. I'd gone flying and scraped my chin on the asphalt. The cut had needed six stitches. What had I been—three, four? I ran my index finger over the scar as the Segway purred smoothly over Fernglen's tiled halls. The tiny ridge of tissue was nothing compared to the massive scarring around my knee, the result of an IED that had killed two of my unit in Afghanistan and gotten me medically retired from the military.

After leaving the wagon with the grateful toy store manager and suggesting that, if she didn't want it to disappear again, she not park it outside the store as an advertising gimmick, I sped up and cut through the food court on my way to the security office, tucked into a side hall near Sears. An ill-lit hallway lined floor to ceiling with white brick tile, its narrowness and dinginess dissuaded most shoppers from venturing down it. A soda vending machine hummed quietly near an emergency exit at the far end. Glass doors fronted the security office, and I pushed through them, leaving the Segway outside. Small, dank, and smelling vaguely of pizza, the office boasted a couple of desks that belonged to whoever was on shift, filing cabinets, and a coffeepot. A short hall led to my boss's office and a storeroom in the back. The office's most prominent feature was a bank of monitors displaying views from the hundred-plus cameras in and around the mall. Actually, only about half the cameras were hooked up, a cost-saving measure I'd fought strenuously. The director of security, Captain Woskowicz, had said, "The cameras are mainly deterrents to shoplifting, Ferris, so as long as the general public doesn't know they're not working, they'll still work." That's what passed for logic in Wosko World.

Joel Rooney, twenty-three years old and thirty pounds

overweight, swiveled his chair away from the screens to face
me as I came in. A smear of cream cheese shone on one
chubby cheek. Soft brown hair curled around his ears. His
ironed white uniform shirt was tucked into his black pants,
but he somehow still looked rumpled. Correctly interpreting
my raised brows, he raised his bagel and said, "It's not as
bad as a donut!"

"A bagel's got just as many calories and not much more
nutritional value," I said. Joel was trying to lose weight and
get in better shape. I'd been helping him by swimming with
him a couple afternoons a week. Swimming was the only
form of aerobic exercise my knee could take now.

He stared wistfully at the bagel. "It's whole wheat."

"Where's Cap—"

"Is Ferris on her way? Didn't you tell her to haul her sorry
ass—" Captain Woskowicz stomped from his small office
into the main room and cut himself off when he saw me.
"It's about time."

With the personality and fashion sense of a third-world
dictator, Woskowicz stood well over six feet tall and wore
a khaki-colored uniform decked with enough medals and
insignia to make Noriega look under-accessorized. The rest
of the security team wore standard uniforms—black slacks
with a white shirt and black Smoky-the-Bear-type hat—but
Woskowicz said that as director of security he needed to
stand out. He'd recently started growing hair back on his
shaved head, and a quarter inch of grizzled fuzz now covered his lumpy skull.

I fought the urge to drop a curtsy and say, "You rang?"
and contented myself with a lifted brow and a quiet
"What's up?"

Woskowicz waited a beat for me to add "sir," but he
wasn't going to live long enough for that. I "sirred" or
"ma'amed" people unless they proved they didn't deserve

it. You do the math. After a second, he popped a breath mint in his mouth and said, "We got a call from the loss-prevention officer at Nordstrom. They've got their eye on a man behaving suspiciously, and they requested our assistance."

"Suspiciously how?"

"How the hell should I know? I'm not there watching the perv, am I?" Woskowicz scowled. "Just go check it out."

"Will do," I said. "Oh, and I called the camera repair company again. They didn't seem to have a record of the service request from when you called earlier. They—"

"You what?" Woskowicz's scowl deepened. "Who asked you to?"

I stared at him. In most jobs, one got kudos for displaying a little initiative. Not, apparently, if one worked for a control freak like Woskowicz. It wasn't hard to figure out why some security officer before my time had christened the director of security "Captain Was-a-bitch." "I thought—"

"Well, stop it. You don't get paid for thinking." He wheeled and tromped toward his office, stopping halfway to glare at me over his shoulder. "When are they coming?"

"It'll be later in the week before they can get here. Something about completing a system upgrade for some bank branches."

He grunted and disappeared into his office, slamming the door behind him.

Joel and I exchanged an expressive glance. "It's good that you called the camera company, EJ," Joel said.

I sighed. A whole wing of cameras had gone black on the midshift two nights ago, and it made me uneasy to have no camera coverage. Woskowicz, who'd been the sole officer on duty that night, swore that nothing unusual had happened, that all of a sudden the screens just blanked out, but it wouldn't surprise me to learn that he'd spilled a cup of

coffee on the computers or something similar. Still, there
hadn't been a break-in or any vandalism, so I had to assume
the outage was an accident. I watched the parade of shoppers
on the screens for a moment, focusing on a young woman
arguing with a man outside a boutique and then on a little
boy trying to wiggle his fingers through the mesh of the pet
store's puppy pen.

Joel followed my gaze. "You need a dog." Joel, the proud
owner of two shelties that he trained for agility competitions,
thought no household was complete without a canine.

"Fubar would disagree."

Nordstrom lay at the opposite end of the mall from the
security office, and I glided down the wide central hall on
my Segway, enjoying the relative quiet of the mall on a
Tuesday. Set out in a large X with anchor stores at each end
of the X, the mall had two levels, multiple garages and parking lots, a food court, and a fountain on the lower floor.
Large planters overflowed with greenery that grew well in
the natural light streaming through the glass-paned roof,
giving an almost greenhouse effect. Located off I-95 in
Vernonville, Virginia, we picked up a lot of customers from
the bedroom communities that fed both Richmond and the
D.C. area. The *bam-bam* of hammers broke into the quiet,
and I looked over the railing to the level below to see workers adding a white picket fence to the enclosure that would
house the Easter Bunny for the next few weeks as he—
she?—posed for expensive photos with fussily dressed boys
and girls. A dolly laden with potted tulips and other flowers
waited nearby.

I passed my friend Kyra's store, Merlin's Cave, and Segwayed into Nordstrom. Wending my way through racks of
ties and men's socks, I found Dusty Margolin, head of the

store's loss-protection division, talking to an employee near his office.

"EJ!" He broke off with a smile when he saw me and dismissed the man he was talking to. In his midfifties, with graying hair and a banker-style suit, Dusty looked like a stuffy businessman until he smiled; then, he looked like someone you'd want to have a beer with at a baseball game.

Getting off the Segway, I said, "You've got a shoplifter problem, Dusty?"

He shook his head. "No, I don't think so. Maybe a pickpocket. I'll show you."

Taking my arm, he guided me around a stack of Spanx for men—who knew?—and pointed out a tallish man casually studying a display of novelty boxers near the dressing room. His back was to us, but I noted improbably black hair and cuffed slacks showing a half inch of white sock above scruffy sneakers. "Looks harmless," I said, crossing my fingers behind my back.

"Watch."

After a moment, an unsmiling man with a blocky build emerged from the dressing room, a blazer and shirt tossed over his arm. He marched to the nearest cash register, paid with a credit card, and lumbered toward the exit. After a moment, the black-haired man moved nonchalantly after him.

"He's been tailing that guy ever since he came in the store," Dusty whispered.

I had a bad feeling about this. "I'll take care of it," I told Dusty, and then moved swiftly to intercept the potential pickpocket as he reached the outer door. "May I have a word with you, sir?" I asked.

"Not now, Emma-Joy," my Grandpa Atherton muttered out of the side of his mouth. "I'm on a job. Don't want to lose my target."

I'd known the stalker was my grandfather from the moment I saw him move. Eighty-two years old, retired from the CIA for over a decade, he still did contract work for various agencies around town and liked to "keep his hand in" between assignments by tailing people at the mall and trying out listening devices or other spy gadgets he got off the Internet or God-knows-where. It was a practice I tried to discourage.

I kept pace with him as we stepped out of Fernglen and into a chilly March day. "The loss-prevention guy at Nordstrom figures you for a pickpocket," I said, wincing at the contrast between the black wig and Grandpa's seamed face.

"Damn," Grandpa said, shooting me a sheepish look from bright blue eyes.

"What exactly are you doing?"

"A little job for a friend at State. Can't tell you more, Emma-Joy—it's classified. But that man"—he nodded to the man levering his bulk into the backseat of a waiting Mercedes—"is a Moldovan diplomat." Without another word, he jogged toward a tan Toyota I'd never seen before, folded himself into it, and pulled out after the Mercedes, giving me a beep from the horn and a mischievous grin as he passed.

I made no attempt to stop him and was merely grateful that whatever trouble he might get into with his Moldovan diplomat wouldn't involve my mall.

The rest of my shift passed uneventfully, although I kept an eye on three teens sporting gang colors of red, green, and white. Two youths of eighteen or so squabbled as they strolled, while a tough-looking girl of fifteen or sixteen walked between them, carrying a stuffed animal. When I first signed on at Fernglen, gangs weren't an issue at our suburban mall. In the past two months, though, we'd seen more gang activity both at the mall and in the town proper. The Vernonville Police Department had gone so far as to set up a gang task force, and they had invited security personnel from nearby businesses to partake in a two-hour seminar. Captain Woskowicz had stuck me with attending, and I learned a lot about gang names, colors, symbols, and rituals, but not a whole lot about how to keep them from meeting up at Fernglen. So far there hadn't been any big trouble, but our maintenance crews were busier than they used to be scraping gang-related graffiti off the bathroom stalls and repainting. I sometimes thought that if I could invent a surface too slick to write or paint on and too hard to carve into, I'd be the richest woman in America overnight.

I swam at the YMCA when I got off shift at three o'clock, gradually relaxing as I did laps—mostly freestyle and butterfly—in the deserted pool. Still self-conscious about the way my knee and leg looked since the IED tore into me, I preferred to swim when there was no one around, and the middle of the afternoon was perfect. After showering, I beat rush-hour traffic returning to my one-story, brick-front home with forest green trim in a community that featured a pool, lush landscaping, and reasonable HOA fees. I tipped my head up to let the sunshine play on my face as I walked up the stepping-stone path from my parking spot to my front door. A glimpse of rusty red gave me warning, and I didn't even jump as a blur of fur leaped out of the shrubbery and attacked my shoelaces. I bent to scoop Fubar into my arms before he could wreak havoc with his claws. Untying shoelaces was one of his favorite games—not one the neighbors thought highly of.

"Stop that," I said, giving him an affectionate shake as

he lay cradled in my arms, face turned toward me so his mangled and mostly missing left ear was evident. The ear and his truncated tail, products of abuse or a run-in with a car or coyote, had prompted me to name him Fubar—the military acronym for "fouled up beyond all recognition"—when I found him slinking around my house shortly after I bought it. Having just been released from the hospital after several surgeries and many hours of physical therapy, I guess I'd felt a kinship with the beat-up cat. He wiggled to get down—cuddling was beneath his dignity—and zipped into the house when I unlocked the door.

The house had served time as a rental before I bought it, and I was hiring handymen to tackle repairs as my budget allowed. I hadn't yet hired anyone to sand the hardwood boards in the small foyer, which looked like someone had practiced Irish step dancing on them, in golf shoes. I'd hidden the worst of it with a pseudo-Oriental rug in blue and white that echoed the colors in the attached living room. Making my way to the kitchen, I found Fubar standing proudly over the remains of a sparrow inside the cat flap cut into the back door. Stifling my distaste, I praised him for his hunting ability, picked the bird up in a paper towel, and deposited it in the outside trash bin.

"I guess this means you won't be wanting dinner." I realized with dismay that I sounded like a mother chastising a kid for snacking too close to dinnertime. Fubar gave me an inscrutable look and wedged himself back through his cat door. "Don't forget your curfew," I called after him.

I experimented with a new ancho chili rub for my pork tenderloin, teased Fubar with his feather toy when he reappeared, chatted via phone with my mom (vacationing with my dad in Cannes), and played my guitar for a while before bed. All in all, a routine evening that gave no hint that a dead body lay in my immediate future.

Two

...

I'm glad I'm not homeless.

That may sound as obvious as "I'm glad I don't have herpes" or "I'm glad I'm not married to Charlie Sheen," but I thought it every time I encountered a homeless person, some of whom, I knew, were vets like me.

We got our fair share of homeless people hanging around the mall, grateful for the warmth of the corridors on cold days and for the air-conditioning in the broiling summer months. As long as they weren't drunk or high, I left them alone, unable to imagine how singularly awful it must be to have no home to retreat to, no place of safety.

When I pulled into the Fernglen lot a bit before seven Wednesday morning, I spotted a homeless person curled up against the wall, apparently asleep. Parking outside the upper level of Macy's, I slung my gym bag over my shoulder and headed for the mall entrance. The parking lot was deserted at this hour except for a few cars parked along the outer fringe of the lot; they belonged to carpoolers who met

up here and made the long trek into D.C. together. The chill
bit through my white cotton shirt, and the scent of the air
promised rain later.

Hustling toward the door, I pulled out one of the fast-food
gift cards I kept in my purse, planning to offer it to the man
slumped on the ground with his back against the rough stone
of the mall's façade. He didn't stir when I called out, "Good
morning." Drawing nearer, I realized that he was younger
than I'd thought, and seemed too clean to be homeless. Oh
no. Something about the quality of his stillness jolted me to
a halt five feet away. His chest didn't rise and fall under the
thin tee shirt he wore, and no muscles twitched. Only a few
silky black hairs trembled, fanned by the fitful breeze.
Knowing what I would find, I knelt and touched his cheek
lightly, ready to spring back if he awakened. His skin was
ice cold. He'd been dead for hours.

I drew in a breath and held it deep in my lungs for several
seconds before releasing it slowly. Damn. Standing, I backed
off a few steps, using my cell phone to call 911 and then the
security office to let Edgar Ambrose, the officer on duty last
night, know I was going to be late. "There's a dead body
outside the east entrance," I told him.

"Bad," Edgar said in his laconic way.

"Agreed."

"Junkie?"

"Maybe." I didn't see any blood or other sign of trauma,
but the young man lay on his side, crumpled over, so most
of his front and the left side of his head were hidden. I knew
better than to disturb the body before the police arrived. His
right arm was stretched out, his hand resting on the sidewalk. A tattoo of a cross lying horizontal was inked onto
the webbing between his thumb and forefinger, and I wondered if it was a gang symbol.

"I guess you didn't see anything?" I asked Edgar. The

night-shift officer was conscientious and fearless, roughly the size, bulk, and color of a walrus, and I knew he wouldn't have hesitated to investigate if he saw something funky going down. In fact, he would have welcomed the break in routine.

"Cameras are still out."

Damn. I was standing outside the wing with the malfunctioning cameras. If the guy had shot up out here, Edgar wouldn't have seen it. "Gotta go," I told him as two Vernonville Police Department squad cars and an unmarked pulled up, lights flashing.

Uniformed cops emerged from the squad car, and a tall blond man got out of the unmarked car. My heartbeat quickened—what was that all about?—as Detective Sergeant Anders Helland strode toward me. He moved with the grace of an athlete, and I could picture him clad in ski gear, poised at the top of a black diamond run. Maybe it was his Nordic-blond hair and name that brought downhill skiing to mind. His handsome face was as expressionless as always, his eyes more gray than blue today as they swept the scene, cataloging every little detail.

"Officer Ferris," he greeted me. "Do you realize I haven't even had a cup of coffee yet this morning?"

"Poor planning," I said.

A muscle at the corner of his mouth twitched. "Wait here." He knelt beside the body, examining it without touching it, then straightened to issue orders to the six uniformed officers now present. When a sixtyish woman got out of a vehicle marked "Coroner," Helland hooked up with her and they returned to the body together, chatting in low voices as a crime-scene photographer took photos. When the photographer cleared out and the coroner squatted beside the dead man, I inched closer to overhear their conversation, hoping they'd say something about cause of death.

As it turned out, I didn't need to eavesdrop; as soon as the coroner shifted the body onto its back, the bullet hole in the blood-drenched tee shirt became visible. I realized two things almost simultaneously: the victim hadn't been shot on this spot, and I'd seen him before.

Detective Helland rejoined me fifteen minutes later, blowing on his cupped hands to warm them.

"Let's talk inside," he said, taking me by the elbow and steering me into the mall. Welcome warmth flowed over us as he held the door for me. "Tell me about finding him," Helland directed as soon as we seated ourselves on one of two benches halfway up the hall. Luxuriant ferns and hostas flourished in huge cement urns at either end of the back-to-back benches, one frond tickling the back of my neck. The faint scent of orange drifted from the dirt, and I figured someone had emptied a beverage cup into the planter, not an unusual occurrence.

My hands were frozen, so I tucked them between my thighs as I gave Helland the few details I had related to discovering the body.

"We'll need the images from your cameras—"

I was shaking my head before he completed the thought. "They're not working." I explained about the outage in this wing.

"Damn."

"Any ID on him?"

Helland hesitated a second, looking down his nose at me, then said, "None. No wallet or watch. It might've been a robbery gone bad."

"He was in here yesterday with two other kids." I described them as Helland took notes. "Maybe it's a gang thing."

"Possible," Helland said. He wasn't much for sharing information.

"Although," I continued, "I can't see why gangbangers would've moved the body."

"How did you know the body was moved?" Annoyance flickered in the detective's eyes.

I sighed. "I was a cop, remember?" I'd been an air force cop, first enlisted and then an officer, before the IED forced my retirement. "I know what it means that there was no pool of blood on the sidewalk, even though his shirt was soaked. He was shot elsewhere and then moved."

Helland stood. "Well, you're not a cop now," he reminded me brutally, "so don't go sticking your nose into this investigation. Other than the fact the body was left on mall property, it probably has nothing to do with Fernglen, so you can continue busting shoplifters and leave the homicide detecting to my team."

Anger lanced through me, and I stood as well, hating that I had to look up at him; he had at least nine inches on my five foot six. "Anything else?" I asked icily.

"I'll let you know." Without a good-bye or a thank-you, he strode toward the door through which I could see TV vans gathered in the parking lot. Realizing I was almost an hour late for my shift, I hurried toward the security office, saying quick "hellos" to mall walkers I passed on the way.

"Sorry, Edgar," I said, pushing through the glass doors.

Big, black, and bald, Edgar looked like an aging boxer or bouncer or cop with enough hard muscle under a layer of fat to telegraph "Don't mess with me," despite being in his fifties. "No sweat, EJ." He rolled up the graphic novel he'd been reading and picked up his old-fashioned aluminum lunch pail.

I checked the logbook we used for passing information

from one shift to the next, but found no entries. "Anything happen last night?"

"Besides the murder?" He grinned, showing a gold-plated incisor. "Nah."

"Did you call Captain Woskowicz?" The boss would be seriously pissed off if he learned about a murder at "his" mall on the morning news.

"Didn't want to wake him." With a wink, Edgar slid out the door, and I picked up the phone to call Woskowicz.

His reaction was predictable: profane and loud. I cut him off by saying, "I believe the media are still outside. If you hurry, you might get here in time to comment." He rang off without another word, as I suspected he might. For reasons I couldn't fathom, Woskowicz craved publicity and never missed an opportunity to schmooze with reporters.

I was entering my discovery of the body into the log, when the door swung open and Curtis Quigley—director of mall operations, the big kahuna in charge of renting the retail space, resolving tenants' gripes, luring customers into Fernglen, and ensuring the mall turned a profit for its investors—came in. He hurried toward me with the prissy walk that Joel could imitate to great comic effect. In his early fifties, I guessed, Quigley favored European-style suits tailored to hug his tall, narrow frame and regimental ties. Sandy blond hair was slicked back from his forehead and tucked behind his ears, brushing his collar. He always wore starched dress shirts with French cuffs and had a set of cuff links for every day of the week. Today's were jade.

"There are cops outside the east entrance, EJ," Quigley said, his expression that of a man waiting for a blow. He spoke with a quasi-British accent, which, rumor had it, he'd adopted during a college semester abroad in England.

"Yes, sir. I found a dead body outside the east entrance when I came in."

"Damn," he said faintly, closing his eyes. He opened them again. "Someone who works here?"

"Not as far as I know," I said.

"Natural causes, I hope?"

I shook my head. "He was shot."

"So sordid," Quigley muttered. He licked a forefinger and slicked it across one eyebrow. "Please let the police know I'd appreciate it if they finished up before opening. It looks bad for the customers, you know, having coppers lurking everywhere. Gives the wrong impression."

"I'll keep you posted, sir," I promised, not bothering to tell him that the police would leave when they'd finished with the crime scene and not a moment before. I also kept silent about my belief that the dead young man was a gang member; I didn't need Quigley obsessing about the possibility of a gang war played out at Fernglen.

Joel and two other officers came in as Quigley left. We staggered our shift starting times so the bulk of our officers were on duty between ten a.m. and six p.m., when we had the most customers in the mall. After greeting them, I left to patrol on the Segway, my knee aching from standing around in the cold earlier. Cruising the mall corridors as shoppers began to trickle in, I kept an eye out for the teens who had been with the murder victim yesterday. I couldn't help thinking how satisfying it would feel to present Detective "Stay Out of My Case" Helland with two potential witnesses. But nada.

As I glided past the food court, Jay Callahan, proprietor of the Legendary Lola Cookies, flagged me down. "EJ! Come tell me about the body you found."

I shushed him with a finger to my lips as a shopper turned to stare at us. "Don't broadcast it to the world," I said, dismounting near his counter. "Quigley thinks it's bad for business."

"Of course he does."

"How'd you hear?"

"It's on the news," he said, gesturing to the kitchen from which issued faint TV or radio voices. Jay leaned his forearms on the glass countertop, a sprinkling of dark red hairs standing out against his pale skin. With matching wavy hair on his head and hazel eyes, he looked like he belonged in a pub in Dublin instead of a mall in suburban Virginia. And the muscled chest and shoulders underneath his orange "Legendary Lola Cookies" tee shirt, not to mention the way his eyes seemed to take in everything, suggested he had once pursued a more active career than cookie baker. Federal agent? Soldier? International jewel thief? Investigative reporter? I'd several times found him lurking in the garage after hours, waiting around for something or someone, and he'd helped me capture a murderer waving a gun awhile back. In short, Jay Callahan was something of an enigma.

"What do your sources tell you?" I asked, accepting the chocolate chip cookie he held out.

He widened his eyes innocently. "Sources? I'm just a dude trying to sell cookies. I don't have sources, other than the television."

I snorted my disbelief and told him what little I knew about the dead young man.

"A gangbanger, huh?" He looked thoughtful. "Interesting. I hadn't heard anything about a gang war. Maybe it's some new gang initiation rite?"

"Could be, I suppose." My stomach lurched at the idea of gangs making new members kill someone to prove themselves. Leaving the bodies on public doorsteps reminded me too much of what Fubar did with his victims when he wanted to get noticed.

"It'd be interesting to know what kind of weapon was used," Jay mused.

I shot him a look as I paid for the cookie. "Yeah, that's what every John Q. Public is wondering," I said. "Just a cookie dude, my eye." On that skeptical note, I mounted the Segway and zipped away, not giving him time for rebuttal.

Three

...

No mass murderers or terrorists roamed Fernglen's halls, I assured merchants throughout the morning.

I helped a woman find her car keys, called maintenance for a malfunctioning toilet in the men's room, and chatted with shopkeepers, all of whom wanted the skinny on the dead body. Word of the murder had zipped around the mall faster than news of a swine flu pandemic. I kept my conversations on the matter brief and factual, trying to tamp down people's curiosity and fears. No, I didn't think it was the work of a serial killer, I told one nervous store manager. Yes, I was sure the police would catch the shooter soon, I told another. By the time I could take a break, I was heartily sick of the whole topic.

Despite that, I found the Segway taking me to the wing with the malfunctioning cameras. The cops were gone. The reporters had moved on to other stories. Customers flowed in and out of the stores. The wing was down a side hall, not one of the major spokes ending at an anchor, and it only held eight stores, four on either side. Down the left were Nailed It, a mani-pedi salon; the Herpetology Hut, a reptile store; Rock Star Accessories, which catered to the teeny-bopper crowd; and Pete's Sporting Goods, a comprehensive sporting-goods store with everything from canoes to pedometers, guns to basketballs. On the other side were the Make-a-Manatee store, which allowed kids to pick out the "skin" of a plush animal and have it stuffed just as full as they wanted it; a sunglasses emporium; a dress boutique called Starla's Styles; and Jen's Toy Store with the cheery red wagon still parked out front holding a sign that read "50% Off All Games!!"

Leaning forward a tad to set the Segway in motion, I traveled the length of the short hall down to the doors and then back up the other side. Plate glass windows gleamed, an acrid smell drifted from the salon, and my friend the bearded dragon, Dartagnan, scrabbled at me through the display window at the Herpes Hut. Business as usual. I didn't know what I was looking for . . . nothing, really. I wondered if the dead young man had exited the mall this way, possibly with his two friends. Had they been surprised outside by a robber? Members of a rival gang? I wrinkled my brow. Probably not, since the victim had been moved after he was shot. I couldn't come up with any reason why someone would go out of their way to drop a dead body at the mall, so I sped up and returned to the main hall.

Joel summoned me on the radio then, suppressed excitement in his voice, and told me to report back to the security office, stat. He'd been watching too many medical dramas. Minutes later, I parked the Segway and pushed through the glass doors to find Detective Helland standing in front of the camera screens talking to Captain Woskowicz. The contrast between the two men went deeper than the difference between Helland's razor-cut, white-blond hair and

Woskowicz's stubble, or the detective's elegant (expensive) suit and my boss's dictator-wannabe uniform. They were roughly the same height, but Woskowicz was much bulkier; he had help from steroids, I suspected. Helland had a confidence Woskowicz lacked; he took it for granted (annoying man) that people would respond to his orders and didn't need to resort to the bluster and threats Woskowicz employed. I'd worked for a colonel once with the same natural air of command.

Helland turned as I came in, and I thought I caught the merest hint of an eye roll as Captain Woskowicz said, "We've got your back on this op, Helland. Gangs will discover that Fernglen Galleria is not the place to play their stupid-ass games." He barked a laugh, and I wondered just how he planned to convince gang members not to hang out at Fernglen. Get the merchants to stop selling clothes in gang colors? Close down the food court? Sprinkle anti-gang dust around the perimeter?

Detective Helland turned to me without replying to Woskowicz's remark. "We've ID'd the victim," he said, holding out a sheaf of papers.

I took them automatically and looked down at a younger version of the victim's face in a formal photo that might have come from a high school yearbook. Brown eyes fringed with thick lashes regarded the viewer seriously, and the closed-lips smile looked perfunctory, at best. His chin rested on his hand in one of those corny poses school photographers seemed to like, and the horizontal cross tattoo was clearly visible. I looked a question at Helland.

"His name's Celio Arriaga. His mother's Nicaraguan, his father Mexican." Helland shrugged. "The father's not around. Celio is the oldest of six, according to the mother, and he dropped out of school last year as a junior. His mother has seen him only a handful of times since then. She had some choice words for the Niños Malos."

"Bad boys?"

"Roughly. It's a gang affiliated with La Gran Familia. We've seen an upswing in their activity lately, here and in Richmond."

"We ought to shoot 'em all on sight," Woskowicz broke in, hand going to his belt where a holster might be if the consortium that owned the mall allowed us to carry weapons. "Anyone wearing gang colors or flashing those dumbass hand signals"—he held up his right hand and contorted the fingers into various configurations—"pow-pow!"

Mr. Sensitivity. "I suppose you want me to show these around, find out if anyone remembers seeing Celio yesterday?" It wasn't much of a guess on my part—Helland wouldn't be here showering me with information about the victim if he didn't want help with something.

"Exactly." Helland smiled. "You were a cop—you know the drill."

"Funny how you remember I was a cop when you need me for something," I said drily.

"Military cops aren't real cops," Woskowicz put in. "Standing at a gate saluting generals is about all they're good for. Officer Ferris, here, though—she's a hero." He put a sneer into the word. "Got the medal to prove it. That and a fiver'll buy her a cup of coffee." He laughed.

I was furious, but Woskowicz would delight in any rebuttal I made, and I refused to give him the satisfaction. I didn't know how he'd found out about my medal—earned in the action that cost me my knee—because I sure as hell hadn't told him. Helland looked at me with new interest, but I cut him off before he could ask for details. "I'll spread these around today and get back to you if I learn anything concrete."

"Thanks." Helland walked with me to the door, his long legs covering the distance in two strides. Once the door swung shut behind us, he said, "Sorry about that."

I gave him a level look. "Why? You're not responsible for Woskowicz's stupidities." I got on the Segway, placed the photos of Celio Arriaga in the foot well, and took off.

Figuring I deserved a break, and needing time to recover my temper before interacting with any of the mall's customers, I headed to Merlin's Cave, which sold an assortment of magic tricks and magician's paraphernalia, New Agey crystals and fantasy figurines, and books on everything from alien visitations to feng shui. My friend Kyra Valentine was managing the shop for a year while her aunt Harmony, the shop's owner, did a sabbatical in Tibet. The store smelled faintly of sandalwood when I entered, and water burbled in a small, countertop fountain. Kyra, six feet tall with smooth dark skin and curly hair that fell to mid-back, was draping a black cape around a mannequin's shoulders.

"Finally!" Kyra exclaimed when she caught sight of me. She let go of the cape, which slithered to the floor. "Damn."

"Finally what?"

"You've finally showed up to tell me about the body. I heard it was riddled with bullets, a gang execution." Her eyes were alight with interest.

I sighed, not too surprised by this evidence of how rumors got exaggerated until they bore only a slight resemblance to the truth. "It might've been a gang thing, or it might not. As far as I know, he was only shot once."

"I guess once *is* enough." Kyra stooped to retrieve the cape.

"Huh?"

"Don't you remember that old Jacqueline Susann book, *Once Is Not Enough*? Hold this."

I obediently clamped the cape to the mannequin's shoulder while Kyra secured it with pins. "There." She stood back to survey the effect. "So, is Detective Helland on the case?" She gave me a sly look.

"Yes." Before she could say anything cutesy about how attractive Helland was—if you liked the icy Nordic type— or how long it'd been since I'd been on a date, I shoved one of the flyers at her. "He wants me to pass these around."

"Is this him?" She studied the photo of Celio Arriaga. "The dead guy?"

"Um-hm. Seen him around?"

She shook her head. "I don't think so. Good-looking kid."

Not anymore. There's something about death that steals the beauty from even the most classical features and flawless skin. Maybe it's the lack of vitality. "I saw him yesterday."

"Here?"

I nodded. "He was with another guy about his age and a slightly younger girl. I kept an eye on them for a while, but they didn't seem to be causing trouble, so . . ."

Kyra crossed to the counter and taped the photo to her cash register. "I'll ask customers about him. This Sunday's the last bout of the season. Are you coming?"

Kyra, an Olympic-medal-winning track star, had taken up roller derby a couple years ago in an effort to stave off middle-age weight gain (she was barely thirty) and keep in shape via a routine less boring than running on a treadmill during northern Virginia's cold winter months. She kept trying to get me into skates, insisting it'd be easier on my knee than I suspected.

"Wouldn't miss it," I said.

She fiddled with a rack of chains, clinking the crystal pendants together. Fiddling was so un-Kyra-like that I stared at her. "My brother Bobby almost got sucked into a gang," she said finally, looking at me with eyes darkened by the memory of something ugly.

"Really? I didn't know that." I'd known Kyra since I was eleven; we'd met when my family came east to vacation with Grandpa Atherton, and our friendship had grown during subsequent visits and phone calls. Bobby was several years older than Kyra, so I hadn't been around him much, but last time Kyra had mentioned him he was a CPA in Boise with three teenage daughters.

"It happened before I met you. I was little, so I don't remember all the details—I'm sure I never knew them—but I remember Mama crying, and Daddy and Bobby fighting, and the police coming a couple of times. I do know that Bobby stole Daddy's car and crashed it, putting himself and a couple of his homeys in the hospital. He was only fifteen. As soon as it was safe to move him, Mama and Daddy sent him off to Boise to recuperate with my aunt Connie and her husband. A couple of scary dudes came around looking for him once or twice—one of them tried to bribe me with a candy bar to tell him where my brother was—but then they went away."

"Thank goodness."

"Yeah. Did I mention Aunt Connie's husband was a prison guard?" Kyra smiled.

We said good-bye, and I returned to showing Celio's photo to mall shopkeepers and their employees. I did it on autopilot, mentally contrasting my own privileged upbringing in a gated community in Malibu with Kyra's. If there'd been gangs in our high school, my friends and I had been unaware of them, buffered as we were by our parents' wealth. Despite high-profile divorces and families as dysfunctional as any you'd see on reality TV, the kids I hung with weren't drawn to gangs. One girl I knew slightly had run away our sophomore year to join a religious cult, which, now that I thought about it, was essentially a gang minus the emphasis on guns and killing.

A couple of clerks thought they might have seen Celio in the mall the day before, but they wouldn't swear to it. The male assistant manager of a cell phone kiosk was more certain.

"Yeah," he said, studying the picture. "He was here, hanging around in the early afternoon yesterday. With a buddy and a hot chick. She had on a pair of stretch jeans and a tee shirt that didn't leave much to the imagination." He licked his lips. "Hot."

Since he was clearly in his midtwenties and the girl had been no more than fifteen or sixteen, I found his fascination with her distasteful. "Did you hear them talking?"

"Not really." He shrugged skinny shoulders under a button-down shirt that gaped at the neck, a size too large. "They seemed to be arguing about something, at least the babe and this guy"—he pinged the page—"were getting into it. I wasn't really paying attention—I had a customer, you know?"

I thanked him, told him to call the security office if he saw either of the two again, and turned into the cameraless hall. I hit pay dirt in the Pete's Sporting Goods.

"He was in here yesterday," the owner said. His name was Colin Garver, not Pete. In his late fifties, he was only a couple of inches taller than me, but wiry and fit, built like some of the special ops guys I'd known in the military. Deep crow's feet around his eyes and skin like tanned cowhide spoke to many hours in the sun. I didn't know him well; he'd bought the store from Pete only a few months earlier. I'd waited while he explained the differences between two brands of in-line skates to a customer and then shown him Celio's photo.

"He was looking at the guns," Colin said, gesturing to the racks of guns—rifles, pistols, shotguns—in locked cabinets behind him.

"Alone?"

Colin nodded. "Uh-huh."

I wondered where the girl and his buddy had been. "What time?"

"I don't know exactly . . . maybe four thirty?"

That was considerably later than I'd seen him and proved he'd still been hanging around the mall in the late afternoon. "Anything special about him? Did he say anything?"

Colin's eyes narrowed. "He was carrying."

"A gun? Are you sure?"

His thin lips slanted up on one side. "I'm sure. Left-hand pocket of his jacket. He kept both hands dug into his pockets, like he was cold, but I could tell."

I believed him. This put a different complexion on things. Maybe Celio had tried to mug someone, someone who also happened to be armed and shot him. That didn't explain why the someone had bothered to move the body, though. "Do you get a lot of gang types in here wanting guns?" I asked Colin.

"Not so many," he said. "They've mostly got sheets and aren't going to pass the background check, or they're too damn young. I get more hunters, or homeowners looking for a piece for personal protection. I've got a nice Beretta here I recommend for women." He pulled a key from his pocket and made a move toward one of the glass-fronted cabinets, but I stopped him with a smile and a head shake.

"Thanks anyway."

He gave me half a wink that told me he suspected I already had a weapon. I did. I practiced regularly with it at the range, wanting to keep my skills sharp for when I got back on with a police department.

"What'd you do before becoming 'Pete'?" I asked.

"Owned a house-painting company."

"Around here?"

Colin shook his head. "Texas."

That explained the complexion like overcooked rawhide, if not his aura of awareness, the feeling he gave off of being half-cocked, ready to explode into action. "What brought you east?"

"Have you ever tried to use a paint sprayer while swaying atop a twenty-foot ladder in a west Texas wind?"

I shook my head, mildly amused by his sour expression.

"Take my advice: don't. There's a reason there are more wind farms than ranches in the Lone Star state, most of 'em in the west. Thirty-plus-mile-an-hour winds, six and a half days out of seven. I don't miss Dumas one little bit."

"So, selling guns and basketballs suits you?"

"It pays the bills," Colin said somewhat grimly. "It pays the bills."

Four

. . .

Going store to store like this reminded me of the house-to-house questioning I'd done a few times as a military cop. Then, as now, it was tedious and largely pointless, but I belonged to the "leave no stone unturned" school of investigation, so I got on with it by Segwaying to the stuffed animal store, Make-a-Manatee. Walking under the huge pink whale just inside the entrance, I looked around for the owner. I spotted him midway back, surrounded by kids clamoring to get their animals stuffed. Mike Wachtel was about five-nine, with male-pattern baldness and his left leg in a cast from foot to midthigh.

"What happened to you?" I asked as he seated himself by the stuffing machine, a huge glass rectangle full of white fluff. A foot treadle pumped the fluff into the limp skins of soon-to-be-stuffed animals. "Skiing accident?"

"It's a pain in the butt," he said, wincing as a careless four-year-old bumped his leg.

When I asked about Celio, he apologetically said he

noticed children more than adults. Since he had a line of kids waiting to have their animals stuffed, and a rowdy birthday party had reached the cake-and-candles stage in the corner, I left. Across the hall, the nail salon's owner said Celio didn't look like the kind of guy who went in for mani-pedis, and my friend Keifer at the Herpes Hut looked doubt-ful. His bead-decorated, midback-length dreadlocks clicked as he shook his head. "This the dude that got killed?"

"Yes. The police are trying to build a timeline of his whereabouts before he got shot."

"Can't help you, EJ. Sorry," he said, handing back the flyer. "When are the cameras going to get fixed? I'm tempted to short my rent unless they're up and running by the first of the month." A group called Lovers of Animal Freedom, LOAF, had "liberated" all Keifer's stock earlier in the year, and he was justifiably concerned about the weak security. I told him the cameras should be online later in the week, and he offered to let me hold Dartagnan. I petted the bearded dragon with one finger for a few minutes before easing him back into his terrarium. I hadn't much liked reptiles when I first started visiting the Herpes Hut, but Keifer had taught me to appreciate them, and I might actually have thought about owning one if it weren't for Fubar. I suspected my cat would see them as hors d'oeuvres or especially entertaining kitty toys—no batteries needed—rather than as step-siblings or housemates.

Leaving the Herpes Hut, I tried Rock Star. The clerks in the crowded store pulsing with a loud pop score were too busy trying to keep tweenage girls from shoplifting cheapo necklaces, purses, and hair accessories to more than glance at Celio's photo. When I insisted, the manager, who didn't look much older than her customer base, glanced at the page. Her name was Carrie, and she was wearing half her product line, so she jingled, tinkled, and rustled with every movement. "Well, maybe," she said. "Could he have been with a girl?"

"Possibly."

She nodded with more confidence, swiping magenta-tipped bangs off her forehead. "I think I saw him in here yesterday with a girl, maybe his girlfriend. Right after I came back from my dinner break, so about five? She bought a pair of earrings. They're on special: buy one pair get the next one free." She pointed to a basket near the register.

I felt faint pricks of excitement. If the girl had used a credit card, I could get a name and have something concrete to give to the condescending Detective Helland. "How did she pay?"

"Cash," Carrie said, dashing my hopes. "I remember because she asked that guy"—she nodded toward Celio's photo—"for money, and he pulled out a roll of bills with a rubber band around them. I don't see that every day. Little girls counting nickels and dimes from their piggy bank—yeah. Guys with rubber-banded money rolls—not so much."

"Thanks anyway," I said. "Can you let me know if you see the girl again?" I gave her my card with the security office's phone number on it.

"Sure," the manager said, tossing the card in a drawer beneath the register with a motion that told me I'd never hear from her. "You know," she said as I turned to go, "it's getting so I don't feel safe here anymore. My dad totally wants me to quit this job. What with that man getting shot at Diamanté awhile back, and now this dude getting gunned down right outside our door practically, it's like working in a war zone."

I debated reminding her that neither Jackson Porter nor Celio Arriaga had been shot on mall property, or giving her a graphic word picture of what life in a war zone was *really* like. But then I focused on the worry in her mascara-rimmed eyes and bit my tongue.

"Me and Malia"—she nodded toward a Hawaiian-looking girl restocking a headband display at the back of the store—"are thinking about taking a self-defense class."

"That's not a bad idea," I said, giving it some thought. "Maybe we could even start one here."

"Really?" Her eyes lit up. "That would be beyond cool."

The more I thought about it, the more the idea appealed to me. "Let me run it past Mr. Quigley," I said, "and I'll get back to you. Mornings, before the stores open, might be a good time to hold classes."

A customer came to the register to purchase a boa molting purple feathers, and I left, pausing to think for a moment outside the shop. So, Celio Arriaga had been carrying a healthy amount of cash. Maybe his death was a robbery gone wrong after all. In which case the police should be doubly interested in interviewing the girl and guy who'd hung out with Celio in the mall; they'd undoubtedly known about the money, and that made them suspects numeros uno and dos, in my book.

Before I could finish canvassing the stores in the wing, Captain Woskowicz swaggered around the corner and beckoned me with a peremptory head jerk. I knit my brows, not used to seeing my boss actually patrolling the halls. He mostly spent the days holed up in his office, allegedly "doing paperwork" and "liaising" on the phone, but more often playing computer games or watching DVDs.

"Why the hell do I have to track you down to get a report, Ferris?" He jiggled a container of breath mints in one hand as he spoke. "Anyone see the punk?"

Somewhat reluctantly, I told him what I'd found out. A Captain Woskowicz who seemed interested in doing his job made me vaguely uneasy because it was so out of character.

"Did the Pete's guy actually see a weapon?" Woskowicz demanded.

"No, but—"

"Then what the hell makes him think the gangbanger was carrying?" Woskowicz snorted. "He probably had his hand around that roll of soft you mentioned."

It wasn't worth arguing about, but I was convinced that Colin Garver knew what he was talking about.

"Did the police tell you what kind of gun was used?"

I gave him a puzzled look. "You heard everything Helland said. I haven't talked with him since."

Woskowicz harrumphed and tossed half a dozen breath mints into his mouth. "I don't know why the cops want to waste resources on this case anyway. Gangbangers offing each other. NHI."

I looked a question at him.

"No humans involved."

I fought down anger at his callousness. "Something else came up this morning," I said, changing the subject. "One of the women who works here mentioned that she's been thinking about signing up for a self-defense class. What would you think about my putting together a class?"

He snorted. "Waste of time," he said. "Woman wants to protect herself, she should get a gun." His eyes slid sideways as he checked out the legs of two women entering the nail salon. He turned back to me. "If you want to waste your time teaching self-defense to a bunch of nervous Nellies, it's no skin off my nose. Just make sure you do it on your own time because it's not coming out of my budget." He walked away.

I finished canvassing the merchants, getting exactly what

I expected in Starla's Styles and Jen's Toy Store—nothing—grabbed a quick lunch from the Wok My World in the food court, and returned to the office to type up my notes. Telling Joel I'd take over the dispatch duties so he could patrol, I sat down in the seat he vacated and began composing an email for Detective Helland. I stared at the scant half page with discontent when I was done. I hadn't come up with much: Celio Arriaga had flashed a lot of cash, might have had a gun, bought earrings, and was still in the mall at about five o'clock. No one was going to be making an arrest based on that information. For all I knew, Helland and crew had already rounded up a likely suspect, or gotten a solid lead from a snitch, and didn't even need my paltry bits of information. My mostly unacknowledged hope that I could make enough of an investigative contribution so that the Vernonville PD would overlook my disability and offer me a job dwindled. With a sigh, I sent the email.

Hope sprang to life again that evening when I walked into my house, hair still dripping from my swim. An official-looking letter lay under the mail slot, half covered with advertising circulars and a reminder that I was due for a dental checkup. The return address was Galax Police Department, a small PD in a small town in the southwestern part of Virginia. I'd applied with them a couple months back and gone for an in-person interview almost three weeks ago. Maybe, just maybe . . .

I took the envelope into the kitchen with me and pried the top off a local microbrew. After a couple sips, I slit the envelope with a paring knife. "Dear Ms. Ferris: Although we were impressed . . . blah, blah . . . wouldn't hire you if you were the last sentient being on earth."

Okay, it didn't really say that last bit, but it might as well have. They didn't want me. My knee would keep me from meeting their physical-fitness standards. The same old story I'd heard from almost twenty other police departments around the state since I was medically retired. Rather than cry, I tore the letter into strips, piled them into a cast-iron frying pan, and lit them with a kitchen match. Fubar emerged from the hall as smoke wisped out of the kitchen. "Mrrowf?"

"Sometimes a woman's just got to set something on fire," I told him. "Want to snuggle?"

With a twitch of his lip that seemed to indicate that snuggling was not on his agenda—Fubar's a big proponent of the "suck it up" school of dealing with disappointment—he leaped onto the counter and nosed around the canisters as I rinsed the ashes off in the sink and ran the garbage disposal for good measure.

A knock at my back door made me whip around, feeling like I'd been caught out in some illicit activity. Grandpa Atherton stood on the back stoop, grinning in at me, his own white hair visible under a plaid motoring cap.

Unlocking the door, I invited him in and hugged him. "Done chasing Moldovan diplomats?" I asked.

"For the moment," he replied with a smile that showed slightly age-yellowed teeth. He seated himself at my kitchen table, pulling off the hat. "What's this I hear about another body in your mall?"

"Don't make it sound like we have one a week," I said, pulling ingredients from the fridge and pantry to make a shrimp pasta. "And this one was technically outside the mall, not in it. The cops think it's a gang thing."

"Nothing for me to work on?" Grandpa asked, disappointment in his voice. "I found these grand new gadgets—listening devices that look like insects—that I've been wanting to field test."

"That gives new meaning to the word 'bug.'"

"I bought a fly and a spider. You plant them in the target's office or home; no one ever suspects that the fly on their wall is a wonder of modern microtechnologies."

"What happens when your fly gets swatted?" I asked. "Or sprayed with insecticide?"

"The website says they withstand pressure up to a hundred psi."

"How does that compare with your average swat?" I asked, curious despite myself.

Grandpa shrugged, "Fill me in on the murder."

To humor him, I told him what I knew about Celio Arriaga, his death, and his last day at the mall. Grandpa listened and sniffed appreciatively as I sautéed fresh garlic in olive oil before dumping in frozen shrimp and some spinach. He waggled his bushy eyebrows when I mentioned the body was moved after the shooting.

"That's going to be at the crux of the case, you mark my words," he said, pushing to his feet to set the table. "Gangs' modus operandi lean more toward drive-by shootings and letting the corpses fall where they may.

Gangbangers don't move bodies, unless it's to leave a message of some kind like 'Stay off our turf' or 'This is what happens to people who rat.' Do gangbangers say 'rat'?"

"Beats me. I get your point, though." I narrowed my eyes against the steam as I slid linguini into a pot of boiling water. "A warning, huh? You could be on to something." While the linguini cooked, I told him I was thinking about starting a self-defense class at the mall.

"Count me in," he said immediately. He went into a half crouch, hands uplifted in a martial arts pose.

"For what?"

"Your co-instructor, of course," he said, abandoning his Jet Li pose to rasp a chunk of Romano cheese across a grater.

"I don't think I'd be going out on a limb to say I've had more hours of hand-to-hand combat training than anyone in Vernonville."

"Undoubtedly," I said, trying to think of a tactful way to decline his offer. I shuddered at the thought of some over-zealous student throwing my grandpa, with his brittle, octogenarian bones, to the ground. My mom would shoot me if Grandpa ended up with a broken hip or fractured spine. "I'm not sure when we'll start," I added, hedging. "I've got to clear it with Mr. Quigley and find some place to hold the class."

"Well, don't let the grass grow under your feet, Emma-Joy." Grandpa dished up generous helpings of linguini, which I topped with the shrimp and spinach sauce. We sat and began to eat. "In fact, if you're too busy, I can make the arrangements, if you want. I'll bet Theresa would come."

Theresa Eshelman was his day-care-owning lady friend. "I'll talk to Quigley tomorrow," I said, knowing that I had small chance of derailing Grandpa once he got excited about a project. I was preoccupied throughout dinner, grappling for an idea that would make Quigley put the kibosh on the whole plan, or insist that it be ladies only, or something else that would keep Grandpa out of the ER, where I was pretty sure he got "frequent visitor" discounts.

Five

...

In any event, I saw Curtis Quigley much sooner than I
had anticipated. He called me midmorning and sent me
searching for my boss, wanting an update on the murder
case. When I knocked on Woskowicz's office door and got
no reply, I turned the handle.

"Captain Woskowicz?" Easing the door wider, I poked
my head around and saw that the office was empty. The desk
was uncluttered—more a testament to his lack of work than
his neatness—and the computer turned off. A lidded stainless steel mug sat atop a two-drawer filing cabinet. The air
smelled faintly of breath mints.

I returned to the main office and asked Joel, "Have you
seen Captain W today?"

"No." Joel smiled at me hopefully. "Do you suppose he
quit?"

I gave him a "we should be so lucky" look and then dialed
Quigley and told him I couldn't locate the director of
security. He ordered me to come brief him on the Arriaga

investigation; before I left, I directed Joel to call Wosko-wicz's home phone and cell while I was gone. I returned six minutes later, having cheered Quigley by telling him there was no further information and no evidence of mall involve-ment, and gotten his enthusiastic endorsement of the self-defense class. "Great idea, EJ!" Quigley had said. "Makes us appear proactive, like we're looking out for our employees."

Joel shook his head at me. "No answer either place."

My brows knit together. Woskowicz certainly wasn't going to get my vote for Boss of the Year, but he hadn't missed a day of work since I started at the mall. Maybe he had a medical or dental appointment scheduled and had forgotten to tell us.

"Do you think it's connected to the murder?" Joel asked, eyes round.

"Unlikely," I said. Joel had some good analytical abilities but was attracted to lurid, interesting, or outrageous explana-tions for events rather than the humdrum, more likely ones. I was trying to break him of that tendency. Sending him out on patrol, I stayed in the office, fielding calls that would've gone to Captain Woskowicz and putting together a flyer for the self-defense class. When my boss still hadn't shown up by noon, I called in an off-duty security officer so our staff-ing would be adequate. About an hour before my shift ended, a knock on the glass door brought my head around.

A redheaded woman wrapped in a full-length, faux-cheetah coat stood outside. I gestured for her to come in. She looked around curiously and patted the red hair teased out a good three inches from her head. I guessed her to be a well-preserved fifty or so. Coral lipstick slicked her wide mouth, and pointy black boots covered her feet.

"Can I help you?" I asked when she didn't say anything.

"Is Beaner around?" Her voice was a low-pitched, Joplin-esque growl with a distinct New York accent.

"Beaner? I don't know anyone by that name."

She huffed an impatient sigh. "He's the boss of this place?"

I stared at her, noting a stiffness to her face that suggested a botched Botox treatment. "You mean Captain Woskowicz?"

"Yeah, him. Tell him I need the check. And I didn't appreciate getting stood up last night. Damn, it's toasty in here." She cocked one hip and unbuttoned the coat to display a mega-tight white tee stretched so taut ripples corrugated the fabric between her large breasts. "That's better. Look, is he back there? I'll just tell him myself."

I stood and blocked her path. "I'm afraid Captain Wos-kowicz isn't in yet today. I can give him a message that you stopped by, Ms.—?"

"A likely story," she said, a sneer in her voice that didn't show up on her immobile face. "You tell him I want that alimony check right this minute or he'll be hearing from my lawyer. I've got bills to pay, you know."

Alimony? So this was one of Captain Woskowicz's ex-wives. Rumor said he had three. "He's really not here, Ms.—" I tried again.

"Nina Wertmuller," she said. "What do you mean he hasn't come in yet?"

"He's not here," I said. "I'll tell him—"

"That's not like him."

I got the impression that if her facial muscles had worked, she'd have had a line between her mostly penciled-on brows. "Where were you supposed to meet?"

"At McGill's. We meet there every month. He gives me the check, we have a couple of drinks and . . ." She trailed off coyly, and I had no trouble imagining what happened next—for old time's sake, I was sure.

"If he's playing least in sight because he's trying to stiff me on the check . . . I'll go by the house and see if he's there," she announced.

"Will you ask him to give the office a call if you find him?"

"Sure thing. Hey, this looks like fun." She picked up one of the self-defense class flyers stacked on the corner of my desk. Before I could tell her the class was for mall employees only, she spun on her booted heel, cheetah coat flapping, and brushed past Joel, who politely held the door for her.

"Who was that?" he asked, gazing after her.

"A former Mrs. Woskowicz," I said.

"She looks a little like my mother."

I didn't know what to say to that, so I kept quiet, handing him a message slip from Sunny, the girl he was trying to lose weight for.

"What did she want?"

"Sunny?"

"The ex–Mrs. W." He tucked his uniform shirt more securely into his slacks; no matter what he did, Joel always managed to look a bit rumpled.

"Her alimony check. Apparently, she and Captain W were supposed to meet last night and he didn't show up." I tapped a finger on the desk, more perturbed than I was letting on about the captain's disappearing act. I wasn't exactly worried, but the man was definitely acting out of character. I couldn't see him passing up the chance for a little nookie with his ex-wife, not without a good reason.

"What'll happen if he doesn't come back? You could have his job!" Joel's brown eyes lit up.

I gave him a look. "Did you finish the inspection of the fire extinguishers?"

"Yeah. What's this?" He reached for one of the flyers I'd printed on bright pink paper. "Self-defense? Cool." He balled his hands into fists and jabbed at an invisible body bag, shuffling his feet like he was trying to scuff a mark off the floor.

"It's self-defense, not boxing," I said, snatching the flyer away. "And it's for women."

"EJ!" Joel actually looked hurt.

"Oh, I suppose—it doesn't matter . . . you can come." I sighed. So much for telling Grandpa Atherton he needed two X chromosomes to participate.

"Great. I'll pass these out while I'm patrolling." He helped himself to a handful of flyers and pushed through the glass doors, still shuffling his feet as though channeling Sugar Ray Leonard.

By the time my shift ended, Captain W still hadn't shown up or called in. After a moment's debate, I crossed the hall to the management offices and asked to speak to Curtis Quigley. The receptionist, a lovely dark-haired girl named Pooja, buzzed him and then said he'd see me. "Is it true that Captain Woskowicz has been kidnapped?" The smile that went with the question told me she thought the idea was utterly ridiculous, and she laughed when I rolled my eyes.

Quigley, seated behind his desk when I entered, immediately asked if the police had arrested someone for the murder and if Captain Woskowicz had shown up.

"No and no," I said, seating myself.

He flapped his hands in a gesture somewhere between annoyance and worry. "This is not a good time!"

I resisted the urge to ask when *was* a good time for murdered bodies to turn up on mall property and senior managers to be no-shows.

"I'm giving my quarterly report to the FBI board this afternoon"—FBI was not the law enforcement agency; it stood for Figley and Boon Investments, the company that owned Fernglen Galleria and several other malls.—"and they are not going to be happy about this. A dead body on the doorstep doesn't play well with the stockholders. It tarnishes our image as a family-friendly mall." He fussed with one of his cuff links, then gave me a penetrating stare. "You're in charge, EJ, until Captain Woskowicz turns up."

I sat up straighter, startled. "But I'm not the most senior—"

He waved away my objection. "This isn't the military. I can put whoever I want in charge and I want you. You seem to have a good working relationship with the Vernonville police and that's important right now. In fact, why don't you go over there this afternoon and poke them about the murder. While you're there, you can tell them that Captain Woskowicz is missing." He scooped up a handful of files and came around the desk.

"Woskowicz is an adult, Mr. Quigley," I said, wondering how to break it to him that the police were going to be monumentally uninterested in hearing about a grown man who'd been missing for maybe twenty-four hours, if we counted from when he'd been supposed to meet Nina Wertmuller.

"Just fill them in," Quigley insisted. "I'm late." He hurried past me and out the door, leaving me alone in his office.

Central Vernonville consisted of two blocks of shops and restaurants in Colonial-era buildings fronted by brick sidewalks. Words like "quaint" and "historical" peppered the chamber of commerce brochures about the downtown shopping district. The police department fit right in, occupying the former Town Hall, a lovely two-story building surmounted by a white cupola. Although the exterior looked like something out of Colonial Williamsburg, the interior had been modernized and was so generic it could've been a police department in Tucson or Augusta: counter staffed by a uniformed officer, waiting area with virtually indestructible molded chairs, wear-resistant carpet in a color between dark green and gray.

As a young officer escorted me back to Detective Helland's office, I took the opportunity to once again admire the photographs spaced along the hall walls. Last time I'd been here, I'd realized that the atmospheric landscapes were all signed "A. HELLAND" in tiny gold type. It interested me to think of Detective Helland turning his analytical brain to photo composition as he tried to capture a mood or a moment; he was just so darn un-artsy on the job.

"I got your email," he greeted me when the officer knocked on his door. His gaze flicked to me for a split second and then returned to the document on his desk. I paused on the threshold. More landscape photos—black-and-white studies of trees—decorated the beige wall behind his desk. An empty fish bowl sat on a credenza near a computer printer; last time I'd been here, it had held a Siamese fighting fish. Perhaps he had moved on to the Big Fishbowl in the Sky. File folders, case binders, a computer, and other office paraphernalia took up most of the available space on the desk and bookshelves. He had no personal photos on his desk—no smiling wife, no tow-headed kids, not even a dog—which I tended to think meant he wasn't married. Not that it mattered to me, I hastily reminded myself.

"Good work," Helland said. "You didn't have to come down here."

His slightly condescending tone raised my hackles immediately. "My boss asked me to check in and see what

progress you're making." I wanted to make sure he understood I hadn't come of my own accord. "And," I added reluctantly, knowing Helland would be dismissive, "he wanted
me to tell you that Captain Woskowicz is missing."

"Missing? I talked to him yesterday." He looked up at
me, raising brows a few shades darker than his white-blond
hair.

"I know, but he didn't show for an appointment with his
ex-wife last evening and he didn't turn up for work today."

"So he had one too many last night and he's sleeping it
off," he said, just as dismissively as I had known he would.
Standing, he shrugged into a pin-striped jacket. "I've got a
meeting."

What was it with men walking out on me today? "I'll
walk with you," I said. He didn't object, so I preceded him
out of the office and we fell into step. Our shoulders brushed,
and I put another couple of inches between us, too aware of
him. From the almost imperceptible hesitation in his step,
I thought he'd felt the jolt, too. "About the Arriaga case. It
would be helpful to locate either the guy or the girl he was
with at Fernglen, right? Have you talked to them yet?"

"No," Helland admitted. "We've managed to touch base
with the *mero mero*—leader—of the Niños Malos, and he's
assured us that no gang member had any involvement in his
homey's death. Cross his heart and hope to die." Heavy irony
laced Helland's words. "He's told the Niños not to talk to
us, so they're not. He suggested we haul in some Latin Kings
for questioning."

"A rival gang, I presume?"

"Exactly."

"Think there's anything to that?"

"It doesn't look like a gang hit to us," he said, pausing
outside a conference room door. "And our gang task force
hasn't heard about a Latin King or Blood taking credit for

it. That doesn't prove it wasn't a gang thing, but—" He shrugged.

People trickled past us into the conference room, giving me curious stares. I knew I was about to lose him. "Look, I can describe the pair he was with at the mall. If you have an artist—"

"We don't. Budget cuts. We'll handle it." He strode into the conference room. I was dismissed.

Six

...

Word had trickled through the security force by the next morning that Captain Woskowicz was AWOL and Quigley had put me in charge temporarily. A couple of the old-timers seemed inclined to resent my being appointed over them, but most of the officers were okay with it. For many of them, working mall security was just a job that paid the bills; they wanted to work their shift and go home with no worries about staffing or funding or other management functions. For others, it was a stepping-stone (they hoped) to a job with a police force. For me, it was a combination of the two: a pseudo law-enforcement job to augment my puny medical retirement from the military until I got back on with a real police force. I didn't mind taking on the director of security responsibilities until Woskowicz showed up, but no way did this job represent the pinnacle of my ambitions.

Joel, however, was enthused by my temporary ascension. "You can fund the operation of all the cameras now," he said when I'd chatted with each of the officers as they came on shift and sent them on patrol.

"I'm the *acting* director of security for a couple days," I told him, sitting at my regular desk; it seemed presumptuous to move into Captain W's office. "I'm supposed to keep the office functioning, not rearrange the funding priorities."

"Oh." He sounded disappointed. "Will you have time to swim today? I lost another half a pound." He patted his still round belly.

"Good for you," I said encouragingly. "Have you asked Sunny for a date yet?"

"No," he mumbled. "But she's bringing her golden retriever to my agility class now, so I get to see her twice a week."

"Ask her out."

"I want to lose five more pounds first."

"Joel, you sound like a girl," I said. "Sunny either likes you or she doesn't. Five pounds one way or the other isn't going to make a difference."

"You think? Well, maybe," he said, clearly not convinced.

If his reaction was anything to go by, it looked like I didn't have much of a future as a dating advice columnist. Before I could urge him further, the radio crackled.

"EJ?" It was Harold Wasserman's voice. He was the oldest of our security guards, a sixty-something retired engineer who had returned to the workforce primarily to avoid having to take care of his twin four-year-old grandsons. "We've got a rabbit issue. Can you come down to the fountain?"

"On my way," I said, resisting the impulse to ask what kind of bunny issue could come up in a mall. Visions of a mass escape from the pet store filtered through my mind, and I hoped it wouldn't create the chaos that a few loose lizards and snakes had generated not that long ago. Shoppers wouldn't object to a cute kitten or beagle puppy playing in the halls, would they? Although, I thought as I mounted the Segway and headed for the elevator, the janitorial crew might have a bit more work.

By the time the elevator bumped to a stop on the lower level and I motored toward the fountain, a small crowd had gathered. Geez, how could a long-eared, fluffy-tailed mammal generate so much interest? When I pushed through the onlookers, I understood. I found myself confronting a six-and-a-half-foot-tall bunny wearing a polka-dotted bow tie and swinging a chair around by two legs. Harold Wasserman stood several feet back, trying to calm the hyped-up rabbit.

"Look, buddy—" Harold caught sight of me and broke off, hurrying to my side. "It's the Easter Bunny. He's drunk. He tipped that little girl out of his lap." He pointed to a ringletted tyke watching big-eyed from within the Easter Bunny's tulip-decked enclosure. "The mother"—he lowered his voice—"smelled beer on his breath and flagged me down. When I suggested that he go home and sleep it off, he got off his chair, picked it up, and took a swing at me." He rubbed his forearm. The odor of cigarettes leaked from him.

"Are you okay?"

"Yeah, sure." Harold grinned behind his luxurious gray mustache. "The twins do worse than that to me three times a week."

"Okay. You get the crowd to move along, and I'll see if I can't persuade Mr. Bunny here to simmer down."

I approached the man in the Easter Bunny costume cautiously, trying to figure out where the eye holes were so I could make eye contact. They clearly weren't in the bunny's head, which was adorned with plastic disks for eyes. Approximately the diameter of a baseball, the eyes were a strange lavender shade with black insets for pupils, and were fringed with two-inch-long lashes. I finally decided a mesh screen below the critter's bow tie hid the performer's face.

"Sir, can you put the chair down, please?" I asked, wondering how he maintained his hold on the wooden chair with his rounded rabbit paws. "What's your name?"

In answer, he hefted the chair a foot higher and said, "You can sit on my lap, pretty lady." A very un-bunnyish snicker issued from the costume's big, round head.

"Mr. Bunny," I said sternly, having no other name to use, "you're scaring the children."

"Good."

We were not off to a promising start. I didn't want to have to subdue him physically—how many kids would be traumatized by seeing the Easter Bunny taken down by a couple of mall security officers?—so I resorted to bribery. "Look, why don't you take off that costume—I'm sure it's uncomfortable and hot—and we can talk about this over a beer at Tombino's. I'm buying."

He thought for a moment, swaying. "Okay, then." He dropped the chair with a clatter and wiggled his hands free of the mittlike paws. Attached to the arms of the fuzzy white costume with a length of cloth, they dangled like a toddler's mittens secured to a parka. I was congratulating myself on my strategy when his hands went to a hidden zipper beneath the bunny's chin and he yanked it to his waist with a metallic whizzing sound. A scrawny bare chest appeared, matted with graying hair.

"No, wait!" I said as a few of the watching mothers gasped or covered their children's eyes. But it was too late. He continued unzipping and shrugged out of the costume, almost falling as he kicked off the clumsy bunny feet that must have been three feet long.

"There, that's better," the man said, wearing the round

bunny head with its one upright and one drooping ear and nothing else but a pair of plaid boxer shorts. I'd never been so happy to see a pair of underwear in my life. I became aware that many of the onlookers had pulled out their cell phones to take photos, and groaned. "Naked Easter Bunny at Fernglen Galleria" was not the kind of headline that would make Quigley happy. I moved forward to help the actor remove the bunny head, which had gotten stuck, and Harold borrowed a coat from someone and laid it around the man's shoulders. It covered him to his knobby knees.

"Good thinking," I told Harold.

He grinned. "What's up, doc?"

It took an hour to get Hiram Dabney, aka the Easter Bunny, dressed, sobered up, and out of the mall in the company of a police officer who seemed to know him from his overnights in the local drunk tank. I arrived back at the security office, hair disheveled and knee aching, to find Joel grinning like a fool, obviously having heard all about the bunny striptease.

"Not one word," I warned him.

Before he could reply, two people arrived simultaneously, and I turned to greet them, hoping they weren't reporters. The first, a man wearing coveralls and carrying a toolkit said, "I'm here to fix the cameras?" The second, a statuesque redhead said, "I need to talk to Denny."

"Thank heavens," I said to the camera guy. I pointed to the bank of monitors. "Do your thing." Joel cleared papers and office-supply clutter out of the way so the repairman had somewhere to spread out his tools.

"Sorry," I said to the redhead. "Denny?"

She sighed heavily, rounded bosom rising and falling

under a zip-up knit jacket. "Denny Woskowicz, the security guy."

I stared at her. Talk about déjà vu all over again. She was taller and a few years younger than Nina, and her hair was a more coppery red, but she was enough like yesterday's visitor to be her sister. It dawned on me a bit late that Captain Woskowicz's first name was Dennis. "He's not here," I said. "He hasn't been in since Wednesday."

"Nina called me last night and told me he was missing, but I didn't believe her," the newcomer said. "This is just great." She sounded put out.

"I'm sorry," I said, holding out my hand. "I'm EJ Ferris. You are—?"

"Paula Woskowicz." She shook my hand, the multiple rings she wore digging into my fingers. "I kept Denny's name when we divorced. You wouldn't think any name would be worse than Woskowicz, but my maiden name was Poupére"—she gave it a French pronunciation—"and I just hated getting called Paula Pooper, so you can see why I held on to Denny's name."

"Uh—"

"Anyway, I bet he's here, right?" She winked a turquoise-gilded eyelid. "He just didn't want to be bothered by that Nina. Anyone can see why he left her for me. I mean, all you have to do is talk to her for thirty seconds. It's all Nina, Nina, Nina. A man needs to feel like he's important, that he's the center of a woman's world."

There was a feminist message if ever I heard one.

"Anyway, I just wanted to make sure that we're still on for tonight."

Captain Woskowicz had hidden depths I'd never suspected. Apparently he was dating at least two of his ex-wives, in addition to a reporter for a local TV station he'd been seeing recently. Now that I came to think of it, she had reddish hair, too. "He's really not here," I said. "Did he ever do anything like this when you were together? Not show up for work?"

"Never," she said. "Denny was all about work. Well, work and . . . you know." She winked again.

Yuck. I didn't even want to think about "you know" with Woskowicz. "Is his car at his house?"

Paula's eyes widened. "Why, I don't know. I haven't been over there, and Nina didn't say. She stopped by yesterday, she said, just to make sure he wasn't ducking us, you know, and to feed Kronos."

"Kronos?" I pictured a slavering Doberman in a spiked collar.

"Denny's hamster." She giggled at my expression. "Yeah, I know. I mean, he doesn't seem like a hamster kind of guy. Aggie gave it to him for their second anniversary. There were two of them, but Cerberus died last year. Kronos just keeps going on and on. Kind of fitting, if you think about it, since he's named for a god. Immortal. Was Kronos a Roman god, or maybe Norse? I can't remember."

An immortal hamster sounded like a shoo-in for whichever Hollywood studio had put out a "squeakquel" about chipmunks. "Aggie?"

"The little home wrecker who filched Denny from me." Her tone, sort of "easy come, easy go," didn't match the words.

Before I could ask more about Aggie, she said, "Look, would you come with me? To check on the car, I mean. It kind of gives me the creeps to think about going over there by myself, when something might have happened to him and all."

"Didn't you say Nina visited the house yesterday?"

"Yeah, but still . . ." She gnawed on the cuticle of her mulberry-painted thumbnail.

I glanced at my watch. My shift had ended long ago, and things were running smoothly.

"Ahem."

I turned, raising my brows questioningly, to find the camera repair guy standing at my shoulder. Medium height, with glasses and thinning hair, he held a tiny screwdriver in one hand and some sort of gizmo in the other.

"I'll keep this simple," he said, his voice a surprisingly pleasant baritone. "See this?" He held up the gizmo from which dangled two wires. "Someone deliberately disabled these cameras. No way did this happen by accident."

Whoa. I exchanged a quick glance with Joel and then told Paula, "How about if I meet you at Captain Woskowicz's place in an hour, okay?"

"Yeah, great," she said, nodding. "I can get some papers graded." With a waggle of her fingers, she left.

I turned back to the repairman, relieved that Captain Woskowicz's ex-wife was no longer listening in, and said, "What do you mean? By the way, I'm EJ Ferris."

"Brad Eaton," he said as we shook hands. "And I meant what I said: someone sabotaged the cameras."

All sorts of questions ran through my head, starting with "Who?" dashing past "How?" and ending with "Why?" but I only asked, "Can you fix it?"

Brad gave me a pitying look. "Piece of cake." He returned to the monitor bank and went at it with his screwdrivers, canned air, and other miniaturized tools.

I drew Joel away, out of earshot, to stand by the credenza that held the coffeemaker. The scent of stale coffee hovered in the air. Joel's eyes were big with excitement as he said in an explosive whisper, "It had to be Woskowicz! He was on duty when the cameras went belly-up."

"Let's not jump to conclusions," I cautioned, although the same idea had immediately leaped to my mind; that was why I'd wanted to get rid of Paula Woskowicz. "And let's keep this between us for now, although I guess I have to tell Curtis Quigley."

"Should we call the cops?" Joel asked.

I shook my head. "As far as we know, no crime's been committed. None of the merchants on that wing have reported any losses or break-ins."

"Maybe the heist is set to go down tonight, or later this week," Joel suggested, clearly eager to volunteer for stakeout duty.

"I suppose it's possible," I said, "but no one had any way of knowing the cameras would still be out, that it would take so long to get them repaired." Or maybe someone did. I remembered that the camera-repair company had been surprised to hear from me, had had no record of a service request from Fernglen. I'd written it off to poor record keeping on their part, but what if Captain Woskowicz had never called them? That would explain why he was pissed at me when I told him I'd gotten in touch with them.

The whizzing of a cordless screwdriver and a clang told me Brad had finished securing the console cover. I thanked him and pointed him across the hall to the mall operations office for payment. Strolling over moments later to let Quigley know about the sabotage, I found he was out of the office, so I wrote a brief note and left it with Pooja, feeling cowardly and relieved at the same time. Retrieving my gym bag from under my desk, I checked in with all the officers on duty to make sure there were no crises brewing, rifled our files for Captain Woskowicz's home address, and left to rendezvous with his second ex-wife.

Seven

· · ·

I pulled up in front of Captain Woskowicz's house to find Paula waiting out front in an aging green sedan. The shadows had lengthened, and when I killed the ignition and the heater cut off, I noticed the air was definitely chillier than it had been earlier. The calendar might say one week shy of spring, but it still felt plenty wintery. Pausing to assess the building before I got out of my car, I noted a snug, two-story brick house with a steep roofline and small front yard. Frankly, it was homier than I'd expected from Captain W. From his lurid tales of his sexual conquests, I'd pictured him in whatever the modern-day version of a bachelor pad is—a high-rise condo with a swimming pool and hot tub?— not this cul-de-sac home with trimmed shrubs just beginning to bud out and a red-painted mailbox at the curb. I wondered which of his wives, if any, he'd been married to when he bought this place.

Paula exited her car and was halfway to my Miata when

I climbed out and locked it. She dangled a key on a P-shaped keychain. "Have you been inside?" I asked.

"Oh, no," she said, brushing a strand of coppery hair off her face. "I waited for you."

"So, you're a teacher?" I walked beside her up the concrete walk to the front door. She didn't look much like a teacher to me, but she'd said something about grading papers.

"Eighth-grade social studies," she said.

"Do they still make the kids memorize the Preamble to the Constitution in middle school?" I asked. Rote memorization had fallen out of favor in educational circles, I'd heard, but I still remembered the Preamble from when I was thirteen and had to recite it in class. " 'We the people, in order to form—' "

"Oh, yeah," Paula said. "I get them to memorize it by encouraging them to text it to their friends."

I looked at her with respect. "That's thinking outside the box."

She shrugged. "You have to meet the kids where they are, you know?"

We had reached the door, and she bent to insert the key. "Wait a minute." Leaving her on the stoop, I crossed to the attached garage, wanting to see if Captain W's car was inside. The garage door was rolled down and locked, however, and had no windows. I rejoined Paula, who was shivering in her rib-knit sweater, and motioned for her to unlock the door. The key clicked in the lock, and the door swung open soundlessly.

Paula stepped in without hesitation and I followed after a brief pause. It felt weird to invade Captain W's space like this, without an invitation and with him gone. We stood in a small, vinyl-floored entryway that was essentially a toehold within a carpeted living room. The furniture was a strange mix of what I'd expected—black leather sofa and big screen TV—and the unexpected: a chintz-covered wing chair and an upright piano.

"It was his mother's," Paula said of the piano, following my gaze.

I didn't ask if he played; I didn't think my image of him could stand it if she announced he was a concert-caliber pianist or played jazz piano with a combo on Tuesday nights.

"The garage door is in the kitchen," Paula said. She strode across the living room and I followed, noting some peanut shells and an empty beer can on an end table. Its single drawer gapped slightly, and the TV remote lay on the floor.

The kitchen was more in line with my expectations: a bland space with black appliances, fridge magnets featuring insurance company and beer logos, a few dishes in the sink, and a couple browning bananas in a bowl with those miniscule fruit flies flitting around them. Most of the cabinet doors were slightly ajar, and none of the drawers were completely closed. I was about to comment on the sloppiness when a whirring sound suddenly broke the silence and I spun, looking toward the hall.

Paula laughed. "That's just Kronos," she said, "on his wheel."

Feeling like a total moron, I crossed the room to what I assumed was the garage door. Pulling it open, I found myself staring into a pantry stocked with enough canned soups to sustain a family of four—much less a man and his hamster—for several weeks. Cheddar cheese and bean with bacon predominated. Ugh. I backed away and tried an identical door two feet to my left. Success, of a sort. Weak fluorescent lights stuttered to life on the ceiling, illuminating the garage. The neatly swept, tool-filled, carless garage. Wherever Woskowicz was, he'd driven there under his own steam. I turned

off the light, closed the door, and told Paula, who was looking a question at me, "No car."

"Huh." She nibbled on her cuticles again. "Well, what do
we do now?"

Before I could answer, a muted thud sounded from the
direction of the bedrooms. Adrenaline spurted through my
veins. "That was definitely not Kronos," I said, "unless he's
the size of a baboon." I wished I had the gun I'd carried as
a military police officer. Confronting a possibly armed
intruder without a weapon of my own would be sheer
stupidity.

"C'mon," I said, beckoning Paula toward the back door.
"Let's get out of here and call the police."

"No way," she said. "This is—was—my house, and I'm
not letting any lousy, opportunistic thief ransack it. Hey, you
back there," she called, raising her voice to a shout before I
could stop her. "We know you're here. We've called the
police."

I pulled out my cell phone and dialed 911 on the words.
I couldn't leave Paula alone to face the intruder, so I wanted
backup on the way. The operator asked, "What is the nature
of your emergency?" at the same time I heard footsteps in
the hall.

"Paula? Is that you?" a woman's voice called.

"Oh my God! Aggie?" Paula's voice went from avenging
Valkyrie to exasperated in two seconds flat.

"Never mind," I told the operator, hanging up.

A short, plump woman emerged from the dark hallway,
flame red hair spiraling to her shoulders in a thick, springy
mass. Mrs. Woskowicz Number Three, I presumed.

"You about gave me a heart attack," she complained to
Paula. She entered the kitchen and went straight to the
fridge, extracted a beer, popped the top with a bottle opener
she pulled from a drawer, and took a healthy swig. She was

forty-fiveish, with skin dark enough to suggest some African-American or Hispanic heritage, small features, and designer jeans spray painted over rounded hips and full thighs. Red platform pumps peeped from beneath her jeans.

"Me? You took five years off my life, Aggie. What are you doing here anyway?"

"Feeding Kronos," the shorter woman said with a sniff that wrinkled the skin on her pug nose. "Who are you?"

I introduced myself and said we were sorry for scaring her. "I don't suppose you have any idea where your ex-husband might be?" I asked.

"He's dead," Aggie announced flatly. She tilted the beer bottle to her mouth and drained it.

Her announcement startled me, and I gazed at her with a mix of suspicion and doubt.

"And you know this how?" Paula asked skeptically. "You're so doom and gloom, Aggie, always focusing on the negative."

"He'd never willingly leave Kronos to fend for himself," Aggie said. "Never. He loved that little guy."

The slight catch in her voice and the tears starting to her eyes seemed overdone to me. Apparently, Paula thought so, too.

"You're such a drama queen, Ag. No wonder Denny divorced you. No man could put up with that 'woe is me, the sky is falling' mopeyness from his cornflakes clear through to bedtime."

Aggie drew herself up to her full height, maybe five-one, and glared at Paula. "Well, at least I held on to him for six years, Miss Sunlight Shines Outta Your Ass. You barely lasted three. So who around here needs an attitude adjustment, huh? Huh?" She thrust her chin forward pugnaciously.

Before the confrontation could degenerate into a catfight, I asked, "Aggie, do you have any proof Woskowicz is dead?"

After a moment's thought she reluctantly said, "No. But he is."

A *ding-dong* from the front door brought all our heads around. Paula and Aggie jostled each other trying to get to the door, and I followed more slowly. Without even looking to see who was on the stoop, Paula fussed with the dead bolt before realizing it wasn't engaged, and then pulled the door wide while Aggie muttered, "What gives her the right? It's more my house than hers because I just moved out last year. I don't know where she gets off acting like she still lives here. I mean, I'm Wosko's most recent wife. Just because she was married to him when he bought this place doesn't give her any special rights."

I made soothing noises and stopped midstep at the sight of the cop on the doorstep. Tall, rangy, and young, he sported a serious expression.

"Hello!" Paula greeted him with a welcoming smile.

"Oh no, what's happened?" Aggie asked. "Is it Wosko?"

I stayed silent. The young officer looked at each of us in turn, somewhat confused, then said, "We got a report of an interrupted 911 call. Is everything okay here?"

"Absolutely," Paula said, "but thank you for coming by."

"No, it's not," Aggie said, shouldering her way forward. "My husband's dead."

"I'm sorry for your loss, ma'am," the policeman said politely. "When—"

"Ex-husband," Paula put in. "And he's not dead. At least if he is, she has no way of knowing it. Unless . . ." She trained a suddenly suspicious gaze on Aggie. "Maybe you'd better come in," she said to the policeman, her eyes never leaving Aggie.

"Are you implying—" Aggie began.

I took that as my cue to leave, sidling past Woskowicz's former wives and the patrol officer as he stepped reluctantly into the mini foyer. I didn't blame him for looking wary.

"Let me know if either of you hear anything from Wosko-wicz," I said. "You know where to reach me."

Midway through the next morning I stood in front of the camera screens in the security office, watching as the views changed. The system was timed to show ten seconds of footage from each operational camera before automati-cally jumping to the next view. With each screen divided to show views from four cameras at a time, it made for a busy display. I watched as a gaggle of little girls—a birthday party, I'd bet—streamed out of the Make-a-Manatee store, each clutching a new stuffie. Behind them, a woman emerged from Nailed It, flapping her hands to make her manicure dry faster.

"What are you looking at?" Joel asked, peering over my shoulder.

"Let's look at Wednesday's footage and see if we can at least figure out when Captain W left the mall," I said. He'd been missing more than forty-eight hours now, and I was actu-ally feeling a bit concerned. It took Joel a few minutes to find the files and load them on his computer screen; when he had them up, I sat down to watch them, Joel hovering behind me.

Apparently, Woskowicz had spent most of the day holed up in his office, because he didn't show up anywhere until early afternoon when the cameras caught him stalking through the halls to disappear into the cameraless wing. That was probably when he found me canvassing the mer-chants with Celio Arriaga's photo. He reappeared moments later, talking on his cell phone. Setting up a date with one of his ex-wives, I thought wryly. He stopped to buy a coffee at Lola's and chatted with Jay Callahan. Then he returned to the office and didn't appear again until quitting time.

Strangely enough, he turned down the same corridor again. Hm.

"What's he doing?" Joel asked from behind me.

"He was probably parked out there," I said.

"Or maybe he had a lead on the Arriaga murder," Joel offered. "He was following up on it and . . . and . . ." He stumbled to a halt, unable to flesh out his theory.

"And what? The murderer, probably a gangbanger, kidnapped him? And how would he have stumbled over a clue when he spent virtually the whole day in his office?"

Joel exhaled on a noisy sigh. "Okay. Look!" His finger stabbed at the screen, and I watched as Captain W appeared in the main corridor, easily recognizable in his uniform despite the grainy black-and-white images, and strode toward the security office. He seemed to be carrying a shopping bag, but I couldn't make out a logo or even estimate the size since his body hid it from the camera. We lost him when he left the field of view of operational cameras, but caught a glimpse of him near the security office hall. Eight minutes later, a camera showed him turning into the Dillard's wing and heading straight for the anchor store. Switching to a parking lot cam, we watched a black Chevy Tahoe that might have been Woskowicz's drive toward the exit. Halting the images, I sat back, thinking. I finally had to admit I had nothing. Captain W spent the day in his office and then left. He could've been headed to the gym, to the grocery store, anywhere. I pushed back from the desk, frustrated.

"Were you here when Woskowicz came back on Wednesday afternoon?" I asked Joel.

Doubt and apology creased his face. "Probably. But I was on the phone a lot. I don't remember noticing him. Oh. You know what? That was the day I left early to help my brother move into his new apartment, so I wasn't here." He looked slightly happier. "Harold was doing dispatch. Maybe the boss said something to him when he left?"

I realized with a tiny nip of surprise that I was actually

worried about Captain W. The man was annoying, border-line incompetent, sexist, and egotistical, but he must have some redeeming qualities or his three ex-wives wouldn't still care about him. His two-day absence was way out of character, and I couldn't help thinking something had happened to him. "I'm as bad as Aggie," I muttered, standing.

"Who's Aggie?" Joel asked.

I filled him in on last night's encounter at Woskowicz's house. "Were there any signs of a struggle?" Joel pushed a brown curl off his forehead.

"None. The place was neater than I'd expected." An image of the cabinets and drawers hanging open popped into my mind. "You know," I said slowly, "I'm wondering if someone searched the place."

"Really? Cool."

"It was probably one of the ex-wives looking for something," I said. Although Aggie had certainly seemed to know just where everything was . . .

"You should tell the police."

I shook my head, remembering Detective Helland's reaction to my visit yesterday.

"Then we should search his place," Joel said, enthused by the idea, "to see if we can figure out what someone else was looking for. It might help us find out what happened to the boss."

"That would be breaking and entering," I said in a discouraging voice. "Illegal." And I knew someone who was very, very good at it . . .

I didn't even have to go looking for Grandpa Atherton. When I walked into the mall operations office twenty minutes later, summoned by Curtis Quigley, Grandpa stood in the middle of the reception area, one arm around the Easter

Bunny head, the rest of the costume draped over his other arm.

"Wha—?"

Before I could get the question out, Pooja gave me a radiant smile. "Meet our new Easter Bunny, EJ," she said.

Grandpa's spying habits were embarrassing and potentially a threat to my continued employment—witness the recent incident in Nordstrom—so I'd gone out of my way to ensure few of the mall's administrators and merchants knew we were related. I responded as if I'd never met him.

"I hope this one intends to stay sober on the job," I said with a darkling look at Grandpa. What was the man up to?

"Never touch alcohol," he lied.

"Isn't it kind of Mr. Atherton to fill in so the kids won't be disappointed about not meeting the Easter Bunny?"

"Very kind," I said, still suspicious of Grandpa's motives. "How about I show you where the Bunny Station is?" I suggested, taking his arm and steering him toward the door.

"How kind of *you*," he murmured.

After asking Pooja to tell Mr. Quigley I'd be right back, I let the glass door close behind us.

"Okay, Grandpa," I said. "What are you up to?"

"Up to?" he asked, keeping pace with me as I glided on the Segway. "I heard there'd been a contretemps with the Easter Bunny yesterday, and I volunteered to fill in. I'm not even getting paid," he added virtuously. The bunny head threatened to escape from his grasp, and he shifted it to clutch it with both arms in front of him. "And you know I'm a people watcher, Emma-Joy," he said. "What better place to watch all the world go by than from the Easter Bunny's enclosure?"

His seraphic smile didn't fool me for a minute, but it was clear he wasn't going to fill me in on his plans. "Fine," I said. "Just try not to promise the kids they'll all get spy gadgets and decoder rings in their Easter baskets."

He chuckled and held the elevator door for me. "I saw the flyer for the self-defense class," he said. "Monday morning at eight thirty. I'll be there."

Drat. I'd been hoping that if I didn't mention the class again, he'd forget about it. Sheer dumb luck that he'd seen a flyer in Quigley's office. As we descended, I told him about my visit to Woskowicz's house the night before and my suspicion that someone had searched it. I also told him about the camera sabotage and the possibility—likelihood?—that Woskowicz was the saboteur.

Grandpa's blue eyes lit up. "What do you suppose he was into, Emma-Joy?"

"I really have no idea," I admitted. "I'm going to go through the stuff in his office later today, see if I can turn up a calendar or a notebook or anything that might give me an idea."

"And I'll have a look-see at his house," Grandpa said, "as soon as I'm done Easter Bunnying."

I didn't try to talk him out of it; after all, I'd gone looking for him, hoping for just this response. "Be careful," I said.

"EJ! When have I ever not been careful?"

Eight

...

I got my chance to go through Captain Woskowicz's office when Joel went to lunch. I had every right to be in here, I told myself as I entered the office, a ten-by-ten-foot space with a wooden desk, a two-drawer filing cabinet, a swiveling desk chair, and a ladder-back chair for visitors. I was the acting director of security, after all. Curtis Quigley, in our brief meeting, had hinted that he might consider making the appointment permanent if Woskowicz continued to be a no-show. "Of course, we'd have to advertise the position," he'd said, smoothing his striped silk tie, "but you'd be the front-runner."

His words played in my head as I closed the office door behind me and approached the desk. Would accepting the job as Fernglen's director of security mean I'd given up on my dreams of returning to police work? Not necessarily, I decided. It wasn't like I'd have to sign a five-year contract or anything. If—*when*—I landed a real police job, I could give my two weeks' notice, help train my replacement, and move on. In the meantime, being director of security would mean a healthy bump in my paycheck. Finding my train of thought vaguely distasteful—it was as if I were conceding that something had happened to Woskowicz that would preclude his return—I studied the desk. The surface was nearly bare, except for a computer and the usual desk tools: stapler, electric pencil sharpener, digital clock. Woskowicz's stainless steel travel mug sat just off a calendar blotter, the only semipersonal item in sight. I powered up his computer and pulled open the middle desk drawer while I waited for it to boot.

Nothing but pens, pencils, paper clips, and a tube of Bengay. Probably for soothing all those steroid-stretched muscles. The drawer on the right yielded a bottle of Wild Turkey, a girlie magazine—I'd thought they were solely for the titillation of adolescent boys at convenience store magazine racks—and two pairs of socks I hoped were clean. Wishing I'd thought to put on latex gloves, I opened the left-side drawer. A black cassette recorder—practically an antique in these days of MP3 players and iTunes—rested on a pair of odiferous athletic shoes. I pulled it out and a cord dangled from it. Not the kind you plugged into an outlet, but a thin, flexible cord with a suction-cup thingie at one end. It was the sort of item you could get at RadioShack. By attaching it to your phone, you could record phone calls. Hm. Did Woskowicz record all his calls, or was he looking to record specific calls? I thumbed the Eject button and the lid popped up. No tape. I moved the shoes aside and felt around the bottom of the drawer but didn't find any cassettes. Maybe the recorder had been sitting there for fifteen years, unused.

Putting it back in the drawer, I turned my attention to the computer. The standard desktop icons were arranged on the screen's left, but a request for a password left me stymied. I didn't know Woskowicz well enough to hazard an intelligent guess. I typed in his first name, then "Kronos," then

each of his wives' names, and finally "alimony," but had to
admit defeat when the system continued to tell me "incorrect
password." Shutting down the computer, I swiveled the desk
chair to face the file cabinet behind the desk. The top drawer
slid open easily and held files related to security office
operations—work schedules, budget documents, security
directives from the FBI head office. I tugged on the bottom
drawer. Locked. I felt a quick spurt of interest but quickly
suppressed it; in all likelihood, the drawer contained only
personnel evaluations and disciplinary documentation. Nev-
ertheless, I searched for the key, hoping Woskowicz had
hidden it here somewhere. If he had it on his key ring, I was
screwed.

When I lifted the phone to look beneath it, it rang, star-
tling me so badly I dropped it, knocking the electric pencil
sharpener off the desk. The little plastic bin that held the
shavings popped off, spewing graphite particles and enough
wood shavings to give the impression that a termite colony
had moved in. What a mess. I took a deep breath, then
answered the phone. "Fernglen Galleria Security Office.
Officer Ferris. May I help you?"

A woman looking for a pair of prescription glasses she'd
left in a dressing room asked if anyone had turned them in.
Putting her on hold, I walked out front to check our lost-
and-found log. "We have them," I told her. I gave her directions to the security office, told her she'd have to show ID
and sign for the glasses, and hung up on her "Thanks."
Tearing a sheet of paper out of the steno pad on the desk, I
bent to scoop the pencil shavings onto it and funnel them
into the trash can. My fingers brushed something cold, and
I leaned over to blow the pencil dust away from a shiny
metal key. Very sneaky hiding place, I mentally congratu-
lated Captain W.

I picked it up and swiveled the chair to face the filing

cabinet. The key slid home, and I felt a brief moment of triumph as I turned it. The drawer eased out with a well-oiled lurch, and I found myself looking at a shoe box. Not for one minute did I think I'd find a pair of shoes in that box. No one took so much effort to secure a pair of shoes. I lifted the box out with one hand, disturbed by a solid weight that slid to one end when I tilted it. Setting the box on the desk, I used one finger to tip the lid up. Surprise, surprise. I found myself staring at a gun. A length of dark metal with a cross-hatched grip. A Kel-Tec P-32 semiautomatic pistol with a short barrel, frequently recommended for women because of its light weight. I'd considered buying one but decided on something with more stopping power. I didn't dare touch the gun for fear of messing up fingerprint evidence. Why the hell did Woskowicz have a gun in his file cabinet? The scent of gunpowder filtered to me, and I had the uneasy feeling that the gun had been fired not too long ago.

"What are you doing?"

I jumped and looked up, automatically sliding the lid back onto the shoe box. Joel Rooney stood in the doorway, his expression one of curiosity, not condemnation.

"Looking to see if I could find any hint about where Captain W might have gone," I said. "Or why."

"What's in there?" Joel nodded at the shoe box.

I couldn't think of a reason not to tell him. "A gun."

He made a disgusted noise. "So, we're not allowed to have weapons at the mall, but he is? Not fair."

This didn't seem to be the moment to enlighten Joel about life's fairness in general or the relative fairness of policies related to bosses and minions. I didn't share my suspicions with him; I simply returned the gun to the bottom file drawer and relocked it. I needed to think about what to do with it. Should I tell the police? Leave it be? Wait for Captain Woskowicz to return and ask him about it?

"Did you find anything else?" Joel asked as I joined him and we returned to the front office.

"Nothing interesting. No pocket calendar with a notation for a vacation to Daytona that he forgot to mention." Suddenly feeling antsy, I told Joel he could handle dispatch while I patrolled for a while. I might only be the temporary boss, but I wanted to do it right by getting out to talk to the mall merchants and the security officers on duty. And I'd start with cookie king Jay Callahan . . . with whom Captain Woskowicz had chatted mere hours before disappearing.

When I rolled my Segway to a stop by Lola's, Jay was serving a string of customers five deep. I watched him as he worked, appreciating his efficiency, the way he actually listened to his customers, and his bright smile. He caught me watching him and smiled wider, mouthing, "Just one sec." I nodded and loitered until he dispatched the last customer with a two-foot-in-diameter cookie frosted to look like a volleyball with the words "Way to go, Norton Netters" scrolled in blue icing.

"Where'd you learn to do that?" I asked, nodding at the cookie.

"From a book."

I thought he might be serious.

Without asking, he poured me a cup of coffee and proffered it with a flourish. Pouring himself a cup, he joined me at the counter. "This feels like a professional visit, not a social one."

I thanked him and blew on the coffee, wondering how he knew. As if he'd read my mind, he said, "I keep an eye on you, you know."

I didn't know what to read into that, so I stayed silent, slightly flustered by the look that went with the words. "I noticed you chatting with Captain Woskowicz on Wednesday," I said, stirring my coffee even though I hadn't put anything in it.

"You 'noticed'?" The look he gave me told me my casual act wasn't fooling him.

"Okay." I put down the coffee stirrer. "Don't spread this around, but Captain Woskowicz hasn't shown up for work the last couple of days. Some friends he meets regularly haven't seen him. He's not answering his phones. I reviewed the camera footage and *noticed* him stopping by here. So, I'd like to know what you talked about Wednesday afternoon."

Jay whistled softly. "Missing, huh? His vehicle?"

"Gone."

"Police?"

"Uninterested."

Jay nodded. "Couldn't expect them to get excited yet, not without evidence of foul play."

He looked a question at me, and I shook my head. I wasn't ready to tell him I thought someone might have tossed Woskowicz's house. And I certainly wasn't going to bring up the recently fired gun.

"I wish I had something helpful to tell you, but we were just shootin' the shit, you know? March Madness. He's picked Duke to go all the way. I like UCLA."

"Are you from California?" I interrupted.

A smile crept across his face at this evidence of my interest. "I spent some time there as a kid growing up."

"Me, too." I'd done more than spend time there; I'd been raised in a ten-thousand-square-foot house on the beach in Malibu and lived there until I graduated from high school and joined the military. Now my time in California seemed like another life, almost like a book I'd read or a movie I'd watched long ago.

"I know."

I kicked myself mentally; I'd forgotten he'd met my dad, Ethan Jarrett, the actor. "Of course you do. Anyway . . ."

"Anyway, that's about it. He got coffee and put in about fifteen packets of sugar. He ordered two peanut butter cookies to go."

"Two?" That piqued my interest. Could he have been planning to meet someone?

Jay gave me an indulgent look. "Don't go reading too much into that, EJ. Half my customers order two or more cookies for themselves. Not everyone's as into health and fitness as you are."

And as he was, I had noted before. Strong biceps showed beneath the short sleeves of his orange tee shirt, and the way he moved, the way the shirt strained across his chest and back, told me he'd put in some serious hours at the gym and/ or competing in some sport. I halted those thoughts and said, "How did he seem? Happy? Nervous? Upset?"

Jay shrugged. "I don't know him that well. A little agitated, maybe. He spilled a sugar packet on the counter and went after it before I could wipe it up, letting loose with the kind of language you'd hear in a biker bar."

"You spend much time in biker bars?"

"Hardly any now." He grinned. "I put it down to the caffeine and sugar."

"It looked like he was carrying a bag—did you see what was in it or notice what store it was from?"

"Sorry, EJ."

I shrugged it off. "It was a long shot."

"So." Jay looked a little ill at ease. "Do you have a boyfriend? Significant other?"

I tucked my hair behind my ear like I do when I'm nervous. "You mean besides my husband?"

"Husband!" He yelped the word, then looked around sheepishly. "I'm sorry. You don't wear a ri—"

My grin clued him in, and he gave me a mock glare. "You don't have a husband."

I shook my head, pleased to have gotten under his skin. "Nope. You?"

"No husband," he said. He relented when I gave him a look. "Or wife, girlfriend, significant other, or any friends with benefits."

"That's comprehensive," I said, slightly startled.

"Thought you might as well know." A customer with four kids under ten was approaching, and Jay cast them a look as he asked hurriedly. "You?"

"None of the above."

With a satisfied smile, he turned to serve the harried-looking woman, and I got on my Segway, resisting the urge to look back as I glided away.

My next task was to locate Harold Wasserman and see if, by chance, he'd had any meaningful conversation with Captain Woskowicz on the day the latter disappeared. Checking in by radio with Joel, I learned that Harold was down by the movie theaters. The theaters were on the ground floor, between Sears and Macy's, so I rode the elevator, stopping to hold the door for a woman in a wheelchair. We both faced outward on our wheeled vehicles as the elevator descended, watching the activity below us through the elevator's glass walls. I glimpsed Grandpa Atherton, suited up as the Easter Bunny, with a little boy on his lap, and a gaggle of teens wearing the red, green, and white of the Niños Malos just passing the fountain. The dark-haired girl in the middle looked familiar . . .

Mentally urging the elevator to go quicker, I pivoted the Segway and faced the door, ready to charge out the moment it opened. The elevator landed with a gentle thump, and I whizzed through the doors, speeding past startled shoppers as I sought to catch the girl. I was fairly certain she was the one I'd seen with Celio Arriaga. I was conscious of Grandpa Easter Bunny turning his head as I went past, of the lush greenery around the fountain riffling in my wake, and saw that I was closing in on the five teens. One of them stepped into a store and the remaining four—

A toddler wandered into my path, headed for the fountain. I jolted the Segway to a stop, skewing it to the left so it squealed in protest. The child's mother snatched her son out of danger by grabbing him by the back of his overalls and hauling him to her chest. Her eyes were big.

"I'm sorry—" I started. I climbed off the Segway and approached the pair, tucking a strand of hair behind my ear. The teens I'd been hoping to catch up with turned into a side hall.

"You almost ran over Micah!" The mother's voice hovered between anger and panic, and Micah began to bawl, more because he'd been prevented from reaching his destination than out of fear, I thought.

"I'm sorry," I said again, knowing I shouldn't have been going so fast. The Segway's top speed is about twelve miles an hour, and I'd been doing close to that, far too fast for a mall crowded with people on a Saturday.

"Ride!" Micah suddenly demanded, stretching out his arms to me.

I was shaking my head even before the mother turned hopeful eyes to me. "I can't," I said. "Mall policy. Insurance. And I'm on duty." I pulled a coin from my pocket. "Micah, would you like to throw the nickel in the fountain and make a wish?" His grasping little hand closed over the nickel and his tears stopped. He studied me cautiously, blinking wet lashes.

I was congratulating myself on successfully distracting the kid and doing my part for customer relations when the little hellion flung the coin at me.

...

By the time I parted from Micah and his mom, the teens had disappeared. I prowled a couple of corridors, but they were goner than a genie sucked into his lamp. With a sigh, I turned and motored back toward the theaters, hoping Harold was still there. The Fernglen Galleria Cinema occupied a wing plastered with film posters advertising the current films and coming attractions. Glass-fronted ticket booths faced the corridor, with a concession stand visible behind them. The scent of popcorn hit me as I rounded the corner and passed an advertisement for a movie that seemed to feature vampire zombies.

The reason for the heavy popcorn smell was immediately obvious: a white lake of popcorn buried the floor to a depth of an inch or two. The Segway's wheels crunched over some kernels, and I got off, kicking the popcorn out of the way as I walked. It was like scuffing through autumn leaves. I wondered briefly if the theater was engaged in some weird advertising ploy, but then noted Harold talking to a couple of sullen-looking adolescent boys and an angry man in a red vest who clearly worked for the theater. He thrust a broom into one boy's hands and gave the other a large dustpan.

"And if you're done before the next show starts, I won't call the police," the manager said.

He was still giving the boys a talking-to as Harold left and came over to me. "I think we've got it sorted," he said. A smile quivered behind his gray mustache. "In my day, it was cherry bombs down the school toilets. Now—" He gestured toward the popcorn explosion.

"How did they do it?" I asked, envisioning the boys hijacking the movie theater's popcorn machine. Had they parked it in the hall, filled it with Orville Redenbacher, and left the lid open?

"Brought in garbage bags full of the stuff," Harold said. "One of their brothers works here, and they thought it would be funny."

"Used to work here, I'll bet."

We paused by the Segway and Harold asked, "Any word from Captain Woskowicz?"

I shook my head. "No. But I've got a question for you."

"Shoot."

"Were you in the office when the captain left on Wednesday?"

Harold thought for a moment, scratching his nose. "Yeah, I was," he said. Beating me to my next question, he added, "But he didn't say anything like, 'Hold the fort, Wasserman, while I catch some steelhead out in Montana,' or 'See you in a week when I get back from having my appendix out.'"

I laughed but asked, "Did you notice if he was carrying anything? A shopping bag or a shoe box, maybe?"

Harold scrunched his eyes almost closed. "Now that you mention it, I think he did have a bag with him. He left, and I thought he was gone for the day, and then he came back, oh, ten minutes later. He popped into his office and was back within a couple minutes. I figured he'd forgotten something. It seems to me he might have had a bag with him when he came in, but I don't remember seeing it when he left again. But I don't remember *not* seeing it either, if you get me."

I understood. "Let me know if you remember anything else," I said.

"You think the boss is in trouble? Real trouble?" Harold's forehead wrinkled.

"I hope not."

Nine

• • •

I walked back into the security office late that afternoon to see Joel on the phone. "Here she is now, sir," Joel said. He thrust the phone at me, whispering, "Helland."

"Officer Ferris," I said formally.

Without preamble Detective Helland asked, "You said something about a Mrs. Woskowicz when you dropped by here on Thursday. Do you have her name and contact number?" His voice was clipped, all business.

"There are three ex-Mrs. Woskowiczes," I said. "As far as I know, there isn't a current Mrs. W. Why?"

"We need someone to make a formal ID."

The news hit me like a horse kick to the gut. "He's dead?" I felt rather than saw Joel jerk his head toward me. "How?"

"Shot." Helland seemed disinclined to say more.

"Where?"

"Just give me the name and number, EJ," Helland said impatiently.

Subdued, I gave him Paula Woskowicz's name. "I don't

have her phone number," I said, realizing I hadn't gotten a number from any of Captain W's wives and didn't even know Aggie's last name.

"I can find her," Helland said. "Thanks." He hung up without saying more, and I banged the receiver down.

"The boss is dead?" Joel asked in a hushed voice, as if we were standing in a funeral home.

"Apparently," I said. Hearing the anger in my voice, I added, "Sorry. I'm pissed that Helland wouldn't tell me anything."

"Was it, like, a car accident or something?"

"Helland said he was shot. I suppose it could have been an accident." The thought hadn't occurred to me; I'd been focused on suicide or homicide. "Was Woskowicz a hunter?"

Joel shrugged.

"Grandpa!"

Joel gave me a funny look, and I shook my head, reaching for my cell phone. Grandpa was planning to search Woskowicz's house after his bunny shift today. If I didn't warn him, he might walk smack dab into a house full of police officers. I dialed Grandpa's number but got no answer. Of course not. The Easter Bunny couldn't have a cell phone ringing in his pocket while posing for photos. "Back in a minute," I told Joel, hurrying to the Segway.

But when I reached the ground floor, the Easter Bunny's little house was empty and a velvet rope barred entrance to the garden area. Damn. Should I drive over to Woskowicz's house and try to head Grandpa off, or would that complicate matters? If the police were already there . . .

If the police had already arrived, there was nothing I could do, I decided. If Grandpa was in the house when they pulled up, he'd have to hide or slip out without being seen. He'd spent over forty years in the spook business—he was good. If he wasn't in the house, he'd see them and abort.

With any luck, he'd gone home after playing bunny to shower and change, waiting for dark to start his B and E. But then why wasn't he answering his phone? I had a niggling feeling his phone was off because he was in Woskowicz's house. Hoping the police had only just discovered Woskowicz's body and hadn't yet gotten around to searching his house, I pointed the Segway toward the exit where I'd parked my Miata that morning, called Joel to tell him I was clocking out and ask him to retrieve the Segway, and headed into the lot at a brisk trot that annoyed my knee.

I tried Grandpa's phone three more times on my way to Woskowicz's place, drumming my fingers anxiously on the steering wheel every time a red light held me up or an indecisive driver slowed me. His phone automatically rolled to voice mail each time. Rounding the corner onto Woskowicz's block, I took in a deep breath and blew it out in a relieved gust. No police cars blocked Captain W's driveway or idled at the curb. They weren't here yet. I didn't see Grandpa's car either, but that didn't mean much. He could be using a car I didn't know—he had access to a seemingly inexhaustible supply of nondescript vehicles—or he could be parked a block or two away. Good tradecraft dictated that he not signal his presence by parking directly in front of the target house. With that in mind, I cruised past the house and down a few blocks, not spotting any cars I recognized. Leaving my car one street over and two blocks down, I slipped a purple hoodie over my uniform shirt and walked back toward Woskowicz's, hands dug into my pockets.

With dusk falling, few pedestrians were out and about, although a steady trickle of cars heralded the return of commuters. Headlights crept up to me and skimmed me time and again, and I kept my head lowered, my hood up, and my sunglasses on, hoping I looked more like a neighbor out for a little exercise before dinner than the Unabomber on a recce mission. I approached the snug house. No stray beam of light in the windows betrayed a flashlight inside, no hint of movement suggested Grandpa was there. Still, I had to warn him, if I could. Hesitating only a moment, I walked up to the front door and knocked, for all the world like I was an expected guest. Not surprisingly, no one answered. Reluctant to holler his name or make myself suspicious by peering into windows, I knocked again, using a three-short, three-long, three-short pattern, Morse code for SOS. If Grandpa were there, he'd get the message.

I started back down the sidewalk, speeding up as another car turned the corner. It had a familiar profile, identifiable even from several blocks away. A squad car. I quickened my step. Struggling to keep my pace even, so my limp wouldn't be obvious, I resisted the urge to turn and see what was happening. My muscles contracted as I tensed, afraid to hear the sounds that would signal Grandpa Atherton had been discovered: the whoop of a siren, a yell of "Stop! Police!" or the thuds of running footsteps. None of those sounds had reached me by the time I crossed to the street where I'd parked the Miata.

My car gleamed a dull bronze under the light from a streetlamp that had sprung to life while I was gone. I bent to unlock the door. A *skritch* sound made me whip around.

"Boo!"

I jumped back, clanging my elbow against the side mirror. It took a split second to realize that the black-clad figure standing there, a huge grin lighting his face, was Grandpa. The relief and the scare, not to mention the stinging pain from my funny bone, made me mad. Rubbing my elbow, I said, " 'Boo'? What do you think this is? Middle school?"

"Sorry, Emma-Joy," he said sheepishly. "Thanks for warning me. I got clear through a back window just as the police were coming in the front door. A neighbor must have spotted me going in and called them. Damn, I'm losing my touch." He looked chagrined.

"You're not losing it, Grandpa. The police were there because Woskowicz's body turned up. He's dead."

Grandpa let out a nearly soundless whistle. "Where? Who did it?"

I shot him a look. "What makes you think he was murdered?"

He shrugged, bony shoulders hunching under the black sweatshirt. "I've met the man, remember?"

"What . . . he had 'murderee' stamped on his forehead in invisible ink?"

"More or less," Grandpa said, unperturbed by my sarcasm. "I'm sorry I worried you, Emma-Joy."

"Hmph." I refused to admit I'd been worried and had already been rehearsing how I'd tell Mom he'd gotten arrested. The fact that I'd goaded him into it—not that he'd needed much nudging—only made it worse. "What did you fi—never mind. Let's talk back at my house. Want a lift to your car?"

"No thanks. I'll meet you there." With a wave of his gloved hand, Grandpa melted into the darkness.

In my kitchen, clutching a mug of hot tea doctored with a healthy shot of bourbon, Grandpa stroked Fubar, who had deigned to leap onto his lap.

"Stupid cat," I said. "Why won't you ever cuddle with me?" Giving me a look that said he couldn't risk his reputation by getting friendly with just anyone, Fubar sprang down and nosed the catnip-filled mouse that had gotten wedged partially under the refrigerator. Deciding it was not as lively as the real thing, he pushed through the cat door and disappeared, stubby tail held high.

I topped off Grandpa's mug with hot water from the kettle and settled in the chair across from him as he tried to brush off the rust-colored hairs that peppered his black sweat suit.

"So, what did you find?" I asked.

He tented his upper lip and blew on the tea. "What I *didn't* find is more interesting," he said after taking a healthy swallow.

I looked a question at him.

"No computer," he elaborated, "even though there were cables for one and a monitor and printer. No calendar or date book. No address book."

"Maybe it was a laptop and he had it with him," I suggested, "and maybe he keeps his appointments and addresses on the computer."

"Possible, but I don't think so."

"Why not?"

"Woskowicz was what—in his mid to late fifties? Most men in that generation don't keep their lives on computers the way the younger generation does. And I didn't find any of the other gadgets that would suggest he was the kind of technophile who'd be comfortable storing his life on the computer: no iPod, no PDA, no video game setup, no fancy docking station for recharging gizmos, not even a decent stereo system on his television."

"Makes sense," I admitted. "So you think someone tossed the place and made off with his computer?"

"Someone definitely tossed the place, and they weren't very careful about it. Sloppy. So either they didn't care if Woskowicz knew they'd searched his house—"

"Or they knew he wasn't coming back," I finished. Scooping up our now empty mugs, I crossed to the sink and rinsed them, thinking. My mind explored scenarios that might explain why someone would steal Captain W's computer, calendar, and address book. Obviously because they were afraid he'd made note of something incriminating, but what? "Did I tell you I found a gun in Woskowicz's office?" I asked.

Grandpa's eyes narrowed, a deltalike mass of winkles crinkling from the corners. "No."

I gave him the details. He looked thoughtful as I concluded, "No doubt the police will search his office tomorrow, especially if his death was a homicide. They'll find the gun. I'll put the file cabinet key in his desk drawer where they can't miss it."

Grandpa rose with a *cree-ick* from his knees. Leaning over to kiss my cheek, he said, "Be careful, Emma-Joy. Woskowicz always struck me as a wily operator. Not Mensa material, but street-smart. I'll bet you next month's Social Security check he was into something dodgy and it bit him. Let the police figure out what happened. I don't want you getting bit, too."

Ten

• • •

Sunday should have been my day off, but I went to Fernglen anyway, knowing the police investigation into Woskowicz's death would be going full throttle, even on the weekend. My white shirt was crisply ironed, black slacks free of lint and cat hair, and my chestnut hair brushed to a shine and pulled off my face in a French braid. I expected a visit from the police today, probably Detective Helland, and I wanted to look my professional best. At least, that's what I told myself. I was proven right as soon as I arrived at the mall parking lot: Helland pulled up in his car just as I shut the Miata's door.

"I thought you'd be here early," he greeted me, offering a cup of coffee. His white-blond hair shone as the rising sun struck it, creating an almost halolike effect. Fjord gray eyes appraised me when I hesitated before taking the cup.

"Thanks," I said. "To what do I owe this?" I hefted the cup. "No, wait, let me guess. You're here to delve into Captain Woskowicz's movements, and it'll go faster if I can set you up to talk to the people who might have seen him the day he disappeared. Close?" I eyed him sardonically as aromatic steam curled from my cup.

"Bang on," he admitted with a smile that conceded me a point.

Damn, he was attractive when he smiled. "What did the autopsy on Arriaga show?" I asked.

Helland gave me an assessing look that showed he knew I was asking for a little quid pro quo, some information in return for my help. "Nothing we didn't expect. Shot with a .32-caliber bullet, probably between nine p.m. and four a.m., body moved after death."

"That's it?"

Helland shrugged. "He had traces of cocaine in his system, and the GSR test was negative."

If the gunshot residue test was negative, Celio hadn't fired a gun recently. "Thanks." I smiled my appreciation for his information. "You know there won't be anyone here yet, don't you?" I said, leading the way into the mall. "The stores don't open until eleven on Sundays."

"That'll give us time to look at the camera footage before starting our interviews."

I felt an involuntary hiccup of pleasure at his use of "us" and "our." Suppressing it—the man had undoubtedly taken many interrogation classes where instructors taught you how to bond with suspects—I told him I'd already reviewed the camera data. "There's nothing much there," I said. "He spent the bulk of the day in his office and talked to only a couple of people. I've already spoken with them," I added, forestalling the comment on the tip of his tongue. "He didn't say or do anything out of the ordinary."

"Quite a display of initiative," Helland said, looking down his aquiline nose at me. His tone was not appreciative.

I pushed through the office doors and said over my shoulder, "At the time, you were totally uninterested in Woskowicz's disappearance."

A brief head tilt acknowledged my point, and I concentrated on not feeling smug. Edgar rose as we entered, and I introduced the two men. Edgar's softball-mitt-sized hand swallowed Helland's when they shook.

"So," Edgar said, rubbing the top of his head, "Woskowicz, huh? Dead. That's something."

"Indeed. When did you last see him?" Helland asked. "Did he say or do anything unusual?"

Edgar shook his head slowly. "Tuesday night."

"That's the night Arriaga got shot!" I said.

"Was Woskowicz in the habit of coming by at night?" Helland asked.

Edgar snorted. "Not."

"So what did he want?"

"Said he'd forgotten to put together a report Mr. Quigley's office wanted. He had me pulling data off the computer for an hour or so. Put me behind on my patrols." Edgar's tone made it clear he thought keeping to his schedule was more important than helping Woskowicz do paperwork.

"When did he leave?" I asked. Helland frowned at me but let the question stand.

"Tennish? Ten thirty?" Edgar shrugged, shoulder muscles looking like tumbling boulders.

"Maybe he ran into Arriaga on the way out and confronted him about something. Drugs?" I suggested. "Vandalism?"

"You're suggesting your director of security shot a gangbanger in the parking lot and dumped his body on the mall's doorstep?" Helland asked, his tone politely disbelieving.

I'd forgotten he didn't know yet about the gun in Woskowicz's file cabinet. "It's possible," I said lamely.

Helland turned back to Edgar. "So Woskowicz wasn't in the habit of coming by during the night shift? Before Tuesday night, when's the last time he showed up during your shift?"

"A couple months back, at least. He brought a date, and they spent some time in his office." Edgar waggled his brows suggestively.

I tried to block the image of Woskowicz and some redhead going at it on his desk, but my expression must have revealed my distaste because Edgar grinned.

When Helland continued to stare at him, Edgar added, "He wasn't the kind to show up just to shoot the shit with the troops, you know?" Edgar's grin stretched at the idea, displaying a gold canine tooth.

"What type was he?" Helland asked.

Edgar gave it some thought while he gathered his lunch box and crossword puzzle book. "An operator," he said finally. "Yeah, the dude was an operator. Always had something going."

"Really?" I was surprised. I hadn't seen Woskowicz as much of a player. Disgruntled, womanizing, tough-guy wannabe, but not an operator.

Edgar shrugged massive shoulders. "He let me know, subtlelike, that he could hook me up with a bookie, if I wanted, and I'm pretty sure he and Weasel had something going with merchandise that 'fell off a truck.' " He winked. "He offered me a deal on a plasma TV once."

Weasel was the previous night-shift guard, a pal of Woskowicz's, who'd gotten himself killed when he tried to blackmail a murderer. "He never hinted at anything like that with me," I said.

Edgar chuckled, a deep rumble. "EJ, everybody knows you're a straight arrow." Still chuckling, he bumped the glass door open with his shoulder and left. I stood staring after him, hands on my hips.

"That's a good thing," Helland said. He kept a straight face, but the corner of his mouth dented in.

I rounded on him. "It makes me sound like Dudley Do-Right or some kind of Goody Two-shoes," I said.

Wisely electing not to pursue the subject, Helland turned to the bank of camera screens and said, "Where do we start?"

As we sat side by side and fast-forwarded through the hours of jerky camera footage, I asked Helland, "So, how did he die? You haven't asked about suicide notes or his state of mind, so I'm guessing he was murdered."

"Good guess." Keeping his eyes on the monitors, he said, "He was shot in his car. A hiker found the car off a dirt road about ten miles from here as the crow flies. Blood was spattered all over the driver's-side window, so the hiker called it in. It was supposed to look like suicide, but there are too many inconsistencies. We're treating it as a homicide."

"Inconsistencies? Like what?"

Helland shot me a sidelong glance. "Like Woskowicz had a nine mil in his pocket. The .38 that did the deed was on the floor in the passenger-side foot well. Why would a suicide take two guns with him? And the passenger-side door, dash, seat had no prints."

"Wiped clean?"

Helland nodded.

"So he met with someone, or drove out there with someone, and that person killed him." I spoke half to myself, but Helland nodded. "Do you know when he died?"

"Sometime between when he left here Wednesday evening and noon Thursday. Given where he was found, and the fact that he missed his rendezvous with Ms. Wertmuller, I'd bet it was Wednesday night."

"So he's been dead this whole time." It made me sad to think of Woskowicz dead and alone in his car while I visited his house and searched his office. The thought made me say, "I suppose you want access to his office." How was I going to slip the file cabinet key, which I had returned to the pencil sharpener, into a desk drawer with Helland right here? I couldn't, I decided. I had to hope his team was sharp enough to find it.

Helland rose. "There's nothing here," he said with a disgusted gesture toward the monitors.

I resisted the urge to say, "Told you so."

"Where's the of—" He stopped as Joel, Harold Wasserman, and another day-shift officer walked in, chatting. They broke off and stared at Detective Helland, leading me to think they'd been discussing Captain Woskowicz's death. Before I could make introductions, the phone rang and I snatched it up.

"EJ," Pooja said, "Mr. Quigley would like to speak to you."

"The police are here about Captain Woskowicz's murder," I said.

"That's what he would like to talk to you about," Pooja said, her voice telling me I'd better trot over to Quigley's office now.

"Is that why you're working on a Sunday?"

"I had plans with my boyfriend," Pooja complained, tacitly answering my question.

"Officer Rooney can show you Captain Woskowicz's office," I told Helland. Joel puffed his chest out. I left before Helland could reply.

Curtis Quigley was standing by Pooja's desk when I came in. "EJ! Finally." His brown eyes scanned my face. "Is it true?"

"That Captain Woskowicz was shot? Yes. I was just

talking with the police detective in charge of the case." Hint, hint.

"This is awful, just awful," Quigley said, ignoring my implication that my time would be better spent helping the police. He ran a hand nervously over his slicked-back hair. An onyx and silver cuff link caught the light. "An accident, I presume?" Hope lit his thin face.

I shook my head. "The police are treating it as a homicide."

"Gaagh." Quigley made a sound like a choking walrus. "We do not. Need. This." He threw up his hands. "Think of the publicity! First the naked Easter Bunny, now this."

I didn't think the Easter Bunny's antics were on par with a murder, but I didn't say so.

"The FBI board of directors was already unhappy about the gangbanger left on our doorstep, so to speak. What in the world will they say about this?" He paced the length of the room while Pooja and I watched. "Have the police arrested anyone?"

I hated to dash his hopes, but I had to say, "No. As far as I know, they don't have any suspects." Not that Helland would necessarily share the info with me if he did have someone in his sights.

"Well, that is unacceptable," Quigley said, thinning his lips. "Since you are now the acting director of security, it is incumbent upon the police to share the results of their investigation efforts with you. You will, of course, report directly to me so I can determine how best to spin—ah, present—the information to the media and to the board. Pooja"—he wheeled to face his administrative assistant—"you'll need to be on top of the funeral arrangements. Find out when it is and send a suitable flower arrangement from Fernglen. Also, draft an announcement that I can disseminate to the mall employees and a position notice to advertise the job. I don't want to seem disrespectful to Dennis's memory, but we can't operate for long without a director of security. You'll be applying, of course, EJ?"

I made noncommittal noises and escaped back to the security office after promising to keep Quigley posted. I found Helland in Woskowicz's office, about to unlock the file cabinet. I raised my brows, impressed that he'd found the key. A uniformed cop crouched by the desk, disengaging the computer from printer and monitor cables. "Find anything interesting?" I asked nonchalantly.

"We're taking the computer with us," Helland said. "We've got computer forensics types who can break the password and get into Woskowicz's email and Internet history."

"Was there anything interesting on his home computer?" I hoped my tone didn't betray the fact I knew his home computer was missing.

Helland's blue-gray gaze fixed on me. "What makes you think he had a home computer?"

I waved away the question. "Everyone has a home computer or laptop these days," I said. "Amazonian jungle dwellers have PCs. Reindeer herders in Lapland travel with MacBooks."

Helland turned his attention to the file cabinet, and I let my breath out slowly. Slipping the key in the lock, he turned it and slid the top drawer out. He riffled through the folders, then pushed the drawer back in and opened the bottom drawer to reveal the shoe box. I edged further into the office as he withdrew it and placed it on the desk. With one latex-gloved finger, he flipped the lid off, revealing the gun. Only a slight wrinkling of his brow revealed his surprise. "Ever seen this before?" he asked, lifting the gun by its trigger guard so it swung from his index finger.

"We're not authorized to carry weapons," I said, dodging the question.

Helland sniffed at the barrel. "It's been fired recently."
The other officer handed him a plastic bag, and he slipped
it over the gun and sealed it. "We'll run ballistics on it."
Standing, he stripped off the gloves and shoved them in his
pocket. "Who's in charge now that Woskowicz is dead?"

"I am."

"Congratulations. Or maybe condolences would be more
appropriate." One corner of his mouth quirked up. "At any
rate, don't count on moving in for a couple days. I'll conduct
my interviews here; it's as good a place as any."

Moving into Woskowicz's office wasn't at the top of my
priority list, so I didn't mind that Helland was staking a
claim. "It's all yours. Let me know when you're ready to
start, and I'll work the schedule so you can talk with all our
officers. I'll also get the camera data downloaded to a CD
so you can let your team study it."

"That's helpful. Thanks. But don't think that just because
I'm conducting the investigation out of this office that you're
a participant," he added disagreeably, "because you're not.
Homicide is police work. Civilians only endanger themselves and others."

His words started a slow burn inside me, but I'd heard it
before from him, so I didn't react, and I didn't remind him
I'd been with the military police for over ten years before
the explosion that led to my medical retirement. I also didn't
remind him that I'd cracked the case—and boosted his arrest
record, incidentally—when a local developer's body had
shown up in a mall display window. Instead, I asked, "Do
you think there might be a link between Captain Woskowicz's death and Celio Arriaga's?"

"Now, why would you ask that?" Helland asked.

Oh, maybe because the gun he'd just found matched the
caliber used to shoot Celio. Not wanting to admit that I'd
had the opportunity to examine the gun, I said, "Doesn't it

strike you as strange that there would be two murders associated with the mall in less than a week?"

He rose. "Given the number of gangbangers, teenagers, stressed-out soccer moms, and garden-variety nut jobs roaming the halls, I'm surprised there isn't a murder a day in this place."

Detective Helland left, saying he'd be back early that afternoon to conduct his interviews with the security staff, and I drew up a quick schedule that would let each of the guards rotate in to talk with the police, and I called the off-duty staff members to request their presence. That accomplished, I turned to Joel, who had scored a copy of the local newspaper.

"Listen to this, EJ," he said. The newspaper rustled. " 'A local mechanic, Ernest Finkle, discovered the body of a dead man in a car while hiking on the south edge of the Wilderness Battlefield area with his dog yesterday afternoon. The man, whose name is being withheld until next of kin can be notified, was shot in the head, the coroner's office confirms. "Sam Adams had run ahead," Finkle said, referring to his Labrador, "and I knew by the way he was barking that there was something wrong. I wasn't expecting anything like that, though. A man in his SUV with blood and brains all over the window. I hauled Sam Adams away and called the police." The Vernonville Police Department spokesman refused to comment on manner of death . . .' Yada-yada." He lowered the paper. "What do you suppose Woskowicz was doing out there?"

"Meeting someone." I wondered if Mr. Ernest Finkle would tell me exactly where he'd found Woskowicz. It might not be my job to find his murderer, as Helland had so testily pointed out, but it couldn't hurt for me to examine the scene.

And if I happened to find something the police had over-looked, it would be my pleasure to share it with them, in a completely unsmug spirit of cooperation, of course.

"Who?" Joel leaned forward with his forearms on his thighs. "A woman?"

"He had a perfectly good house—he didn't need to make out in his car in the middle of nowhere. That's for teenagers."

"Maybe she was married," Joel said.

I pursed my lips thoughtfully. "Not a bad idea."

Encouraged, Joel expanded his theory. "Her husband suspected she was having an affair and followed her. When he saw her with Woskowicz, he lost it and shot him."

"And the woman—what? Just sat there?"

"She ran into the woods," Joel said, nodding rapidly as his story gained momentum, "and the husband went after her and shot her. Or," he plowed on before I could raise objections, "she and Woskowicz did the nasty and she left in her car. *Then* her husband, who had been lurking nearby, shot Woskowicz."

"Not totally implausible," I admitted, "but it doesn't explain why Woskowicz had a gun on him. Why take a nine mil to a romantic tryst?"

"Woskowicz probably always carried concealed," Joel said, "because he was the kind of guy who liked to pack a weapon. That way, he could break up a bank heist if he happened to be making a withdrawal when one went down, or shoot a robber trying to rip off the Quik Mart when he went in to pick up a six-pack."

Joel's observation was surprisingly astute. Woskowicz was the type to fantasize about playing the hero and then doing the talk-show circuit. More than once I'd heard him applaud the actions of a vigilante who'd made the news for taking the law into his own hands. Still, I wasn't buying Joel's scenario. It didn't account for the gun in the file drawer or for Celio Arriaga's murder. Despite Helland's skepticism, I had a hunch the two deaths were connected.

Eleven

...

When I managed to get hold of him, Ernest Finkle obligingly provided GPS coordinates for where he'd found Woskowicz. "I never hike without my GPS," he said, apparently not even curious about why I wanted the information. "Why, I get turned around in your mall."

I thanked him and went to ask Kyra if she'd like to go for a little hike after her roller derby bout. "What about the cops?" she asked when I explained why I wanted to check out the site.

"What about them?" I asked, my expression daring her to suggest that I didn't have a prayer of discovering something the cops had overlooked, or that the police might object to my inspecting the crime scene. The Wilderness Battlefield Park was open to the public . . . Why shouldn't I stroll along its southern border if I wanted to?

Evidently reading the determination in my face, Kyra didn't press the point. "Sure, I'll go with you. Then you can buy dinner."

I agreed, and three hours later, after the Vernonville Vengeance, Kyra's roller derby team, trounced the Harrisburg Hornets, we stood in a copse of trees beginning to bud, the setting sun ruddying the dried grasses in an adjacent field and the Civil War–era artillery piece pointing at us from the far end. The chill of approaching night nipped at me as I pulled the GPS unit from my pocket, grateful for my leather gloves. Kyra slipped on an ear-warmer headband and fluffed her thick hair around it.

"Just over here," I said, moving forward and to my right.

"Not much to see," Kyra observed as she joined me.

Unhappily, she was right. I could barely make out tire tracks on the verge of what was intended to be a walking trail. A crushed pine sapling released its pungent scent and bore mute witness to the path Woskowicz's SUV had taken. We were only about fifty yards off the road, where I had parked the Miata, but the trees and dense undergrowth of vines, saplings, and ferns effectively blocked the road from view. Keeping an eye out for poison ivy, I shone my powerful flashlight on the ground and followed the tire tracks from where they first broached the trail to a set of deeper impressions where Woskowicz had apparently parked. Kyra quickly lost interest as I played the beam back and forth across the ground, and she wandered to the edge of the copse to stare across the meadow.

"Do you believe in ghosts?" she asked out of the blue.

I snorted. "What? You think Captain Woskowicz's ghost is lurking here, waiting to avenge his murder? I can't imagine the murderer is likely to come back to this spot, so he's in for a long, fruitless haunting."

"Not Woskowicz," Kyra said. "Them." She lifted her chin to point at the field.

"Them?" I joined her in staring at the field, wondering if she'd spotted some tourists draining every last minute from a day of battlefield tramping. March wasn't exactly the height of tourist season, but dedicated Civil War enthusiasts showed up year-round. I saw nothing but lengthening shadows and a fox skirting the tree line as she began her evening's hunt.

"The soldiers."

Kyra's husky voice gave the words unusual weight, and I leaned forward, almost expecting to see men in ragged gray or blue uniforms surging forward or scattering at the whistle of incoming artillery. No whiff of cordite stung the evening air, and no screams echoed. I'd been in a couple of firefights in Afghanistan, and it was my considered opinion that no soldier's ghost would willingly stick around a battlefield, the site of terror and confusion and chaos. I told Kyra as much.

"Who said they were willing?" She asked the question almost under her breath and then, after a moment, turned her back on the field. We resumed our scan of the area, and I picked out what looked like another set of tire tracks on the other side of the trail behind where Woskowicz's SUV had parked. These were set closer together, suggesting a smaller vehicle.

"Someone opened their door here," Kyra said, pointing to waist-high breakage on a holly bush. "But it could've been last October for all we know."

"No," I said, sniffing the branches. "This is new. It still smells sappy, and the twigs show green inside."

"So, someone—man, woman, or alien—arrived in his, her, or its own vehicle and climbed in with Woskowicz for a chat or a make-out session or whatever. They argue, the newcomer pulls out a gun, and pow!" She made a gun out of her index finger and thumb and mimed shooting me in the head.

"I think whoever it was came here planning to kill him,"

I said. "Otherwise, why the gun? It was premeditated. And Woskowicz either trusted the person or wasn't afraid of him, because he had a gun of his own but kept it in his pocket. If he'd really been nervous about the meeting, he'd have had the gun out from the get-go."

"Makes sense." Kyra shivered. "Can we go now? I'm getting hungry. I always work up an appetite roller-skating."

"Sure," I said, sweeping the flashlight in an arc one more time. Nothing leaped out at me. Well, what had I been expecting? A monogrammed flask dropped on the ground and overlooked by the cops? A collection of lipstick-stained cigarette butts? A library book that could be traced back to the borrower? I laughed at myself inwardly and trotted to catch up with Kyra, already halfway back to the Miata.

After we ate dinner and Kyra left, I went to bed, setting my alarm clock for midnight. I planned to return to Fernglen and visit with the night-duty officer for a bit, determined to start off on the right foot as acting director of security. If I got chosen to replace Captain Woskowicz, I wanted all the guards, especially those who worked the night shift, to know I valued what they did. Fubar objected with a startled "Mrrow!" when the alarm went off at midnight and I stifled it with a groan. Curling up in the warm spot I had vacated, Fubar watched through slitted eyes as I dressed in jeans and a sweater. "Tell me I'm being a good boss," I suggested. He closed his eyes.

I parked in the deserted lot and waved at the nearest functioning camera atop a light post. Sunday and Monday were Edgar's nights off; Victoria Dallabetta was working the midshift.

If she was in the office, rather than patrolling, she'd see

me, I hoped, and not be startled when I came in. Using my
key to unlock the mall door, I slid inside and locked it behind
me. Security officers didn't have keys to the individual mall
stores—the tenants hung on to those—but we had keys for
the main doors, garages, and elevators.

My footsteps seemed louder in the semigloom of the mall
at night, a gloom heightened by Quigley's insistence on
using the lowest possible wattage bulbs for night-time illu-
mination. My refrigerator bulb provided more light. The
escalators and fountain were turned off, reducing the am-
bient noise, so the squeak of my athletic shoes on the tile
echoed strangely. I turned into our hall just as Dallabetta
emerged from the ladies' room, and she jumped when she
saw me.

"Jesus Christ! You startled me." A stocky woman ten
years older than me with short, dark hair, Vic had been a
Fernglen security officer for five or six years, and I suspected
she resented my being made acting director over her. The
suspicion deepened when she pushed through the glass
doors into the office, saying, "Come to check up, have you?
Well, I'm here, doing my job. Sorry to disappoint." Plopping
into a chair, she turned her back on me to ostentatiously
study the camera screens.

"Actually," I said, refusing to respond to her snippiness,
"I just wanted to bring you some coffee"—I placed the lidded cup I'd brought from home on the desk at her
elbow—"and cookies." I pulled a baggie containing a half
dozen chocolate chip cookies from my purse. "I know the
midshift can get dreary."

"I'm on a diet," she said.

I took a couple deep breaths, determined not to react to
her hostility, and seated myself beside her. "I know when I
worked mids in the military, I was grateful for anything that
broke up the monotony."

"You want gratitude?" Vic swiveled to face me. "Fine, I'm grateful. Consider my monotony broken." She worked her lips in and out. "You should know that I'm going to apply for the director of security job when they advertise it."

"Great," I said. What else could I say? "I'm going to throw my name in the hat, too."

"Like I didn't know that." She turned back to the monitors, carefully studying a whole lot of nothing. "Quigley might have tapped you to fill in, but the hiring decision will be made by the whole board, and they'll have to pay attention to my qualifications."

I didn't ask what her qualifications were, sure she'd see that as an attempt to disparage her or make an end run around her for the job. I rose. "In the meantime," I said, "I hope you'll feel like you can bring issues to me. I know I'm just in the job temporarily, but I want to do it right for Fernglen and all of us on the security team."

Vic's gaze slid sideways to me. "I can't afford 'issues.' I've got a daughter to support."

"I didn't know you had a daughter. How old is she?"

"Fourteen going on forty-two," she said, her face relaxing almost into a smile for the first time since I'd arrived. "Josie Rae. You got kids?"

"Me?" The question startled me. "I've never even been married."

"Me either." Vic turned back to the monitors, the fragile accord between us broken after mere seconds by my careless tongue.

"Well, good night," I said lamely after an awkward pause. I left the cookies and moved toward the door. When Vic didn't respond, I left.

Maybe I should pass up the director of security job and double my efforts to get on with a police department, I thought, walking slowly through the empty halls. My knee had started to ache. Policing was what I really wanted to do. The pay raise that went with the director of security position wasn't enough to make the personnel headaches worth it. I tried to put the brief interlude out of my head. I was tired and cranky and it was one thirty in the morning—not the best time to be making career decisions. As I neared my car, grateful for the chilly air that blew some of the cobwebs from my head, a movement on my right made me spin.

Jay Callahan approached me, his hands held shoulder high, a grin on his face. "Fancy meeting you here." He wore a black leather jacket and jeans and looked . . . dangerous.

"I should have known," I said sourly. "I suppose there's no point in my asking what you're doing here at this hour."

His grin grew broader. "Someone got up on the wrong side of bed this morning. Or haven't you been to bed yet?"

"I've been and now I'm going back." I opened my door.

"I don't suppose that's an invitation?"

I gave him a look. Not that the idea didn't have some appeal.

"I heard about Captain Woskowicz." His expression sobered. "Two mall-related shooting deaths in a week . . . seems a tad unusual. Makes a good case for gun control."

Something in his voice made me look at him closely. The streetlamp several parking spaces over cast a fitful glow on his face, but I felt, rather than saw, his air of alertness or expectation. "Interested in guns, are you?" I asked.

"Oh, no more than the next guy." He came closer, and I was absurdly conscious of the breadth of his chest under a dark sweater and the thigh muscles outlined by his jeans. He reached a hand toward me, but just then the squeal of tires brought our heads around in time to see a Cadillac Escalade burst out of the garage and tear toward the exit. Moments later, a midsized sedan followed it, catching enough air over the speed bumps to score high points in a snowboarding competition.

"What the—" The incident had happened so fast, I didn't even have time to note how many people were in the vehicles or get license plates—not that I could've read them at this distance and in this light. I slewed toward Jay, who stood with the slight breeze riffling his hair, his posture relaxed after his initial stiffening when the cars barreled out. I narrowed my eyes. "So that's what you were doing here."

"Me? What?" He assumed a look of injured innocence.

I had run into Mr. Jay Callahan in the garage before at strange hours, apparently observing meetings between unknown people who remained in their parked cars. "Gimme." I beckoned with my hand.

"Give you what?" He slid his hand into his pocket.

"Aha! I know you've got the license numbers. I want to ask the police to run them."

"What makes you think—oh, all right." He pulled a small notebook from his pocket and ripped out a page with two license plate numbers, one Virginia and one Florida, on it. "They won't tell you anything."

I felt a warm glow at his implicit acknowledgment that he was more than a businessman trying to make a go of a cookie franchise at the mall. He trusted me enough to let down his guard slightly, although I knew better than to expect him to brief me on exactly what kind of an operation he was involved with. As I reached for the page, his hand caught mine. Startled, I met his eyes. "EJ—" A rueful smile curved his mouth as he hesitated. He seemed to think better of what he was about to say. "I know you won't—"

"I won't tell anyone you like to lurk in the mall parking garage after midnight writing down license plate numbers. It's kind of an American suburban version of train spotting," I said.

He laughed softly and released my hand. I still felt the warm imprint of his fingers. "If you hear anything about guns or weapons, either the ones used in the murders or others, will you let me know?"

"If I can."

"Fair enough." He bent and pressed a swift kiss on my lips. Before I could react, he was striding away.

I got into the Miata, thinking hard, and started for home. Jay Callahan had kissed me. True, it wasn't much of a kiss, and I didn't know why he'd done it, but he'd kissed me. It'd been . . . I couldn't remember how many months it'd been since a man kissed me. Bad sign. I fought the temptation to dwell on the kiss and what it might or might not mean. I had more important things to ponder.

Soon after he took over the Lola's stand in the food court, I'd made Jay as a law-enforcement agent of some kind, or maybe an investigative reporter. He knew too much about police procedure, and he'd run to help me when a pair of clever murderers started shooting at me near the fountain some weeks back. He'd brandished a gun and yelled, "Stop! Police!" He'd told me later that he only said that to scare the shooters, but I hadn't bought it.

I drummed my fingers on the steering wheel. His interest in weapons made me wonder if he might be an Alcohol, Tobacco, and Firearms—ATF—agent. Could someone be running guns and using Fernglen as—what? A delivery point? Or maybe he was FBI working a terrorist sting of some kind and had intelligence about a weapons cache the terrorists were planning to use. A shiver skittered up my back. I'd grown complacent since giving up my uniform and badge, my gun and handcuffs. Being a mall cop was dulling my instincts. Where I used to patrol in a state of high alert, ready for small arms fire or a suicide bomber, now I chatted my way around Fernglen, keeping half an eye out for vandals, pickpockets, or shoplifters. Was it possible that a weapons smuggling ring was operating at Fernglen and I hadn't caught so much as a whiff of it?

Grinding my teeth as I pulled up in front of my house, I locked the car and went in, almost tripping over Fubar, who pounced at my feet and clawed at my laces. With a laugh, I scooped him up and carried him into the bedroom. When I loosed him on the bed, he promptly leaped down and headed back to the kitchen. Moments later the *whisk* of his cat door told me he preferred prowling to sleeping. Maybe I'd do some prowling tomorrow, I thought sleepily, sliding under the covers, and see what kind of prey I could scare up at the mall.

Twelve

. . .

Monday was technically my second day off, but I
arrived at Fernglen only slightly later than usual despite my
midnight visit to the mall. Today was the first meeting of
the self-defense class and I needed to set up for it. Harold
Wasserman was already in the office, holding a mug of what
smelled like peppermint tea.

"Casual-dress day?" he greeted me, eyeing my slim-
fitting red sweatpants and loose tee shirt.

"I'm teaching a self-defense class."

"I saw the flyer. Not a bad idea. Lobbying to be the head
cheese, huh?" He grinned in a friendly way when he said it
and I smiled back, relieved he wasn't as against the idea of
my becoming the director of security as Vic Dallabetta was.

"Are you applying for the job?"

"Not me." He waggled his eyebrows. "I don't need the
headaches. This job suits me just fine—gets me out of the
house, puts a little change in my pocket, and doesn't push
my blood pressure into the stratosphere. I had enough of

that in my first career." He gulped some tea. "I quit smoking again, and the mint in this"—he lifted the mug—"is supposed to help with nicotine cravings."

"Really?" Harold had quit smoking at least ten times since I'd worked here and never made it more than sixty days or so. I knew because we ran a pool each time to guess how long he'd hold out. I hoped he would succeed this time. "Good luck. Anything going on?" I nodded at the monitors.

"Quiet as the grave." He winced. "Speaking of which, we got an email from the mall manager's office saying Captain Woskowicz's memorial service is tomorrow morning at nine. Mr. Quigley encourages 'as many employees as possible' to attend."

I nodded. I would certainly go. I hadn't much liked Captain Woskowicz, but I didn't think that mattered. Paying my respects by attending the service was the right thing to do. Since the service was occurring before the stores opened, I could probably get by with keeping only one guard on duty during that time, so most of the security staff could pay their respects if they wanted to.

"I'll hold the fort," Harold volunteered, as if reading my mind. "I'm getting to the age where I go to too damn many funerals as it is."

Segwaying to the Bean Bonanza, I bought coffee and then glided to the open area fronting the food court where Quigley had said I could hold the self-defense class. The maintenance team had already set out a series of mats the mall used when visiting gymnastics groups or cheerleaders performed for customers. I took off my shoes and poked at one of the mats with a toe. Soft enough for our purposes. It wasn't like we were going to be practicing judo throws. At this hour, the area was virtually deserted, with only a mall walker or two striding past, caught up in conversation with a buddy or deafened by earbuds delivering up-tempo music.

A lone janitor swished a mop at the far end of the food court, and I waved at her.

I glanced at my watch just as Grandpa Atherton and Joel Rooney came around the corner. Even though Joel was younger by almost sixty years, Grandpa looked much fitter and tougher in his black tracksuit, with his shoulders thrown back and eyes automatically noting all the details of his environment. His white hair and wrinkles proclaimed his age, but his bearing told would-be robbers that they might be taking on more than they could handle if they picked on him. Joel, in baggy knee-length shorts, had his hands jammed in the kangaroo pocket of his gray hoodie. With his brown hair tousled, he looked half asleep and would have been an easy target for even a third-rate mugger. Grandpa gave me a vigorous hug, and Joel half lifted a hand in a little wave.

"Nothing like hand-to-hand combat to start the day off on the right foot," Grandpa said. "It's almost as good as sex." Putting a hand to his slim waist, he stretched to the side. Joel's brows had climbed toward his bangs at the word "combat" (or maybe at the idea of an octogenarian starting the day with a quickie), but after a moment's hesitation, he did the same. A couple of women straggled up next, and within five minutes we had a ragtag collection of students dressed in everything from coordinated velour lounging wear (Starla from Starla's Styles) to shorts or sweatpants (most of the women), to jeans and high-heeled pumps (Nina Wertmuller, Captain Woskowicz's first wife). I offered my condolences, even though two wives had succeeded her.

When she saw my gaze light on her impractical shoes, Nina said, "It's not like a rapist is going to wait until I'm wearing workout gear to attack, you know. I dress like this all the time, so I figured it'd be smart to practice in what I'll be wearing if I'm ever attacked."

She had a fair point, but I made her take off the stilettos, not wanting her to break an ankle or gouge holes into the mats. The two young women from Rock Star Accessories trotted up a couple minutes late, balancing Starbucks cups, which they set down at the mat's edge; they made the group an even ten. Grandpa and Joel were the only men. When everyone had removed their shoes and found a spot on the mats, I introduced myself and started with a question. "What is always your best self-defense option, when feasible?"

No one spoke at first, but then I heard a few half-hearted answers: "Kick him in the balls" and "Go for the eyes."

"Nope." I waited until I had everyone's attention. "Run away. If you can get away from an attacker, do so. Fighting is the last resort. Your attackers are almost always going to be men, and they're probably going to be bigger and stronger than you are. And they might be armed. Not good odds. So, if you have a chance to run, take it. It is not wimpy or cowardly to run. It's smart."

Some of the women shifted uneasily, their eyes wide, and Grandpa nodded decisively. Joel looked unconvinced. I talked for another fifteen minutes about how self-defense starts before an attacker ever appears, with simple precautions like not walking in dangerous neighborhoods alone or after dark, checking the backseat of a car before getting into it, and keeping home and car doors locked. A few mall walkers glanced at our group curiously as they passed, but continued with their laps.

"Well, duh," Nina Wertmuller said when I paused. "I mean, every woman with a scrap of survival instinct does those things."

The self-conscious and embarrassed expressions several of the students exchanged seemed to argue against that, as did the stats about women as victims of violence, but I didn't dispute her. I raised my brows, inviting her to go on.

"When are you going to show us something *real*? Like how to put down an attacker." She folded her arms under her plump breasts. Her abrasive attitude was wearing, and I caught myself thinking I couldn't totally blame Captain Woskowicz for preferring Paula.

"Right now," I said. "Joel, will you help me?"

Apprehension flitted across his features, but he came forward gamely to stand in front of me. "Grab my wrist," I said.

With a sheepish smile, he reached out and encircled my wrist loosely with his big hand. With a simple roll of my wrist, I broke free. "No, grab it like you mean it."

This time, he braced himself and clamped down on my wrist.

"Better," I said as I launched a side kick at his knee, grasped my captive hand with my free hand and wrenched it free, and sent that elbow thudding into his solar plexus. Despite my only putting about 50 percent power into the moves, he staggered back and clutched at his abdomen. "Now what do I do?" I asked the class.

"Run," they chorused.

"Exactly." I smiled with satisfaction. "You okay, Joel?"

"Sure," he grunted. "You surprised me, that's all."

"You're a good sport." The women clapped for him, and he stood straighter, a pleased smile creasing his face. "Now, if I, with a bum knee, can do that to an attacker who's several inches taller and fifty pounds heavier than I am"—it was probably more like eighty pounds, but I didn't want to make Joel feel bad—"you can do it to almost anyone you come up against. Pair up."

With Grandpa coaching Joel, plus Nina and her partner, and me working with the other women, we spent half an hour practicing side kicks, throwing elbows into knees or abdomens, and breaking wrist holds. Everyone was sweating and panting slightly when we finished.

"This was great!" the Rock Star manager announced enthusiastically when we quit for the day. "Again on Thursday, right?"

"You bet. We'll learn palm-heel strikes."

With a smattering of applause that made me feel surprisingly good, the women scattered, leaving me alone with Grandpa and Joel. "You've got potential, Rooney," Grandpa told Joel. "Good balance."

Joel puffed up with pleasure and said, "I'd be happy to be a tenth as good as you are, sir."

They beamed at each other, a mini mutual admiration society, and I rolled my eyes in pretend exasperation.

Despite the fact that I could have gone home after the class since it was my day off, I returned to the office. It had struck me when I awoke that if Captain Woskowicz had deliberately disabled the cameras to the Pete's Sporting Goods wing, he did it because something nefarious or underhanded was going on there. If I reviewed earlier images of that wing, and looked for Captain W, maybe I'd spot a pattern or see something else that might provide a clue.

The task was mind-numbing. We stored camera data back two weeks, and even though I could fast-forward through a lot of it, I had to go slow enough to spot Captain Woskowicz's distinctive—luckily—figure. I isolated the data from the Pete's wing initially and spotted Captain W in that hall six times in the week before the cameras went belly-up. Of course, he might have been down there more often and not gotten caught on camera. He visited the sporting goods store and the Make-a-Manatee operation three times each, the

nail salon and the sunglasses place once, Rock Star twice,
Jen's Toy Store and the Herpes Hut not at all, and Starla's
Styles six times. I made notes of the dates and times and
circled Starla's Styles.

His presence in the wing could easily be explained as
routine patrols, but he hadn't so much as glanced down some
of the other minor wings, as far as I could tell from studying
the camera data, and he'd never gone out of his way to get
to know all the merchants. What could he want from a
ladies' boutique like Starla's Styles? Was he buying gifts for
all the women in his life? Only one way to find out. Waving
to Harold and another security officer who was chatting with
him, I strolled off through light Monday crowds to Starla's
Styles. Since I wasn't technically working, and didn't have
on my uniform—I was still wearing the sweats and tee shirt
I'd taught in—I left the Segway behind.

I'd been in Starla's several times before, of course, to chat
with Starla and her clerks and, once, to escort out a verbally
abusive woman determined to get Starla to accept the return
of an outfit she'd clearly worn several times. The store featured a sound track by Tony Bennett, soft lighting to flatter
mature skin, and clothes designed to appeal to women of a
certain age and girth. Lots of knits, polyester, and "forgiv-
ing" silhouettes. Let's just say this was not a store a teenager
would be caught dead in. Belts and accessories, including
rings with faux gems as large as drawer pulls, occupied
revolving racks in the center of the maroon-carpeted space.
Three dressing rooms, fitted with solid doors with silver
stars glued to the front, ran across the back of the small
space. A bell dinged as I crossed the threshold, and Starla
bustled out from behind a curtained doorway that guarded
a stockroom or office area.

A plump fifty-year-old, she wore her own stock: dark

blue velour pants and a matching top that brought out the hints of auburn in her overstyled hair. It looked like the same outfit she'd worn to the self-defense class, but she'd clearly applied makeup since then. Her false-eyelash-fringed eyes grew round at the sight of me. "Officer Ferris. There's nothing wrong, is there?" She peered around me as if looking for a handcuffed shoplifter or mall maintenance person who was going to break the news about a cockroach infestation or major plumbing snafu.

"No, no," I reassured her. "Just making the rounds."

"Oh." She sighed. "This morning's class was wonderful. I feel so much safer now."

"Just don't get overconfident," I warned. "How's it going? Business good?"

"Oh, you know, the economy," she said vaguely, looking around at the customerless space. "I'm keeping my head above water. Barely."

"I suppose you heard—"

"About Captain Woskowicz?" She sighed again and tugged at one of the six or seven rings decorating her fingers, sliding it on and off. "Yes. So sad. I'll be going to the memorial service tomorrow. Janice can open the store for me if it runs long."

"I'm helping the police with the investigation"—whether they wanted me to or not—"and I noticed that Captain Woskowicz stopped by here a few times recently."

Her expression froze, her gaze fixed on me. The ring fell to the carpet.

"Can you tell me what he talked about?" I asked. "Was there something on his mind, some issue that he was helping you with? Anything?"

She bent to retrieve the ring. When she straightened, her face was flushed. "Oh! Well, nothing really. He stopped by on occasion—kind of like you do—to make sure things were okay. I've told Mr. Quigley time and again how much I appreciate the security staff at Fernglen." Her words tumbled together, and she seemed unaccountably flustered. "You do such a good job, and you're so *attentive*."

I wrinkled my brow, taken aback by her nervousness. "Thank you," I said. "We try to keep the mall safe for the merchants and the shoppers."

"Oh, you *do*," she said, moving past me to fuss with the chenille sweater and spangly scarf on a mannequin, making it impossible for me to read her face.

"And Captain Woskowicz?"

"He did, too," she assured me. "He made me feel so safe. Was there anything else? I'm expecting a delivery." She faced me, blinking rapidly, and began edging backwards.

"I guess not," I said.

"Well, I'll see you at the memorial service tomorrow, then," she said. "Toodles!"

With no other option, I left the store, glancing over my shoulder when I reached the hall. Starla's face peered at me from behind the curtained doorway but jerked out of sight when she saw me looking.

What in the world was making the woman act so goosey? I didn't know her well, so maybe her scattered persona was normal. Still . . . she seemed awfully nervous. I tried to imagine what criminal enterprise Starla could be operating from the boutique that benefited from having the security cameras disabled. Could she have bribed Captain W to sabotage them? Or had he done it of his own accord for some reason? Maybe she was selling drugs to her zaftig and middle-aged clientele. Prozac and OxyContin? Not impossible. Maybe she smuggled in outlawed ivory or accessories made from the skins and pelts of endangered animals. Blood diamonds disguised as tasteless cocktails rings! I chuckled at the outrageous idea—I couldn't see Starla negotiating with smugglers—and gave up trying to puzzle it out for the moment.

I wandered to the Make-a-Manatee store where I could see Mike Wachtel straightening stuffed animals in the window display. I waved and he beckoned me in. Walking into Make-a-Manatee made me wish I had kids or nieces and nephews to buy stuffed animals for. Although the store specialized in marine mammals, with a large display of seals, dolphins, walruses, and, of course, manatees at the front of the store, they also had lobsters, starfish, sharks, and other ocean dwellers in fantastical colors. Bins of the unstuffed creatures sat waiting for a child to make a choice and bring the animal to "life" with stuffing, a red plastic heart on which they could write "I love Teddy" or some such, and even a voice box that produced generic squealing noises that could be interpreted as whale song or seal barks. A pink whale large enough to swallow a five-year-old hung suspended over the doorway. The stuffing machine made a hissing noise as it circulated fluff in the large glass enclosure.

"EJ." Mike came over to greet me, shaking my hand. His gait was awkward with the cast dragging down his left leg. "Thanks for stopping by. What a week, huh?"

"You can say that again."

"At least the security cameras are working again. But, good God! I was shocked to hear that Dennis had been killed. What are the police doing? Have they made an arrest?"

It was strange to hear Woskowicz referred to as Dennis. "Did you know him well?" I asked. "I notice he stopped by here several times in the last couple weeks."

"I wouldn't say 'well,'" Mike said, scratching his chin. "We chatted occasionally . . . you know how it is. He bought a shark for his nephew—or maybe his godson?—oh, a couple years back, and we got to talking. We both did a little home brewing—beer, you know—so we talked about that. We went pub crawling once or twice, but I've got a wife and family, and Dennis, well . . ."

He trailed off with a sheepish smile. I got the impression Woskowicz's endless quest for dates had made Mike uncomfortable.

"He had a thing for redheads," Mike said, confirming my hunch.

I was silent for a moment, pondering the image of Woskowicz as a man with a family (besides ex-wives) and hobbies. I couldn't remember hearing him talk about anything besides guns, sports, and women. A part of me felt guilty, like I should have made more of an effort to get to know him. The practical side of me pointed out that he was my boss and he certainly hadn't encouraged a friendship; in fact, he went out of his way to insult me and disparage my military experience.

In the quiet, the sound of voices filtered to me from behind a panel at the rear of the store. "Is there someone—?" I nodded toward the back.

Mike laughed. "That's my TV. I like to keep a game on for when it's slow like this."

"NCAA?" Kyra had gone to Duke and would be despondent if they didn't make the Final Four.

"Basketball, baseball, World Cup—I'm a sports junkie."

I changed the subject, not wanting to get caught up in a discussion of favorite sports teams. "Did it seem to you that Captain Woskowicz was hanging out in this wing more than usual?" I asked.

Mike pulled his head back slightly. "That's a strange question," he said slowly.

I explained about reviewing the camera data.

"He might've been here a bit more than usual," Mike

conceded. "Maybe because the cameras were out? He could've felt like he needed to be here to keep an eye on things. He didn't mention it to me, though." Stooping, Mike pulled a bottle of window cleaner from a low cabinet and moved past me to spritz the glass door, rubbing at little fingerprints. "So, what are the police thinking? Was it a robbery with Dennis just in the wrong place at the wrong time? I heard it happened at the battlefield park. Strange. Dennis never mentioned being a Civil War buff." He straightened to watch for my reaction.

"I don't know if the police have a theory yet," I said. "They might be around to talk to you and the other merchants."

"Well, I don't know what I can tell them," he said, turning back to the door. *Squee, squee* went the cloth. "Other than it's a damn shame."

I left Mike still cleaning his windows and headed toward Pete's Sporting Goods, the other store Woskowicz had visited frequently. Before I reached it, though, my cell phone rang and the security office's number popped up. When I answered, Harold's voice said, "EJ, you won't believe who . . . it's . . . you need to get back here right away."

Puzzled by Harold's stammering, I turned and walked at a brisk pace back to the security office, wishing I had the Segway when my knee started aching. I paused outside the doors. Standing with their backs to the glass doors were a man and a woman. I suddenly understood Harold's confusion.

Entering the office, I greeted my mother with pleasure and Ethan with resignation. "EJ!" He swept me into a bear hug.

...

I introduced my parents to Harold.

"Ethan Jarrett is your father?" Harold asked, eyes wide.

Mom, highlighted blond hair pulled into a low ponytail, and dressed in jeans and a cashmere sweater, could have passed for any well-off suburban housewife on her way to lunch at the country club or a board meeting at her kids' charter school. Dad was permanently in actor mode when he left the house (and sometimes even at home), and he radiated a charisma that drew all eyes to his pressed jeans, painfully expensive navy blazer and ostrich boots, and designer sunglasses. He was in his fifties but looked fifteen years younger, thanks to the magic of Hollywood plastic surgeons and his weekly spray tans. He flashed his famous smile at Harold.

"Nice to meet you, Mr. Wasserman. I don't know why it's always a surprise to EJ's friends when they meet us. It's like she never mentions us or something." He shot me a roguish look.

Of course I didn't mention him. All my life, until I joined the military, I'd been "Ethan Jarrett's daughter," befriended by people hoping they could meet my dad or hoping I'd be openhanded with his millions. Now that I finally had a sense of myself and who I wanted to be, I didn't muddy the waters by talking about my famous father. At all. Kyra knew, because we'd met when we were eleven and Mom, Dad, Clint, and I had come east one summer to visit Grandpa Atherton. She'd visited us in Malibu on numerous occasions throughout our teen years and was one of the few people I knew who seemed genuinely impervious to our lifestyle. Jay Callahan knew because he'd bumped into me and Ethan—Dad had insisted Clint and I call him Ethan from the time we were thirteen—and assumed we were romantically involved. I had quickly enlightened him. Other than that, I tried to keep it quiet. Which was going to be damned difficult if Ethan insisted on popping into the mall now that they were temporarily living in Alexandria while he filmed his new action-thriller.

Mom gave me a sympathetic smile. "We were hoping you'd have time for lunch with us, dear," she said, shooting Ethan the "tone it down" look.

"So you can fill us in on the murder. Why do I have to read about your boss being killed in the paper? You never tell us anything," Ethan complained. "I think it's time you joined me in my production compa—"

"Sure, let's lunch," I said, herding them out of the office as Harold watched with a bemused expression.

"My grandsons love the old *Roll Call* reruns," he called after us.

I let my folks drive me home to change before rejoining them in the limo for the half-hour ride to a discreet restaurant in an eighteenth-century inn where no prices appeared on the menus. If you had to ask, you couldn't afford it. The staff were sufficiently accustomed to the rich and famous not to hover over Ethan. Mom and I talked about Clint's latest story—he was an investigative journalist currently writing about politics in Venezuela—until Ethan turned the conversation back to Captain Woskowicz's murder.

"I don't like it, EJ," he said, gesturing with a forkful of quail. "Murder is nothing to mess around with."

"You have more dead bodies in a two-minute scene in one of your movies than a big-city cop sees in a twenty-year career," I pointed out.

He frowned at me with the piercing blue eyes that stared out from many a movie poster. His forehead didn't wrinkle, and I wondered if he'd discovered Botox. "For God's sake, EJ, that's the movies. It's not real."

I was relieved to hear him say that because I sometimes wondered if he knew the difference. "True," I murmured, taking a swallow of the lovely Riesling he'd ordered. Wine during the day felt decadent. "Did I tell you I'm applying for the director of security job?"

My mother looked slightly troubled, but before she could comment, Ethan said, "Do you suppose someone is targeting security guards at Fernglen? If it were one of my scripts, it'd be a former employee with a grudge, or maybe an escaped mental—"

"No one's targeting security guards," I said, exasperated. "The police are focused on Captain Woskowicz's private life." It was standard procedure to suspect a victim's nearest and dearest, so I was sure I wasn't way off in fib land with that statement.

"Even so—"

"Did I tell you Grandpa is the Easter Bunny?" I asked, desperate to distract him from my work life.

Mom sputtered wine over her salad. Grandpa Atherton was her dad. "He's what?"

I explained. Mom shook her head dubiously. "It sounds harmless enough." Doubt born of fifty-plus years' experience sounded in her voice.

"His activities always do," Ethan pointed out, "until something blows up or he lands in the ER with a couple broken bones or the police pick him up."

"Dad hasn't been arrested in at least two years," Mom said with the air of someone trying to be fair.

"Then he's about due."

While Ethan gave the server explicit directions for preparing his after-meal espresso, I rose to visit the ladies' room, and Mom surprised me by rising, too, saying, "Excuse us, Ethan."

The restroom evoked a previous century with gilt-edged mirrors and paintings, two spindly legged chairs upholstered in a cream and gold striped damask, a small chandelier dangling crystals just above our heads, and sconces with bulbs made to look like candles. As Mom and I washed our hands, her gaze met mine in the mirror. "How much thought have you given this director of security job, EJ?" Worry put a slight pucker between her brows.

"It's only until I land a real police job."

Holding her hands under the automatic dryer, Mom spoke louder to be heard over its roar. "If you get too comfortable at Fernglen, you won't want to leave. Every day that goes by makes it harder to break free of the comfortable routine, the rut."

"Trust me: I'd walk away from Fernglen tomorrow if a police department called. So far, they haven't." I tried to keep the bitterness out of my voice, but I knew Mom heard it. "I've only been there a bit over a year; I don't think it's quite fair to say I'm in a rut."

"A rut," Mom insisted. She carefully reapplied the rose-colored Chanel lipstick she'd been using as long as I'd known her. Smooching her lips into a tissue, she said, "You need to challenge yourself, EJ, go out on a limb, get your mojo back, as Clint would say."

I stared at her. "There's nothing wrong with my mojo! In case you forget, I'm the one who broke out of the daughter-of-Hollywood-superstar rut and joined the military. I had enough 'mojo' to go head-to-head with the Taliban, to lead—"

"That was before," Mom said, her voice quiet and as steady as the heater's hum from the vent above us.

Before. Before the IED. Before my injuries. Before the cataclysmic event that divided my life into before and after. I swallowed. Blood thrummed in my ears and I felt a little dizzy. "What are you saying? That I'm a coward?"

"No, oh no, honey. Both you and Clint have always had more courage than I thought was good for you. Certainly more than was good for me, being your mother." Tears glinted in her eyes, but she gave a husky laugh. "And you're still the most courageous woman I know. I'm just afraid that it's taking you too long to give up on an unrealistic dream and find another dream. I'm afraid you're going to *settle* for a job, an environment, a life that is so much less than you deserve and are capable of."

"You're saying I'll never be a cop again."

After a brief hesitation, she nodded. "That's what I'm saying."

"You and Dad didn't raise me to give up." It came out like an accusation.

"No, we didn't. 'Giving up' was the wrong phrase. I should have said 'reevaluating your options' or 'coming to terms with new realities.'"

"Being a cop is my reality. It's who I am."

"No."

Anger infused the word, made it brittle enough to shatter into a thousand tinkling, crystalline pieces on the marble floor.

"You are not your job," Mom said, gaining control again. "What you do is *part* of you; it doesn't define you. When you limit yourself so needlessly, it makes me . . . makes me want to spank you."

Her words startled a reluctant grin from me. "You never spanked me."

"Well, I should have," she said tartly.

"So I should—what? Take Dad up on his offer to make me a VP in his production company? No thanks."

"Have you ever thought about owning your own business?"

"Selling cookies?" It was the first thing that popped into my head.

She looked at me strangely. "You're not the cookie type."

Neither was Jay Callahan, I thought but didn't say.

"What about a security business? Your father and I could bankroll you, help you get started."

I'd never thought about going into business for myself. I didn't know exactly what all a security firm did, but it sounded intriguing. "I'll think about it," I said, feeling emotionally bruised and too confused to think clearly.

"Wonderful, dear." With a final pat to her immaculate blond hair, Mom glided to the door with the air of a tycoon successfully concluding a multibillion-dollar deal or a magician pulling off a new and dangerous illusion.

With a rueful smile, feeling half-grateful and half-resentful, I followed her.

Thirteen

...

After the heavy meal and heavy conversation, I felt logy and unmotivated when my folks dropped me off. I wanted a nap but knew some exercise would be much better for me. Grabbing my swim bag before I could cave in to the bed's siren call, I drove to the YMCA. I was a little later than usual, and there were more people in the pool than I was comfortable with when I walked onto the deck from the locker room with a towel tied around my waist. Moist air heavily scented with chlorine steamed the natatorium's windows. Steeling myself, I dropped the towel and immediately slid into the water, looking around surreptitiously to see if anyone had noticed my leg.

"Hey, EJ!"

I turned, startled, to see Joel Rooney approaching, a broad smile on his chubby face, a roll of fat hanging over the waistband of his Hawaiian-print swim trunks. His bare feet slapped the damp tile, and he plopped into the lane beside me, displacing a wave that earned a glare from a lap swimmer breaststroking past us. I was glad to see him. Somehow, working out with Joel, coaching him as he swam, kept me from being quite so self-conscious about my leg. Maybe, I thought with a little thump of realization, because I was focused on *him* and not *me*. Hm. Something to think about . . . later, like maybe when the time for New Year's resolutions came around.

"I didn't think I'd see you," Joel said.

"Good for you, coming to work out on your own," I told him.

He beamed. "Sunny and I are going to a movie this weekend."

"You asked her out? Way to go! I told you a few pounds wouldn't matter to someone who liked you."

"She asked me."

He seemed a little sheepish, so I said, "That's even better. Ready?"

We swam for nearly forty minutes. Joel's stamina was improving, and he was able to do two whole laps now before stopping for a breather. I felt tremendously better by the time I'd showered and changed and left the Y. So much better, in fact, that I swung by the grocery store and then drove to Grandpa Atherton's, planning to make him dinner. "Surprise," I said when he opened the glossy blue door to his townhome.

"Why, Emma-Joy," he said, kissing my cheek, "that's very thoughtful of you. But I was just about to go bowling. Why don't you come with me?"

"Bowling?" I stared at him. Instead of his usual crisp shirt and slacks he wore dark gray sweatpants and a striped rugby shirt whose shoulder seams fell two inches below his bony shoulders. His white hair was slightly mussed and he patted it down with one hand. "You don't bowl."

He brushed away my observation. "Of course I do.

Everybody bowls. In fact, your grandma and I used to belong to a league. Come on." He shoved my grocery bags into the fridge, herded me out the door, locked it, and headed for a gold Cadillac parked at the curb.

"Whose is this?"

His blue eyes twinkled. "A friend's."

"You're making a drop, or whatever you call it, at the bowling alley, aren't you?" I said, comprehension dawning.

"Nonsense," he said, opening the door so I could slide into the luxurious leather interior. "I might be meeting someone for a brief exchange of information—simple, fast, discreet. You won't even notice." He thunked the door closed and got in on the driver's side, shooting me a grin.

When we walked into the bowling alley, to the sound of clattering pins, a short-order cook yelling about fries, and the *ping* of pinball machines, I said, "I can't bowl." I patted my leg.

Grandpa said, "Those jeans'll work fine, Emma-Joy. We'll rent some shoes."

He was being deliberately obtuse and I glowered at him. "Not my clothes—my knee."

Proceeding to the counter and asking for size-ten shoes, Grandpa said, "Last time you bowled—what was your score?"

I gave him a puzzled look. "It was years ago. Ninety-five or a hundred and three, maybe."

"So," he said triumphantly, "you've always been a lousy bowler. Your knee's not going to make a difference. What size?"

We had a surprisingly good time, and even though I didn't see him meet Jason Bourne or the spy who came in from the cold or whoever, I knew when he'd done it because the slight tension I'd felt from him all evening disappeared. "Everything go okay?" I asked when he returned from the bathroom.

His smile acknowledged my instincts. "You can rest easy tonight knowing that the fate of the free world is in good hands."

I snorted and picked up my bowling ball. My approach was lousy and I lofted the ball so it slammed into the lane, but I knocked over nine pins, so I was happy. "Tomorrow's the memorial service," I told Grandpa when I returned to my chair. He'd been eating French fries and wiped his hands on a napkin before rising to get his ball.

"Want me to come with you?" he asked over his shoulder, crouching for his approach.

By virtue of his earlier career, Grandpa was an acute observer. "Sure," I said, thinking he might spot someone whose behavior was a little off. "I'll pick you up at eight thirty."

Moving with surprising fluidity for an octogenarian, he stalked forward and released the ball with a funny upward flourish of his hand. "Strike!" he announced, pumping his fist.

I rolled my eyes.

Captain Woskowicz's memorial service was being held, strangely enough, on a tennis court in a downtown park in Vernonville. Metal chairs had been set up on the court, the net had been removed, and a folding table laden with candles, flowers, and photos of Woskowicz was at one end. A sparse crowd sat in the chairs, huddled into their coats against the fifty-degree chill, which was magnified, I discovered, by the cold metal of the chairs. Several people cast uneasy glances at the overcast sky.

"Why this place?" I asked the woman seated beside me when Grandpa and I settled two-thirds of the way back. "Was it special to Captain Woskowicz?" Maybe he was a huge tennis buff and I hadn't known it.

She sighed heavily. "Nina's Catholic, Paula's Baptist, and Aggie's Buddhist—this was the only site they could agree on. As far as I know, Dennis wasn't anything."

A sad epitaph, I thought as the memorial commenced with each of the ex-wives going forward to the makeshift—altar?—to lay flowers in front of Woskowicz's photos. The rest of the service was a strange amalgam of traditions with prayers, candle lighting, incense burning, and eulogies in which the three redheads shared their special memories of "Beaner," "Wosko," and "Denny."

"When I go, Emma-Joy," Grandpa whispered to me, "just set my body adrift on a burning boat. Nobody gets to say anything."

I choked on a laugh and hunched my shoulders against glares from the couple in front of us. As it started to drizzle, I looked around, spotting Curtis Quigley seated behind the ex-wives near the front, and several other mall denizens: Starla, Mike Wachtel, Kyra, Dusty Margolin from Nordstrom, and most of the security office staff. A glance over my shoulder showed me Detective Anders Helland and another officer standing in the back, studying the attendees. Helland gave a tiny nod when he caught me staring at him, and I turned around, flushing.

The service ended with a bang—literally—when Aggie tried to plug in a boom box to play John Denver's "Rocky Mountain High" and the rain shorted it out. Jumping back from the electric fizzle, she smoothed her damp skirt and began to sing the song herself in a thin soprano. She gestured for everyone to join in, and several people did, sending the phrase "Rocky Mountain hi-igh, Colorado" quavering over the park. Grandpa Atherton enthusiastically contributed his strong baritone to the mix until I elbowed him. Somehow, I couldn't see Captain Woskowicz as a John Denver lover and suspected he would have made gagging noises or booted the boom box to the other side of the park if he'd been there.

People edged awkwardly away from the tennis court, clearly uncertain about which of the three ex-wives, if any, deserved a widow's condolences, and broke for their cars when the rain began to pound down in earnest. I had beeped open the Miata's doors when Paula Woskowicz caught up with me, rain darkening her coppery hair and anxiety darkening her expression.

"Miss Ferris," she said, casting a curious look at Grandpa where he sat, warm and dry, in the passenger seat. "Could I come by your office later to talk to you? It's important."

"Sure," I said, curious but anxious to get out of the rain. "Any time. I'll be there until four or so."

I hopped into the car and shook my head like a dog, spraying droplets of water onto the windshield and Grandpa.

"Emma-Joy!"

"Sorry," I said, putting the car in gear. I had almost reached the parking lot entrance when a figure appeared in front of me. I hit the brakes hard. Aggie—I realized I still didn't know her last name—stood there, wet as a chunky mermaid, hand extended in a "stop" signal. When I rolled down the window with an exasperated, "What now?" she scurried over and hunched down to stare in at me. Raindrops glinted on her stubby lashes, and she flinched as a rivulet squiggled between the breasts displayed by the deep and unfuneral V of her blouse.

"I called the mall and they said you're head of security now that Wosko's gone. Is that right?"

"For the moment," I said, wondering why she cared. "They'll advertise for a permanent—"

"And you're using his office?"

The words "Not really" hovered on my tongue, but she didn't pause. "He might have left something there. Something important. Something I need. I'll come by this afternoon to look for it."

Before I could ask what the item was or why she thought it was in his office—could she know about the gun?—she darted away, splashing up gouts of water from the puddles already forming in the pothole-pocked lot.

"That man married some strange women," Grandpa observed, watching Aggie climb into a pickup truck, skirt rucking up to show a muscled calf.

"Indeed."

My hair had dried, a hint of curl drawing it up along my jawline, and I was conferring with one of the officers about vacation schedules when Paula Woskowicz entered the office shortly after two.

"School out already?" I asked, smiling at her.

She shook her head. "I got a sub today. I couldn't face the kids, not after Denny's service."

I couldn't face a roomful of eighth-graders on my best day, so I didn't blame her.

"Look, can we talk privately?" she asked, her eyes lingering on the totally uninterested guard watching the camera screens.

"Sure," I said, leading her back to Woskowicz's—my—office. Detective Helland and crew hadn't been back since conducting the interviews, as far as I knew, and I'd personalized it to the extent of lobbing my swim bag under the desk.

Paula remained standing, looking around curiously. "I never visited Denny here," she said. "He was always real serious about his work, made sure I knew I couldn't just pop in and interrupt. Well, I understood that; it's not like he could've dropped by the classroom any time to take me to lunch. Did you box up his stuff already?"

"Nope," I said, wondering where this was going. "This is all there was." I swept my arm out to encompass the virtually barren office.

"No photos?" Paula looked miffed, as if she'd expected her ex would have her photo prominently displayed on his desk.

"The police took a couple of things." She was welcome to assume they'd walked out with a crate of photos. "Look, Paula," I started, impatient to move this along. "I don't know—"

"It's about his will," she said.

Aha. I waited in silence.

"You know he was married to Nina first and then to me—we truly loved each other—and finally to Aggie," she said. "Well, Nina's got a copy of a will signed by Denny, and it names her as the sole beneficiary of his estate." She puffed out her considerable chest with a deep, offended breath. "But it was signed *before* he married me, and I'm sure he made a will in my favor, so I've got to find it."

"And you think it's here?" I wrinkled my brow.

"It's got to be," she said, an edge of desperation in her voice. "I've been all through the house and it's not there."

"Isn't it possible he . . . *forgot* to make a will in your favor after you got married? Lots of people don't like thinking about wills."

"No! We talked about it. I know he—let's just look for it." She surged forward as if she were going to ransack the desk, but I put a hand on her arm to stop her.

"Paula, slow down. Let's be methodical about it. And I've got to be the one to go through any sensitive personnel files."

She nodded, copper hair bobbing, and we set to work. Forty-five minutes later, even Paula had to admit that the document wasn't there. Nothing remotely will-like had turned up. The woman looked near tears, and I wondered if it was because she was counting on the inheritance or because she was saddened that Woskowicz hadn't "loved her enough" to redo his will in her favor. As I said good-bye to her, I forbore mentioning that even if he'd done a new will when he married her, he might have revoked it when he married Aggie. The thought didn't seem to have occurred to her, and I didn't want to be the one to burst her bubble.

When Aggie waltzed in an hour after Paula left, I was pretty sure I knew what she wanted. She'd dried off since the memorial, but her flame red hair frizzed past her shoulders, a victim of the humidity. Tight jeans encased chunky legs, and a black bomber jacket might have been a concession to her grief—or it might have been her usual fashion statement.

Joel had ducked out for a break and I was watching the cameras, but I stood when Aggie came in, watching the screens out of the corners of my eyes. "Let me guess," I said after we exchanged greetings and she took in the office with a curious gaze. "You're looking for a will."

"A will?" Her brow puckered. "What about a will?"

Uh-oh. Me and my big mouth. "Uh . . ."

Dragging a hand through her wiry hair, she shrugged. "I'm not worried about a will. My lawyer's handling that. And since I'm still legally Wosko's wife—"

"What?"

She shot me a triumphant look. "Our divorce wasn't going to be final until this Friday. So if Nina or Paula think they're going to get a dime from Wosko's estate, they've got another think coming!"

I fell silent, digesting this piece of news. If true, Aggie

was clearly going to be the one to benefit financially from Woskowicz's death. And she was the one who'd announced early on that he was dead . . . I studied the short redhead, wondering if she'd had anything to do with his murder. Surely the police had looked into her whereabouts for Wednesday night?

"So what did you want to see me about?" I asked.

"I need to get into Wosko's office," she said airily.

"Why?"

Glaring at me, she hiked her purse higher on her shoulder. "Because."

I stood unmoving, arms crossed over my chest.

"Oh, all right," she grumbled. "I don't see how it's any of your business, but I need to find a key."

"What kind of key?"

She answered me with an uncompromising stare, lips thinned into a straight line.

Shrugging, I said, "It doesn't matter, because there are no keys in there."

Joel returned and I motioned him to the monitors with a nod, then led Aggie down the short hall to the director of security's office.

"How do you know it's not here?" Aggie said, stopping inside the door to survey the small room.

"The police have searched it," I said, "and I've spent a fair amount of time in here since . . ." I carefully didn't mention that Paula and I had ransacked the room an hour earlier. "Maybe Captain Woskowicz kept whatever key you're looking for on his key ring. In which case, the police probably have it." Unless the murderer stole Woskowicz's keys. My eyes widened. Of course he did. That's how he got in to search Woskowicz's house without leaving signs of a break-in. I reconsidered. Knowing that both Paula and Aggie were looking for something, and Nina, too, for all I knew, made me wonder if it had been one of them who searched the house.

"Well, I'll have a look-see, if you don't—"

I stepped in front of Aggie as she prepared to tear the office apart, dismantling the desk and ripping up the flooring, if her expression was anything to go by. "You're going to have to take my word for it, Aggie. The only key I found was to a file cabi—"

"How do you know it wasn't for a safe-deposit box?" She looked ready to mug me on the spot and turn my pockets inside out.

"Because it fit the file cabinet drawer," I said, pointing.

"Oh."

"If I come across the key elsewhere"—I gestured to the outer office—"I'll be sure to let you know."

"Me," she insisted. "Not Nina or Paula. Me. It's mine."

She sounded like one of the seagulls in *Finding Nemo*: "Mine. Mine. Mine-mine-mineminemine."

"Or maybe I should turn it over to the police," I said.

"You'd better not." Her jaw thrust forward, and despite her shortness and her cute pug nose, she looked tough.

"What do you do?" I asked, curious.

She reared back slightly, startled by the question. "Do? I sell cars. At Dealin' Dwight's Used Car Supercenter. You've probably seen our ads on TV."

Hadn't everyone? They came on every fifteen minutes (or so it seemed) and featured Dealin' Dwight himself—a hearty-looking man who bore more than a passing resemblance to former senator and actor Fred Thompson—and a herd of llamas. I'd never yet figured out the connection between the llamas and used cars.

"If you ever need a new—gently used—car, come on down and I can set you up. We're between here and Richmond, just off I-95." She handed me a card. It read "Delia

'Aggie' S. Woskowicz, Senior Sales Associate." I saw that, like Paula, she had retained Woskowicz's name; I guess it made sense if she was still legally married to him.

"Will do," I said, ushering her back toward the front. She cast one longing look over her shoulder but allowed me to see her out with one more reminder about contacting her if I found any stray keys around the office.

"What was that all about?" Joel asked as soon as Aggie departed.

"I'm not sure," I said, staring out the doors long after she was out of sight. I told him about Paula's looking for a will and Aggie's wanting to search for a safe-deposit key.

"Maybe the will is in the safe-deposit box," he said reasonably.

"Could be," I said, "but Aggie didn't seem much interested in a will. She said she's still legally married to Woskowicz, that their divorce wasn't quite final."

"Really?" Joel looked disapproving. "Woskowicz certainly carried on like he was single."

"Yeah, well." I suspected that was Woskowicz's modus operandi, single or married. If what Paula said was true, he'd taken up with Aggie before divorcing her.

"I wouldn't do that," Joel said.

I smiled at him. "Of course not."

Joel hid his pleasure by pretending to study the camera screens. "Do you think she killed him to get whatever's in the safe-deposit box?"

"Maybe."

"I'll bet it's cash. Lots and lots of cash."

The odor of coffee sludge on the verge of burning wafted through the room. Crossing to the coffeemaker, I unplugged it. "It's probably papers: birth certificate, will, other documents. Isn't that mostly what people keep in safe-deposit boxes?"

"Maybe it's jewels," Joel said, ignoring my prosaic interjection.

I gave him a look.

"Okay," he conceded, "Captain W wasn't a jewelry kind of guy."

"Although I bet the exes were jewelry kinds of gals."

"Maybe it's videos of him and her," Joel said, nodding in the direction of the departed Aggie. "You know." He waggled his brows.

"Joel!" Despite my surprise that Joel had suggested it— he came across as sweet and slightly naïve for a twenty-three-year-old—it wasn't a bad thought. "You could be on to something there."

My gaze had strayed idly to the screens as I talked, and now I leaned forward to study two girls exiting a teen clothing store. "It's her!"

"Who?"

"See that girl?" I pointed to the Hispanic teen who'd been with Celio the day he got shot.

Joel peered at the screen. "Yeah?"

"Don't lose her. I've got to talk to her." I was halfway out the door on the words. "Keep me posted on where she goes." I tapped my radio.

"Got it," Joel said.

Luckily, she was on this level, so I didn't have to waste time in the elevator. When I Segwayed to the store she'd been leaving, she was nowhere in sight. "Joel?" I clicked my radio.

"They went into FaceNook," Joel said.

FaceNook sold cosmetics and hair products and was across the hall from where I stood. Zipping across the little bridge that spanned the gap between the two hallways, I paused outside FaceNook and peered through the window. Sure enough, the girl and her friend were experimenting with eye shadows in front of a round magnifying mirror while a clerk hovered at their elbows. I watched them for a moment, unobserved. The girl who'd been with Celio was looking on as her friend, a tall teen who held herself with a confidence lacking in the shorter girl, smoothed eye shadow from lash line to brow. Each had a couple of shopping bags at her feet. Leaving the Segway outside, I walked in.

The clerk, a fortyish woman I'd chatted with before, called, "Hi, EJ."

The two girls looked up and wariness settled on their faces, like fog on a pond.

"I just wanted to chat with these young ladies for a moment," I said, aiming a friendly smile at the teens.

Apparently, they read my expression as something more sinister because the taller girl yelled, "Run, Eloísa!" The girl I'd seen with Celio snatched up her bags and darted around the end of a counter, knocking over a display of lipsticks, which clattered to the tiled floor and rolled in all directions. Clear of the counter, she bolted through the door. Her friend stooped to pick up some lipsticks but thought better of it, straightening to follow Eloísa. Leaving the sputtering clerk to corral the lipsticks, I dashed after the girls.

Hopping on the Segway, I sped after them, clicking on my radio. "A little help, please."

"What?" Joel sounded confused. "Oh. Just passing Merlin's Cave, looking like they're trying to set an Olympic record. What'd you say to them?"

Ignoring the question, I leaned forward to get more speed out of the Segway.

"They split up," Joel said over the radio. "One headed for the garage, and the other went into Nordstrom."

"Who went where?" I really wanted to catch up with Celio's friend; the other girl held less interest.

A moment of silence had me almost humming with

impatience. "I'm not sure," Joel finally admitted. "They both had dark hair and were wearing jeans. It's not like I'm working with high-def here."

"I know," I said, squelching my frustration. Eeny-meeny-miney-mo. I headed for Nordstrom.

Fourteen

. . .

Lily-scented perfume assailed me as I crossed into
Nordstrom. A half dozen cosmetics counters lay in front of
me, laden with face products worth as much as the annual
budget of a midsized city. Dodging a woman who wanted to
spritz me with the perfume, I caught up with a clerk and
asked if she'd seen a dark-haired teen in a hurry. She pointed
wordlessly toward the lingerie department. I knew an exit
door was on the far side of the bras and pajamas, so I zipped
along as quickly as I could. The Segway gave me a little
extra height as I scanned the department, able to see over
the revolving racks and displays. One middle-aged woman
examined undergarments with enough support to hold up
the Brooklyn Bridge. No teenager. Damn. She must have
made it to the parking lot.

I cut diagonally through lingerie and out the row of glass
doors leading to the parking lot. Looking both ways, I didn't
see anyone who resembled the girl I was following. Possibly
she was already in her car, if she had one. Or . . . I spun the

Segway and returned to the dressing room between lingerie
and women's evening wear. It was the only one on the route
the clerk had indicated the girl had taken. There was no
attendant in sight, so I dismounted and walked through an
open doorway. A chime sounded. The dressing room doors,
unfortunately, went to the floor, so I couldn't peer beneath
them and figure out which ones were occupied.

"Eloísa?" I called softly. I began to walk the length of
the dressing room, toward a three-way mirror at the end.
Doors lined both sides of the narrow hall. Rustling sounds
and the clink of hangers came from behind several of them.
With a sigh, I turned the handle on the first door. Empty.
Ditto for the second and third doors. The fourth room held
a skinny woman who clutched a gray chiffon gown to her
chest when she spotted me.

"Sorry," I apologized.

"Well! Cameras in here to prevent shoplifting are bad
enough, but this is ridiculous," the woman said as I closed
the door.

The next two doors yielded nothing but piles of discarded
clothes on the floor and slung on the bench. A woman carrying an armload of bathing suits and resort wear emerged
from the next door before I reached it, stepping past me with
a muttered, "Excuse me." I envied her the cruise I imagined
she was shopping for. Hesitating at the final door, marked
with a "Handicapped" placard, I heard nothing from within.
My fingers closed over the handle, and I eased the door open
an inch. It promptly slammed shut, clearly propelled by a
well-placed kick or shoulder.

"Eloísa," I said, "this is crazy. I just want to talk with
you for a couple of minutes. About Celio. You're not in
trouble."

"I'm not?" The door muffled the voice, but I heard tension and doubt.

"Absolutely not," I said. "I'm trying to figure out what happened to Celio. If he was your friend, I'd think you'd want to know, too."

"I don't know anything," the girl said.

"Would you please come out?"

The middle-aged woman emerged from the other dressing room, garbed in the gray gown, which did nothing for her light eyes and mousy hair. "Teenage daughter, huh?" she asked in the voice of experience.

Did I really look old enough at thirty-one to be the mother of a teenager? Involuntarily, I glanced at my reflection in the three-way mirror.

"Don't you wish you could lock 'em in a closet—with a muzzle on—from the time they hit adolescence until they're about twenty-three?" the woman asked, edging past me to stand in front of the mirror. "When my Suzanne was seventeen, she tried on fifty-four dresses before finding one she wanted to wear to the prom. Fifty-four! Why, I only tried on three to find my wedding gown." She turned first one way, then the other, craning her neck to view her backside. "Does this dress make me look fat?"

"Not at all," I replied truthfully. Drab, yes. Fat, no.

Satisfied, she returned to her dressing room, and I knocked on Eloísa's door once more. "I'm not going away."

Apparently, she believed me because ninety seconds later the door opened. The teenager slid out through the crack, all long denimed legs, dark brown hair, and wary eyes. But she wasn't the girl I'd seen with Celio. She was Eloísa's friend from FaceNook, the one who'd told her to run. "You're not Eloísa." Master of the obvious, that's me.

"No." The girl tossed her hair, clearly pleased at having put one over on me.

"I'm EJ Ferris." I extended my hand. "What's your name?"

Caught off guard, the girl stared at me. "I'm really not in trouble?" She had a soft Virginia accent that was disarming.

Her obviously guilty conscience made me wonder what the girls had been up to. Shoplifting? Playing hooky? Some of the local schools were on spring break, but not all. "I told you, you weren't."

Somewhat satisfied, she grasped my outstretched hand in a weak, brief handshake. "I'm Gilda." She pulled her hand back and thrust it into her jeans pocket.

"Pretty name."

"What do you want with Eloísa?" she asked, curiosity replacing suspicion in her eyes.

I saw no reason not to be honest with her. "I saw her with Celio Arriaga here at Fernglen the day he was killed. I want to talk to her, see if she remembers anything from that day that might help the police figure out who shot him."

"She doesn't." Gilda spoke positively.

"How do you know?"

"Because Enrique says so."

"Who's Enrique?"

"The leader of the Niños Malos. What he says goes." A certain stiffness to her face made me think she wasn't totally in sync with Enrique.

"And you're part of the gang, so you have to do what he says?"

Gilda shook her head vehemently, swishing her hair against her shoulders. "Not me. I stay away from that gang shit. But Eloísa was tight with Celio, and, well . . ."

"Enrique won't find out if Eloísa talks to me," I promised, passing her a business card with my phone number on it. "If she cared about Celio—"

"Cared about him? She loved that poser." Gilda rolled her eyes.

"You didn't like him?"

"I didn't *not* like him, but getting mixed up with the Niños is a bad idea. Eloísa didn't see it, though. Celio was her kryptonite."

"He was her boyfriend?"

She gave me the look all teenagers have perfected, the one that laments the stupidity of everyone over eighteen. "Nah. Her cousin."

"What's her last name?"

The talkative shopper popped out of her dressing room, the gray chiffon draped over her arm. "That looks great on you," she told Gilda in an affirming way. "You should buy it." She left.

The woman's appearance, or maybe my question, disrupted the tenuous rapport between Gilda and me. "These are my jeans, and I've had this sweater for four years," Gilda said, looking down at her attire. "I've gotta go."

Sensing that pushing her at this point would only make her less likely to pass my words along to Eloísa, I walked with her to the dressing room entrance. "Thanks for talking to me," I said. "Please tell Eloísa what I said."

She ducked her head in a funny little bob that could have been acknowledgment, agreement, or teen for "leave me the hell alone." She strode toward the exit without looking back.

I knew I should call Detective Helland with what I'd learned—both from Paula and Aggie, and from Gilda. I was reluctant to sic the police on Eloísa, though, in case they were ham-handed about finding her and exposed her to Enrique's punishment. I compromised by calling from the office and telling Helland that Captain Woskowicz had a safe-deposit box that might hold something of interest. "And I don't know if you knew," I added, "but he was still legally married to his third wife, Aggie."

"Huh," Helland said without inflection. "She gave a different address."

I smiled into the phone, pleased to have one-upped him. "I guess they've been separated for a while. If she inherits his estate, that would give her a good motive for killing him."

"Assuming his estate's worth anything," Helland said discouragingly.

"Did you get anything useful from the gun? The one from the office?" I slipped the question in, hoping he might feel motivated to share with me since I'd given him a useful bit of information.

Apparently not. Ignoring the question completely, he said, "If that's all?"

Before he could hang up, I caved and told him about Eloísa, unable to square it with my conscience to keep possibly important information about a murder from the police. "You can't just barge in and interrogate her, though," I said. "She's afraid of some low-life named Enrique, the big kahuna—"

"Mero mero."

"—of the Niños Malos. I don't know her last name, but she's Celio's cousin."

There was a pause from Helland's end of the line. I expected him to let loose with some comment about me presuming to tell the police how to do their job. Finally, he said, "The bullet the coroner pulled out of Celio matched the gun we found in Woskowicz's office. That information is not for public consumption." He hung up.

I had hardly put the phone down when Pooja stepped into the office, a sheaf of papers in her hand. She thrust them at me, and I raised questioning brows.

"The application for the director of security job," she said, smiling slightly. "The board voted to move ahead quickly, and the first round of interviews is

Saturday—they're anxious to fill the position. I thought I'd give you a head start."

"Thanks," I said, eyeing the application with distaste. "I think." She started for the door, but I stopped her. "Officer Dallabetta wanted to apply, too. Do you have another copy of the application?"

"It'll be online in a minute," Pooja said, "along with the job announcement. As soon as I get back to my office, I'm posting it to the Jobs section of the Fernglen website."

Leaving Joel out front to man the phones and keep an eye on the cameras, I went back to the office and got started on the forms. Why in the world did they need my mother's maiden name, I wondered, filling in "Atherton." The phone rang at my elbow, the little *brrr* that let me know Joel had transferred a call to me. "Officer Ferris," I said absently, trying to remember my address from six years ago to include on the application.

"If you want to talk to Eloísa, be at Phat Cat at ten o'clock tonight," a voice whispered.

"But she's underage." I said the first thing that came to mind. Phat Cat was a twenty-one-and-over nightclub about halfway between here and Quantico.

A laugh ghosted over the line. "Phat Cat. Ten o'clock. One chance."

"Wow," Kyra said when I told her about the phone call. "Cryptic phone calls. Very Nancy Drew. Do you think it might be *a trap*?" She said the last words with mock breathlessness, leaning forward across the table in the food court. Her hair threatened to fall in the barbecue sauce she was using for her chicken strips. "Of course I'll come."

I pointed to her hair, and she flicked it over her shoulder. Taking a bite of my Szechuan green beans, I said, "Thanks."

It surprised me a little to realize I felt more trepidation about hanging out in a nightclub by myself, looking desperate and out of place, than I did about confronting a possibly armed, undoubtedly dangerous gangbanger or two. I had no proof it was Eloísa who had called, although I thought the voice was female.

"What'll I wear?" Kyra asked, tapping a green-painted fingernail against her teeth. "More importantly"—she surveyed me critically—"what'll you wear?"

"Jeans."

"You can't go nightclubbing in jeans!"

"We're not going nightclubbing," I said repressively. "We're interviewing a witness."

"In a nightclub; ergo, we're going nightclubbing."

I rolled my eyes.

"When's the last time you went dancing?" she asked, piling the lunch debris on her tray.

"Senior prom?"

She shook a finger at me. "I'll bet it was before you went to Afghanistan, right?"

"Well, duh. Dancing wasn't high on our list of activities. It fell somewhere below 'Protect the base,' 'Accomplish the mission,' and 'Stay alive.'"

"Yeah, yeah." She brushed away my sarcasm. "What I mean is you haven't been dancing since you got back. You used to love to dance."

"That was long, long ago, in a place far, far away," I said, trying to put a humorous spin on a conversation that was going somewhere I didn't want it to go. "Don't mention my knee or I'll spill this on you." I indicated my strawberry smoothie.

Kyra raised her brows. "I'll mention what I want to mention, girlfriend. But, fine, have it your way. You're letting a nameless body part keep you from doing things you would like to do if you weren't so worried about how you'd look doing them now that the nameless body part doesn't work as well as it once did." Crossing her arms over her chest, she gave me a "top that" look.

Caught between irritation and amusement, I wondered why I'd never noticed how square and stubborn Kyra's chin was. "You might—might!—have a teeny, weeny, minor point. Which doesn't change the fact that I'm wearing jeans. To the nightclub. At which I'm not dancing."

"Who's going nightclubbing?"

Kyra and I looked up to see Jay Callahan standing over the table, eyebrow quirked, warm smile making him look very appealing in a boy-next-door kind of way. That is, if the boy next door carried a gun and led a double life of some sort.

An evil glint came into Kyra's eyes. "We are," she said. "Tonight. And you're invited."

"Great," Jay said without hesitation.

"Wait—" I started.

"You'll have to dance with me, though," Kyra continued, "since EJ doesn't dance anymore."

"I don't think that'll be a hardship," Jay said, smiling down at her. His mischievous gaze shifted to me. "Although maybe we can change her mind."

My abs clenched against the warm feeling his look stirred up. I rose, holding my tray in front of me like a shield. "Don't you have some garage-lurking to do?" I asked.

He pretended to consult an invisible calendar. "Nope, no garage-lurking on the schedule. I'm all yours for the night."

I frowned to stave off the images that leaped to mind. "Fine. Come if you want. But I'm still wearing jeans."

Fifteen

· · ·

In any event, getting dressed at nine o'clock, I couldn't make myself wear jeans. Phat Cat wasn't a trendy D.C. nightclub, but it was a pretty happening place for the 'burbs, or so I'd heard. I tried to tell myself that that was why I didn't want to wear jeans, but I knew it had more to do with Jay Callahan. Sliding hangers aside to reveal some of the clothes I'd worn in my L.A. life, before the military, I pulled a short peach-colored dress from the back of the closet and held it wistfully in front of me. It would probably still fit, I thought, remembering long nights of dancing with the floaty skirt twirling around me. But I didn't wear above-the-knee dresses anymore. I returned the dress to the closet and pulled out a pair of slim, metallic slacks with enough stretch to make them fit close. And I could wear my silver ballet flats with them; my knee definitely didn't do high heels anymore. An ice blue halter top that bared my swimming-toned arms would complete the outfit. A few moments later, a glance in the mirror told me I looked . . . well, hot.

Fubar agreed, twining around my ankles and depositing rusty red hairs on my silver pants. He followed me into the bathroom and leaped onto the toilet tank, nosing at my cosmetics bag and sneezing before leaping down again. Twisting my chestnut hair into a messy topknot and skewering it with a couple of enameled chopsticks, I applied some eye makeup and deep red lipstick, and found myself looking at someone unfamiliar in the mirror. Not totally unknown— more like someone you meet at your tenth high school reunion and know you should recognize.

This slim woman with the smoky eyes and the chestnut tendrils drifting against her cheeks was a ghost from my past. Certainly from before my knee got torn up. Looking at the reflection, I realized I'd spent a big chunk of my adult life in uniforms of one kind or another: military, mall cop. On the one hand those uniforms said I was part of a team, and I liked that. On the other . . . did they steal a bit of my individuality? Impatient with my thoughts, I turned away from the mirror, tucked a credit card and ID into the tiny silver bag I looped over my shoulder, and hesitated. Should I take my gun? No, I decided. They might well have a metal detector at the club, and I wasn't going to put myself in a position where I'd need it. I was meeting a fifteen-year-old, for heaven's sake. Besides which, I didn't have a concealed carry permit. I snorted for even thinking about it. Telling Fubar not to wait up, I locked the door and waited on the front stoop for Kyra.

The parking lot at Phat Cat was half-full when we arrived. We were way too early for the serious partiers, Kyra informed me; they wouldn't arrive until after midnight. "Don't these people have jobs to go to in the morning?" I grumbled as I got out of the car. "Classes?"

Kyra started toward the club door, which was practically pulsating with the techno track beating against it. In a tight red dress that displayed a mile of shapely leg and high heels that took her to over six feet tall, Kyra looked magnificent. I smiled ruefully. I might as well have worn my jeans since no one was going to look at me with Kyra standing nearby. At the door, we discovered it was ladies' night and we didn't have to pay a cover to enter. Kyra flashed a thumbs-up at the news and led the way into the glittery, strobey, loud interior.

Phat Cat had an industrial feel to it with exposed metal pipes big enough for a prison escapee to crawl through, lots of concrete, and glass and chrome fixtures. I got an impression of a long shiny bar, not enough high-topped tables or uncomfortable-looking stools, snaky glass light fixtures, and a surging crowd of mostly twenty-somethings. The club didn't seem to be a gang hangout, I noted with relief, since people of a dozen ethnicities danced, talked, and drank without the kind of "this is our turf" glares I associated with gang members. The dance floor, at the far end of the room from where we'd entered, surged with bodies moving to the hypnotically repetitive beat of some song I'd never heard before. How in the world was I going to find Eloísa, let alone carry on a conversation with her?

Kyra and I maneuvered our way to the bar and ordered, a cosmopolitan for her and a club soda for me. Kyra stared at me in disbelief. "If I'd known you weren't drinking, you could have driven," she said.

"Maybe I'll have a drink after I meet up with Eloísa," I said, my eyes studying the people who passed by. I didn't see anyone who looked underage, or Jay. A tall man in black with garish red shoes asked Kyra to dance, and she cocked a brow at me. I shooed her toward the dance floor with a smile, and she trailed after the man, hips swaying.

Perching on a stool vacated by another woman who'd headed toward the dance floor, I sipped my club soda and tried not to think what the decibels in the club were doing to my hearing. I laughed at myself. I must really be getting old. Such a thought would never have crossed my mind in my hard-partying days.

"Something funny?" Jay Callahan's voice, right next to my ear, made me jump. He'd wedged himself between my bar stool and the one next to me, which was occupied by a man the general shape and size of a sumo wrestler. When I turned, my face was only inches from his. His hazel eyes smiled into mine.

"Dance?"

"I'm waiting—" I cut myself off. I wanted to dance with Jay Callahan. Eloísa could find me on the dance floor. My knee . . . "Okay."

He took my hand in a firm clasp and led me toward the floor. Merging into the mass of writhing dancers, I tried to feel the rhythm and sway with it. My knee twinged but I ignored it, grinning at Jay. This was fun. The floor was so packed that no one could possibly make out the motions of an individual dancer, so I lost my feeling of self-consciousness and began to move with the beat, being careful not to twist my knee. I saw Kyra several dancers away, arms waving in the air, hair flying as she moved. I pointed her out to Jay and he grinned. He danced with the shuffle step so many guys employ, but he seemed to have a decent sense of rhythm and was enjoying it. He leaned closer, and I thought for a moment that he was going to kiss me.

"So, want to tell me what we're really doing here?"

Surprised, I leaned back so I could see his face. I was debating whether to tell him about Eloísa or pretend I hadn't heard him when I caught sight of a woman over his shoulder whose gaze was fixed on my face. She looked vaguely familiar . . . Gilda! With expertly applied makeup, her hair up in a topknot like mine, and a form-fitting dress that revealed a busty figure, the girl looked twenty-four. She gave a tiny jerk of her head that seemed to indicate I should move toward the far side of the dance floor.

"Excuse me," I told Jay, edging toward Gilda.

By the time I had extricated myself from the dancers, I'd lost sight of her. However, a narrow hallway with a "Restrooms" sign and a pointing-finger graphic lay in front of me, so I turned down it. A man with heavily gelled hair erupted from the men's room, bumped into me, and put a hand on the wall for balance. "Sorry," he said before heading back to the bar. I pushed open the door to the ladies' room, expecting to see Gilda.

No Gilda. The relative silence was soothing, and I felt tense muscles relax fractionally. The industrial theme carried over in here with white subway tiles, concrete stalls, and lots of mirrors. A short blonde was applying mascara to lashes already gunky enough to suggest she'd been swimming in the Gulf of Mexico during the oil spill. She eyed me disinterestedly before returning to her task. A toilet flushed and a moment later Gilda emerged from one of the three stalls, shot me a sidelong look, and went to the sink to wash her hands. She waited until Mascara Girl exited and then said softly, "She's outside."

"Is this cloak-and-dagger routine really necessary? Wouldn't it be easier for us to chat at a coffee shop?" I couldn't believe Grandpa Atherton had put up with this sort of thing for decades and still did it for fun.

Gilda caught her breath and looked under the stall doors. Apparently satisfied that we were alone, she said, "You don't know Enrique. This is a good spot because it's not a place we're likely to run into the Niños. My sister works here," she added.

I felt churlish. Yes, the setup felt like teenage drama to me, but I didn't know the gang culture and maybe Eloísa really was putting herself on the line to talk to me. "Thanks," I said.

A couple of women came in, giggling and chatting, and Gilda just nodded at me. I left the restroom and turned to the left where an illuminated "Exit" sign glowed. A placard warned that alarms would sound if I went out the emergency exit, but the door was open a crack, so I pushed through it and found myself in a noisome alley behind the club facing three overflowing Dumpsters. A line of scraggly trees separated the Phat Cat property from what appeared to be a meadow or pasture less than fifty feet away. It was lonely out here, isolated. Stars twinkled overhead in the clear night sky, and I took a deep breath, regretting it immediately as the odors of stale liquor and rotting food attacked me.

"Eloísa?" I called softly.

A figure detached itself from the shadows on my right. I turned as the girl walked toward me, almost invisible in dark jeans and boots and a black sweatshirt with the hood pulled up. Something glinted dully on her chest, and I realized, as she came closer, that it was a crucifix. "Gilda told me I should talk to you," she said in a low voice. Her accent gave the words a melodic rhythm. "About Celio."

"I saw you and Celio and another friend at the mall," I said, "the day Celio got shot. Can you tell me what you guys were doing, where you went?"

Her dark eyes flitted from my face to the Dumpsters, to the trees at the property line. "We went to the mall to hang out, that's all. No special reason. We . . . we just walked around, went into stores, shit like that. Nothing special." Her left hand went to the crucifix, and she rubbed it between thumb and fingers. "We got cookies in the food court."

She had her head bowed, staring at her feet, and I could

barely make out her words. I stepped closer and she jumped back, knocking against the club's wall.

"Sorry," I said, holding up my hands. "I couldn't hear you."

She nodded, but kept a wary eye on me.

"Who was the other guy with you?"

"Enrique," she said after a moment.

The biggest and baddest of the Niños. "Was that unusual?"

She gave me an uncomprehending look.

"For Enrique to hang at the mall with you and Celio?"

"Enrique does what he wants to do."

I was getting nowhere with this line of questioning. I switched tacks. "How did Celio seem? Happy? Nervous? Angry?"

Something sparked in her eyes, and I knew I'd touched on something. "He seemed really hyped up," she said.

Drugs? I wondered.

"Like . . . like something was going to go down. The only other time I've seen him like that was when—just before—he robbed the Gas-n-Go."

Even in the dim light she must have caught my reaction because she said fiercely, "Celio wasn't bad. He wasn't! When we were younger, he used to feed all the stray cats on the street. They recognized his step and would come running whenever he walked down the sidewalk. My mom used to call it 'Celio and the Cat Parade.' And he walked to school with me every day, even though he was older and the other boys teased him about it. And he could make you cry when he played the guitar."

"It sounds like he was special," I said gently, saddened by her recital.

Bitterness infused her voice and she sounded suddenly

older than her fifteen or sixteen years. "It was those Niños. They changed him."

Niños Malos. Bad boys. I didn't point out that Celio had chosen to join the gang. What did I know about the boy and his options?

"I think it was guns," Eloísa said from out of the blue. "I heard Enrique say something about *cuetes,* and then he dragged me off with him, saying Celio had something to take care of."

"When was this?"

The girl shrugged one shoulder. "Late in the afternoon? Three?"

"And did you see him again?"

"Sure. Maybe twenty minutes later he caught up with us by the fountain. We were watching the children visit the Easter Bunny."

She sounded wistful, like she wished she weren't too old for sitting on the Easter Bunny's lap. "We left right after that."

"Celio was with you?"

She nodded. *"Sí."*

I wrinkled my brow. "So he must have come back to the mall later, or whoever killed him chose the mall—why the mall?—as a spot to dump his body." I was mostly speaking to myself, but Eloísa answered.

"He was supposed to eat dinner with us—my family— but he and Enrique just dropped me and left. That was the last time I saw him."

The tears in her voice made me reach out to put a comforting hand on her shoulder, but she ducked away. "You need to tell the police this, Eloísa," I said. "About the guns. About Enrique."

She gasped. "No! No *policía.* Enrique would—" She

couldn't even finish the sentence. She looked over her shoulder, and I could tell she was about to bolt.

"Eloísa, did you see where Celio went in the mall when he sent you off with Enrique? What store?"

"We were in that hall with the nail salon. I wanted to get a manicure, but they didn't want to wait for me. Enrique and I left, but Celio, he stayed there. I think he was going to—"

A truck's headlights swept around the corner of the building, and an engine growled as the vehicle trundled toward us.

"Enrique!" Eloísa gasped, then bolted, clinging to the building's shadow before taking off, fleet as a deer, for the strip of woods bordering the property. I spun and took two strides in the opposite direction, thinking I'd make it hard for him to choose a target. Without warning, my knee, already annoyed by the dancing, collapsed under me. I hit the ground in a crouch and flung up my forearm to shade my eyes from the truck's lights. As I was preparing to roll away from the chrome grille bearing down on me, the truck slowed and stopped.

"Everything okay, ma'am?" a voice called from the cab. The accent was pure Virginia, and I was pretty sure it didn't belong to a guy named "Enrique." The truck's door opened and a lanky man stepped down. As he came closer, I saw he was wearing a gray Phat Cat tee shirt. Club security. I breathed a sigh of relief.

"I'm just getting some air," I said, pushing to my feet. I breathed in deeply through my nose to demonstrate.

He eyed me carefully. "We've got volunteers to drive you home if you're indisposed, ma'am."

He meant drunk. I wondered if he thought I'd been buying—or selling—drugs. Had he seen Eloísa scamper off? "I'm fine." I balanced on one foot using my good leg. "See?"

"Maybe you should come with me—"

The door behind me sighed open, and the security guy and I turned as one. Jay Callahan stood there, sizing up the situation. "You feeling okay, honey?" he asked, crossing to me and putting a solicitous arm around my shoulders. "I've been looking for you everywhere." His hand squeezed my shoulder hard.

I wriggled out from under his arm. "Just fine, babycakes."

"I'll take her home now," Jay told the security guy, a reassuring "I'll keep her out of your hair" note in his voice.

"Thank you, sir," the guard said, climbing back in the truck.

"I am not drunk," I growled at Jay as he walked me out of the alley and around to the front of the club, the truck trailing us—probably to make sure we really left.

" 'Babycakes?' " he asked, a laugh in his voice.

We arrived at the parking lot, and he steered me toward an Audi sedan. "I can't go home with you," I said. "Kyra."

"I already told her I was taking you home," he said, opening the door for me.

"Oh." Since I didn't really want to return to the club and since Kyra would probably dance until closing time, I slid onto the seat. "Thanks."

"You can thank me by telling me what you were up to back there," he said. "That guy was on the verge of busting you for drug dealing."

"Pooh," I said. "I don't even have an aspirin on me."

He gave me a look as he started the car. "Address?"

I gave it to him. Leaning back against the comfortable seat and absently massaging my knee, I told him about chasing Gilda through the mall and the arranged meeting with Eloísa. "She was on the verge of telling me where she thought Celio was going in the mall when the security guy spooked her. She took off like a bat out of hell. I doubt she'll agree to talk to me again." Not that I had any way to find her—I didn't know either her or Gilda's last name.

"Are you going to tell the police?"

The car's motion was making me drowsy. That plus the shot of adrenaline and the evening's tension made me feel like I could nod off. "I should," I said.

Jay tapped long fingers on the steering wheel. He drove fast but competently. " '*Cuetes*,' huh? Now, why would Mr. Arriaga think he could get his hands on some guns at the mall?"

Studying his profile, I got the impression that he wasn't so much speaking to me as working through something aloud. "You tell me," I suggested, more convinced than ever by his apparent understanding of the term "*cuetes*" that he knew a suspicious amount about the illegal buying and selling of weapons.

He slanted a look at me and immediately returned his gaze to the road. "Me? I'm just a cookie ba—"

"Yeah, yeah—you're just a cookie baker, an entrepreneur trying to make a buck, an Average Joe who runs his business by day, watches *Survivor* at night, and plays softball with the guys or waxes his car on the weekend."

Jay chuckled. "Actually, I don't even own a television— can't stand the drivel that's on it, and if I want to watch a ball game I can go to a sports bar; I play softball with guys *and* gals, coed team; and I run my car through a car wash every other month or so. I've never been one of those guys who obsessed over his ride, not even in high school. But now you mention it, maybe I'll tell the car-wash crew to wax her next time I go in." He patted the dash. "If you like softball, you could play with us next Monday evening. One of our regulars had a baby last week and is going to miss the rest of the season. Wuss."

Despite myself, I laughed, feeling a warm tingle of

pleasure at the invitation. Spending some time outside the mall with Jay Callahan would not be totally painful, I realized. "I used to play some, but not in a long time. And you didn't see what happened back there." I jerked my head toward Phat Cat. "Half a dance and my knee gave out on me." I massaged the offending body part, half angrily.

"We're not recruiting for the Orioles," Jay said. "Drue played right field for us Saturday morning and had the baby that afternoon, which ought to give you an idea of how low we set the softball-skills bar. In fact, you meet all the requirements: two X chromosomes."

Was my knee a bigger physical handicap than being nine months pregnant? Probably not. I hesitated, pleased that he'd invited me, that he wanted to spend time with me—although playing coed softball together wasn't really a *date*—but leery of looking like a fool.

"Have you thought about a knee replacement?"

I stiffened.

Jay caught the motion and held up an apologetic hand. "None of my business."

Damn right it was none of his business. I didn't have the inclination or the energy to fill Jay in on the details of the injuries to my knee and the surrounding soft tissue, tendons, and ligaments. He didn't need to know about the metal rod in my femur or the pins in my fibula. Despite that, I said, "The docs aren't sure it would do any good."

Jay only nodded in response and I yawned. Next thing I knew, he was shaking me awake outside my town house. "Your pumpkin coach has arrived, Sleeping Beauty."

"I think you're mixing your fairy tales," I said groggily. Unbuckling, I opened the door and stepped out, keeping my weight on my good leg. I bent to look in at him. "Thanks for playing knight errant—even if I didn't really need rescuing."

"Knight errant?" He feigned disappointment. "Not Prince Charming?"

"You've got to work your way up to that." I closed the door and went into the house, smiling to myself.

Sixteen

. . .

I arrived at Fernglen the next morning determined to figure out what Celio had been up to in the Pete's Sporting Goods wing. I'd go store by store if I had to, and see what kind of response I got when I dropped hints about Celio and guns. I'd had to use my soft brace on my knee this morning and was walking stiffly when I arrived at the security office to find Joel already manning the security cameras.

"Overdid it with the dancing?" he asked with a nod at my leg.

"How'd you know I went out last night?"

"Kyra mentioned it." He'd initially been pretty nervous around Kyra, but after the three of us had worked together to demonstrate how a killer could set up a body in a display window, they'd become buddies.

"Big mouth," I said.

"Her or me?"

"Both of you."

He grinned. "You can still swim today, can't you?"

"Sure."

Before the stores opened, I caught up on paperwork and finished my application for the director of security position, which I walked over to Pooja's desk. "We've already got four applications," she whispered, looking toward Curtis Quigley's office.

"Really?" I don't know why I was surprised; with the economy the way it was, people with fine arts degrees or who'd been laid off from construction jobs were probably applying.

"Yes. Victoria Dallabetta, Dusty Margolin from Nordstrom, and two gentlemen not associated with the mall."

I left the mall manager's office not feeling quite so confident I'd get the job. Dusty Margolin was well qualified for it, and Vic Dallabetta might be, too. And for all I knew, the unknown applicants had spent thirty years each in law enforcement or private security. I shrugged it off. I'd either be the new director of security for Fernglen or I wouldn't.

Kyra came around the corner just as I placed my hand on the security office door. The blinding grin on her face told me she'd had a good time at Phat Cat.

"We need to do that more often," she said.

"Dancing?"

"Going out. Doing new stuff. Meeting new men."

Aha. "So you met an interesting man?"

She nodded.

"Mr. Red Shoes?"

"Uh-uh. I don't think you saw Kyron."

"Chiron? Isn't he a satyr or a centaur or something in Greek mythology?"

"Kyron with a *K*," she said.

"You can't ever marry him. Kyra and Kyron would be just too much. Can't you see it on a Christmas card: 'Happy Holidays from Kyra and Kyron and our little Specials K's.' "

Kyra hooted.

"What's he like?"

"Tall, dark, handsome, fabulous dancer, snappy little Bimmer convertible, nice house in Octagon Park."

I raised my brows. "You went home with him?"

She grinned again but changed the subject. "So, how'd it go with your snitch?"

"She's not a snitch," I said, mildly annoyed. "She's really torn up by her cousin's death. She wants to help catch his killer, but she's afraid of the gang he ran with."

Kyra sobered, and I thought she might be thinking about her brother. "I can relate to that. Did she know anything?"

I shrugged. "Maybe. I'm going to check a couple of things out."

Fernando Guzman came around the corner, dragging a mop and bucket. We all exchanged "good mornings," and Kyra said she had to open Merlin's Cave. I adjusted the brace, which was pinching my thigh, climbed on the Segway, and headed toward the wing where Celio Arriaga had ditched his cousin to conduct some business that might, or might not, have been related to guns.

I'd be methodical, I decided, and go down one side and up the other. I'd check out all the businesses, not making assumptions about any of them. Accordingly, I walked into Nailed It and gagged as a sharp wave of acetone knifed my nostrils. I wasn't much of one for beauty treatments, but the shop seemed similar to the nail salons my mom used to drag me into: rows of polishes to choose from, eight massage chairs poised over foot basins gurgling with hot water, narrow tables staffed by smiling men and women.

"Mani-pedi?" asked the owner, coming forward with a smile that showed a gap between his front teeth.

"Not today, Yong. I'm wondering if you've ever seen this man in here?" I showed him the creased photo of Celio

Arriaga. The other workers, not having any clients this early, watched us curiously and chattered softly in Korean. One woman eyed me uneasily and disappeared into a back room.

He studied it. "Is the murdered man," he said, eyes lifting to my face.

"Yes."

He shook his head sharply. "Is not customer. I told you this last time you asked."

"I know. Can you ask your staff?"

Taking the paper from my hand, Yong showed it to each of his employees. I didn't understand the whispered Korean, but the head shakes told me he was batting zero.

"Thanks anyway," I said when he handed me the photo along with the news I expected. "I don't suppose you keep a gun here, for protection?"

Yong's face closed down. "I have baseball bat," he said. He said something to one of the women, and she obligingly lifted a Louisville Slugger from beneath the counter and held it over her head. "But security very good here. I don't need."

I thanked him and left.

The Herpetology Hut was next down the line, and I went in to find Keifer loosing a live rat in Agatha's enclosure. The heavy python looked like she hadn't even noticed the rodent, but I didn't figure it would be there by the end of the day. I averted my eyes. Keifer noticed and grinned, teeth white against his dark skin.

"Squeamish, EJ?"

"It doesn't seem like a fair fight," I replied. "Not with the rat trapped in there."

"How many of life's fights are fair?" he countered.

"True enough. I don't suppose you're selling guns out of your storeroom or running a 'Buy a snake, get a Colt Python for free' promotion?" Though I'd told myself I'd interview all the business owners in the wing impartially, I knew Keifer too well to believe he was peddling guns.

Keifer looked at me like I'd lost my mind. "What are you going on about, EJ?"

"I don't know," I admitted.

Flipping his dreads over his shoulder, he asked, "Does this have to do with the banger who got killed, or with Woskowicz's death?"

"Maybe both, maybe neither."

Keifer gave me a pitying look. "Leave it to the police, EJ."

His mention of the police made me guiltily aware that I hadn't told Detective Helland about my conversation with Eloísa.

Rock Star was next up, and when I entered the teen accessories emporium, a pair of women in their midthirties were trying on lace gloves—for a costume party or theater event, I hoped. The manager, Carrie, caught sight of me and came clicking, tinkling, and jangling forward. "Oh, Officer Ferris, I forgot to tell you. That girl you were interested in? She was in here yesterday with a friend. I meant to call you, but then it got busy in here. But I'm telling you now." She smiled like a dog expecting praise or a tidbit for performing a task.

"Thanks," I said drily.

"Any time!"

I didn't know how to broach the topic of guns with this barely twenty-year-old girl whose appearance and demeanor suggested that the most lethal weapon she'd ever owned was her car, or maybe a nail file. "Um, do you ever get people in here asking for something unusual?"

"Like what?"

"Well, like—"

"Oh, I know what you mean. Like tiaras and stuff? We don't carry them in stock, but we can special order them. We get a lot of requests for those around Mardi Gras and

Halloween. Or real gems? You wouldn't believe how many men wander in here thinking they can buy their wife or girlfriend a tennis bracelet or something." She rolled her eyes at the thought. "It's not like we're a *jewelry* store—we're an *accessories* store."

Short of tossing the *g*-word into the conversation, I didn't see how I could nudge her around to the topic I was interested in, so I gave it up and left.

"See you in class tomorrow," she called after me. "My little sister wants to come, too."

Call me ageist if you want, but if she was selling illicit weapons, I'd eat my belt. Besides—I gave it more thought—who was likely to buy guns? Probably not teens of the female persuasion. Women, maybe, for protection, or to shoot their husbands, and men for all sorts of reasons. Maybe a woman could get away with sidling into Rock Star, browsing the bracelets, and then asking for a gun on the side. Men? No way. A steady trail of adult men, even a trickle, would stand out in Rock Star like Hannibal's elephant-mounted army in the Alps. Using that logic, I'd also have to eliminate Jen's Toy Store and the Make-a-Manatee shop from consideration, I thought, surveying the wing.

Just as I reached this conclusion, a man in a Windbreaker with trousers a fraction too short strolled into Jen's, bumping the wagon that still stood outside the door. A daddy buying a gift? I sighed. Men could shop for their kids at Jen's or Make-a-Manatee, I guessed, so those stores would have to stay on my list after all. The most man-friendly place on the wing, Pete's Sporting Goods, was next up, and I crossed the threshold to find myself beneath an upside-down canoe that hadn't been there last time I was in the store.

"You've been doing some redecorating," I commented to Colin Garver, pointing to the canoe above my head. "Are canoes the new must-have element for home décor, like granite countertops or stainless steel appliances?"

"I think it has limited appeal as a home accent piece," Colin said, a smile creasing crinkles into his tanned skin. He stood behind a counter near the door, and I joined him, hitching one hip onto the counter. "Although it might work for folks who like the 'lodge' or 'mountain retreat' look. I assume you're not really here to look at canoes. Can I help you with a pair of Rollerblades or a Ping-Pong table?"

I hadn't thought about Ping-Pong in years. Clint and I used to play—the Malibu house had a table in the basement rec room next to the home theater that seated twenty, the wine cellar, and the home gym—and I'd been good. Good enough that Clint refused to play with me anymore by the time I was twelve or thirteen. It might be fun to get a Ping-Pong table. I mentally smacked myself. I was not here to buy sports gear; besides, who would I play with? Fubar had many talents, but I didn't think Ping-Pong was his forte.

Colin was looking at me quizzically. "Sorry," I said, shaking my head to refocus on the present. "The mention of Ping-Pong zoned me out for a sec—childhood memories."

"It's making a comeback," he said, but didn't press for the sale.

"When I was here before, you mentioned that Celio Arriaga had been in here, asking about guns."

Colin nodded but his gaze was on a customer examining sports bras. "Those are among my most shoplifted items," he said, discreetly gesturing toward the bra-browsing woman.

"Do you get a lot of shoppers in here wanting to pick up a gun without bothering with the waiting period or the background check?"

"Define 'a lot,' " he said. "We get a few each month."

"What do you do?"

That snapped his attention back to me. "What are you implying?" With narrowed eyes and the cords on his neck suddenly more prominent, he looked intimidating.

"I'm just wondering what you tell them," I said in a non-confrontational voice.

He wasn't totally pacified, but he responded, "Mostly, I explain the laws to them and they leave."

"And those who persist? What if a woman came in needing a gun to protect herself from an abusive husband or boyfriend?"

"I don't like where you're going with this, EJ." He rotated his shoulders back three times and then forward three times. "Have there been complaints?"

"No. Just humor me."

Comprehension glinted in his pale eyes. "I see. Do you have a 'friend' some man's using as a punching bag? Someone who needs a gun?"

I didn't respond, letting him draw his own conclusions. The shopper disappeared into a dressing room with a handful of bras, and Colin didn't even notice. "I get it. In such a situation, I might—I say I *might*—suggest she visit a gun show, preferably in another state, or check Craig's List."

Interesting. "Aren't sellers at gun shows bound by the same rules you are?"

"In theory. In practice . . . that environment is a whole lot looser and less regulated. No bar codes. No sales orders on record with manufacturers like Beretta or Glock. A lot of the gun show business is cash-and-carry, so no credit card receipts or checks to track. The feds have been trying to keep better tabs on what goes on, but they don't have the manpower. They won't get it until some jerk shoots up a playground or shopping center with a weapon bought at a gun show," he finished cynically.

Asking Colin point-blank if he sold guns under the table would only earn me his hostility, so I thanked him and left, leaving him with the impression that I had a friend who wanted to solve her marital problems with a bullet. His response let me know that, at the very least, he was willing to, if not bend the rules, then point a would-be gun owner toward someone who would.

Sunshine streamed into the wing from the double glass doors leading to the parking lots, and I felt it drape across my shoulders as I crossed the hall toward the sunglasses place. It half blinded me, so I didn't notice Detective Helland approaching until he was almost in front of me.

"Officer Ferris," he said, his voice flinty. "Just the person I wanted to see."

I got the sort of feeling in the pit of my stomach that used to attack me when told the principal wanted to see me in her office. Usually, I hadn't done anything to merit a chewing out by the principal, so the feeling of dread was wasted. Today, however, I was conscious that (a) I hadn't told Helland about Eloísa's revelations, minor as they were, and (b) I was interviewing merchants on a topic he might feel he had a proprietary interest in, so to speak. Consequently, I managed only a strangled, "Hi."

With his tall figure now blocking the sunlight, I could face him without squinting. His mouth was set in an uncompromising line. "A Mrs. Rosita Arriaga reported her daughter Eloísa missing this morning."

I gasped.

He nodded grimly at my reaction. "Exactly. You call me one day to tell me about a fifteen-year-old who may know something about a murder, and the next day she's gone missing. I don't like coincidences. In fact, I don't basically believe in them."

I didn't either, at least not in this case.

"The cop who took Mrs. Arriaga's report recognized the name and clued me in. What do you know about it?"

Tucking a hank of hair behind my ear, I said, "After I talked to you yesterday, I got a call saying that if I wanted to talk to Eloísa I should go to Phat Cat last night. I did and I hooked up with her briefly." I filled him in on what Eloísa had said. "She was terrified of this Enrique, and when a truck came around the corner, she took off for the woods like Usain Bolt headed for the finish line. It was only a club security guy."

"She didn't come home last night," Helland said, making it clear he blamed me for that. As galling and as worrying as it was, he was probably right.

"I didn't see her after she ran off. That would've been a bit after ten," I said. Where could the girl be? I pictured her alone, chilled and hungry, hiding in the strip of woods near Phat Cat.

"You wouldn't hide her?" Helland's tone was marginally less stern.

"I might if I thought there was reason to, but I'm not and I'd've told you if I were."

"You didn't tell me about your conversation with her."

That was unanswerable, so I kept quiet. I didn't think saying "I was going to" would cut much mustard with him. "She's got a friend, a girl named Gilda whose sister works at Phat Cat," I said. "I don't know her last name."

He stopped short of rolling his eyes, but the expression on his lean, handsome face said it all: I'd messed up big-time.

"I'm sorry."

"You should be. You're interfering with a police

investigation, and you've endangered a girl who may be a key witness. If this is an example of the type of 'policing' the military does, no wonder things are so screwed up in Afghanistan."

"That's not fair" hovered on the tip of my tongue, but I bit it. Underneath Helland's hostility, I sensed worry for Eloísa and that kept me quiet. "Where are you looking for her?" I asked quietly.

"I'm not Missing Persons; it's not my case," he bit out. "I just volunteered to come over here and grill you because I was certain you had something to do with her going missing."

"I can help—"

"You've helped enough. Call Detective Angela Barnes in Missing Persons if you see or hear from Eloísa." He scribbled a number on a piece of paper from his notepad, ripped it out, and thrust it at me.

I took it numbly and stuck it in my pocket. Without another word, Helland wheeled and strode toward the door. As he moved away, the sun struck my face again, blinding me, and I turned away to stop the involuntary tears. Caused by the sun, I told myself.

Seventeen

...

Joel took one look at my face when I returned to the office and asked, "Whoa. Who died?"

"No one." Yet. I prayed it was true and that Eloísa was safe. I gave him the *Reader's Digest* version of Helland's tongue-lashing.

"That's ridiculous," Joel said promptly, reaching into a plastic snack bag for a celery stick, which he then crunched down on. "You know what you're doing. It's not your fault—"

I stopped him with a shake of my head. I appreciated his faith in me, but no one could absolve me of blame in this case. "No. I screwed up. I should have called Helland before I ever went to the club. If something happens to Eloísa, it's at least partly my fault."

Silence fell, broken only by Joel's chomping, and I watched the monitors absently, not really seeing what was playing out on the screens. The sound of Joel's teeth grinding against the celery made me feel like I was in a barn with a team of cud-chewing oxen. All that was missing was the smell of dung.

"I don't suppose you've seen this?" Joel asked, pushing the *Vernonville Times* toward me. He pointed toward a paragraph on an inside page.

"New Development in Gang Killing," read the headline. I skimmed the lines beneath it.

A spokeswoman for the Vernonville Police Department today revealed that the police have recovered the weapon used to kill Celio Arriaga, the man found outside the Fernglen Galleria on Wednesday. "We caught a break," Lieutenant Erin McEvoy, VPD public affairs officer, told reporters yesterday. She went on to say that the .32-caliber gun was originally registered in California but had been turned in as part of a gun amnesty program run by the Mantua, New Jersey, police department. That department is investigating to determine how a gun thought to have been destroyed ended up back on the streets, according to McEvoy.

"Interesting," I murmured, my gaze still on the newspaper. The article didn't say where the police had acquired the murder weapon, but it almost had to be the gun from Captain Woskowicz's office, didn't it? I noticed the police PA lieutenant hadn't said anything about an imminent arrest. Was that because they were convinced Captain W was guilty and you couldn't arrest a dead man?

"I thought you'd think so," Joel said, pleased. "So, do you think a crooked cop killed that gangbanger?"

"Why would a cop from New Jersey be interested in a low-life gang minion in Vernonville?" I asked. "I doubt that's what happened. However, maybe a cop or someone connected with the company contracted to destroy the guns saw a way to make a little profit."

"And sold it?"

I nodded.

"Was Arriaga from New Jersey?"

Wrinkling my brow, I tried to remember everything I'd heard about Celio Arriaga from Gilda and Eloísa. "I don't think so," I said slowly. "I got the impression he was from this area, but I suppose it's possible he moved from New Jersey. Why?"

Joel's eyes lit up and he leaned forward, excited as always by speculating about a case. "Well, if Arriaga was from New Jersey, maybe he made some enemies up there. Do they have Niños Malos in Jersey? A rival gang. They got hold of the gun, and one of them came down here to pop him." He must have seen the skepticism on my face because he plowed on. "You're going to say 'Why would they bother?' Right?"

I nodded, a half smile on my lips. He was learning.

"I've got that figured out. He had something on someone, and they were afraid he'd tell. He saw someone kill somebody, or knew too much about someone's drug-ring operations." He bounced in the chair, causing an alarming squeak.

"I'm not saying that's impossible, Joel," I said after a moment's thought, "but it all hinges on Celio being from New Jersey, and we don't have any reason to think he was." Even if he were from New Jersey, I found Joel's convoluted scenario unlikely. More probably, the reason for Celio's death was closer to home: he was in the wrong place at the wrong time and got killed, not an unusual occurrence when one hung out with angry young men who carried guns and thought it was "cool," or a sign of manhood, to shoot people.

"I'll find out where he was from," Joel said, clicking away on his computer keyboard.

I left him to it and went to find Grandpa Atherton. He was Easter Bunnying, and I had to wait for him to finish with a toddler who burst into tears when her mother plopped her onto his lap. In less than thirty seconds, he had jollied away her tears, and by the one-minute mark he had coaxed a grin from her. He had a way with children, and I smiled at his silliness, remembering how he used to entertain me and Cliff with made-up nonsense songs, much the way he was now beguiling the now giggling child on his lap. The photographer snapped a photo, and the tot's mother lifted her from Grandpa. The little girl promptly dissolved into tears again, holding her arms out toward Grandpa, and crying, "Bunny, play Bunny!"

When the mother had hauled the heartbroken girl away, Grandpa turned to me and said, "My, you're quite a big girl. Did you want to have your photo taken with the Easter Bunny?"

I heard the laughter in his voice. "Sure." I climbed over the low picket fence and stood beside him while the confused photographer readied the camera.

"Say 'Bunny,'" the photographer demanded and we complied. "I'm taking a break," he said after accepting my money for the photo. He walked off, pulling a pack of cigarettes from his pocket.

"To what do I owe the honor?" Grandpa asked.

I pulled the photographer's folding chair up beside Grandpa's Easter Bunny throne and sat. It was weird talking to the vacant stare from the Easter Bunny's egg-shaped eyes, and I tried to focus on the mesh screen near his bow tie. "What do you know about gunrunning or gun amnesty programs?" I asked, thinking that he might have some experience from his CIA days.

"You mean like guns for oil? I wasn't involved with any of those ops," he said.

"Not guns for oil so much as gun smuggling into the U.S. or illegal gun sales on a smaller scale," I clarified.

"You know that would be the FBI's or ATF's bailiwicks," he said. "The Company doesn't operate within the U.S."

"I know," I said. "But I thought you might've had some involvement . . ." I tapered off so he could take the question any way he wanted. There was something surreal about discussing gun smuggling with the Easter Bunny.

"Sorry, Emma-Joy," he said. "You probably know as much about that as I do. And all I know about amnesty programs is that some police departments offer to accept guns, no questions asked, from citizens. They think that it'll get guns off the streets and make cops—and other citizens— safer. I've never bought their logic, though, since I doubt the lowlifes who are likely to kill are the ones turning in their weapons."

I was a little disappointed at Grandpa's lack of expertise in this area, but not too surprised. "Thanks anyway," I said, hugging him and landing a kiss somewhere on his furry neck.

I grabbed a quick lunch in the food court, toying with the idea of asking the mysterious Mr. Callahan if he knew anything about gun smuggling. He'd asked me to tell him if I heard anything about guns, and this qualified, surely? A grandmotherly woman with poorly fitting dentures was manning the Lola's counter, however, and I didn't see Jay.

Checking in with Harold Wasserman, on dispatch duty while Joel lunched, I learned there was nothing of note happening in the mall. "I'll be in the Pete's wing if you need me," I told him and clicked off.

That short corridor of shops pulled at me, like waves inexorably tugging grains of sand from the beach into the depths. The key to whatever had happened to Celio, and maybe Captain Woskowicz, too, lay in one of these shops. I was sure of it. I Segwayed past the shops I'd been in earlier, stopping at the outer doors to gaze into the parking lot.

Nothing unusual. Cars parked nose to nose, the gleam of chrome, a trickle of shoppers crossing the lots, either laden with bags as they returned to their cars or strolling empty-handed into the mall. No one hurried because it was a beautiful, warm spring day.

I did a one-eighty and surveyed the wing that spread out before me. Nothing stood out. Planters overflowed with ferns and hostas. One bench was empty, and one was occupied by a bored-looking man maybe waiting for his wife to finish shopping. The sun slanted in at an angle that revealed little handprints and maybe a nose smudge or two on the toy store window. My gaze drifted upward, lingering on the cameras. The cameras . . .

I glanced over my shoulder at the sidewalk just beyond the glass doors. My gaze lingered on the spot where I'd found Celio. If Celio was killed by someone gang-connected and his body was dropped at the mall to keep police from discovering the murderer, how likely was it that the killer, or killers, would happen to dump him at the one entrance with a nonfunctional camera? Not very. That was too big a coincidence for me to swallow. Only a handful of people knew the cameras weren't working, and they all resided in this wing or in the security office.

My eyes widened as a question occurred to me: Was it possible that Celio had been killed *inside* the mall and his body dragged outside? Everyone had been working under the assumption that Celio was killed off mall property somewhere and his body driven to the mall. What if that assumption was wrong?

I tried to rein in my galloping thoughts. If I was right, Captain Woskowicz became the prime suspect. He had means (the gun found in his file cabinet) and opportunity (he knew the cameras were on the fritz). I had no idea what his motive could be, but I knew it wasn't necessary to prove

motive to convict someone. But if Captain W had killed
Celio, who had killed Captain W? A gang member getting
revenge for Celio's death? Or some totally unknown player?

I found myself taking out my cell phone and dialing
Detective Helland's number almost without conscious voli-
tion. A bored voice told me he wasn't available, and I asked
to be switched to his voice mail. After leaving a detailed
message that laid out my analysis, I hung up, feeling I'd done
a little bit to atone for not calling him about Eloísa.

Leaning forward to propel the Segway, I pulled up beside
the red wagon in front of Jen's Toy Store and went in. The
store was bright and cheery with shelves of games, toys,
stuffed animals, and a large Lego table in the middle with
half-built creations rising from the bumpy surface. Resisting
the urge to add a couple of Legos to a lopsided castle, I
looked for Jen, who hadn't been in when I canvassed the
wing before, and spotted her on her hands and knees beside
a shelf, probing beneath it. "Lose something?"

She started and looked up, withdrawing a long piece of
wire—a repurposed clothes hanger, I surmised—from
beneath the shelf. A soft-spoken woman originally from
Oklahoma, Jen was in her mid to late forties, with a spat-
tering of freckles and slightly jug ears that made her look
younger. Standing, she said, "Just doing my weekly Lego
collection." She wiped a wisp of hair from her forehead with
the back of her hand. "Somehow they end up all over the
store, not just around the table. What's up?"

"Had any more problems with disappearing wagons?"

She laughed gently. "No. Not this week. I sold two,
though."

Did that mean the wagon out front was not the one that
had been on display the day Celio died? I felt a twinge of
disappointment because it had occurred to me that the

wagon would make an excellent corpse transportation device in a pinch. "Did you sell the wagon sitting out front and then put out another one?"

Jen gave me a funny look. "No, I usually sell boxed ones from my storeroom. That wagon"—she nodded toward the hall—"has been my display wagon for a couple of months. I'll sell it at a discount in another month or two. It gets a little banged up out there."

I pulled out my photo of Celio. "Was he ever in here?"

She examined it, absently tapping the wire down the length of her leg. "Not that I remember. Why?"

"He's the one whose body was left out front," I said.

"That poor boy. He looks so young." Her gaze lingered on the photo before she looked up at me. "Have the police arrested anyone?"

Shaking my head, I said, "No. But they're making progress. Today's paper has an article about them ID'ing the gun that was used."

"What's that tattoo on his hand?" she asked, pointing at the horizontal cross that was barely visible in the photo. "Does it mean something?"

"That's a good question," I said slowly, wondering why I hadn't thought to research an answer before now. "I don't know."

"Such a shame."

Jen knelt again and resumed her sweeps under the shelves, pulling stray Lego pieces to her with the hanger. A display of realistic-looking cap guns and squirt guns trembled as she jostled the shelf. I doubted most people could tell them from the real thing if they were seen from a distance. "Sell a lot of guns?" I asked.

She laughed. "The boys love 'em."

How easy would it be, I wondered as I left the store, to

insert a real gun into a cap-gun or squirt-gun package and
let customers walk out of the store with the gun in plain
sight? Pretty easy, I'd bet.

Returning to the office, I left another message for Detective Helland to relay my thoughts about the wagon, before sitting down at the computer to do a search on "gang tattoos." I didn't need to scan more than one page of images to find the horizontal cross I'd last seen inked onto Celio Arriaga's hand. Text described the cross as the symbol of the gang member responsible for supplying the gang with guns. I leaned back in my chair, gazing intently at the simple black image now magnified on the computer screen. A gang's division of labor wasn't too different from the military's, I thought; the military had staffs for personnel, intelligence, logistics, and the like. And gangs definitely had a command hierarchy, as well. I closed the tab. I wasn't sure that my new knowledge got me any place. It confirmed that Arriaga was probably interested in acquiring pistols and Mac-10s and rocket launchers, for all I knew, for the Niños Malos, but it didn't tell me where he went in the mall after splitting from Eloísa and Enrique, and it didn't tell me doodly-squat about who killed him or why. With a sigh, I applied myself to paperwork until the shift change at three o'clock. Joel left, saying he planned to swim, and Vic Dallabetta arrived. We greeted each other civilly, and I asked if she'd done anything special the day before on her day off.

"Parent-teacher conference," she said briefly. Bending to pick up a stray piece of paper from the floor, she accidentally cracked her head on the desk. "Ow!" She stood, fingers pressed to her forehead. "Damn it!"

"Sit. Let me get you some ice."

"I don't need—"

I was out the door before she could protest. To get ice, I'd have to go all the way down to the food court. So I improvised and bought a can of Coke from the vending machine in the hallway. I was back in the office within thirty seconds. "Here," I said, holding it out to her.

"Thanks," she muttered, gingerly putting the can to her forehead.

I studied her, noting dark circles under her eyes and tension in the way she pressed her lips together. Of course, she'd just smacked her head, so the tension might be pain, but the dark circles spoke of sleepless nights or worry.

I sat in the chair Joel had vacated. "Is everything okay?"

"I just split my head open, for Christ's sake," she said, looking at me from the corners of her eyes.

"I meant at home, with your health, or with Josie Rae." I persevered, even though I could see she resented my questions. "I don't want to pry," I said, "but if there's something I could help with, I'd be happy to."

She didn't snap my head off as I expected her to. Instead, she leaned sideways so she could support her elbow on the desk and take some of the weight off the arm holding the Coke can to the lump on her forehead. "The swing shift is hard for me," she said finally. "I have to make arrangements for someone to pick up Josie Rae and keep her after school. One of my friends does that. But she's got night classes, so she takes Josie Rae to my sister's for dinner. After dinner, Bree—my sister—makes sure she does her homework and that she goes to bed at a decent time. I pick her up when I get off shift, so it's eleven thirty by the time we get home and I get her into her own bed. Then we're up by six to get her ready for school." Her eyes flitted to me once or twice, but she mostly kept her gaze on the desk.

"I don't see why we can't tinker with the schedule to keep

you off swings," I said, relieved that her problem was a simple one to solve.

"Captain Woskowicz said if I played 'the mommy card' he'd fire me," she said, straightening and putting the can on the desk with a clink. "I don't want favors because I'm a single mom." She tried for a glare, but the hope in her eyes undermined it.

"We all have lives outside work," I said. "Some folks have aging parents to care for or children or pets. Some have hobbies that consume their lives and require time off. Rick Sencenbaugh is running a marathon next week, you know, and we've worked his shifts so he can do it without taking vacation days."

"I thought he was doing a triathlon," Vic said.

"Whatever. One of those races no sane person would tackle."

That earned a small quirk of her lips. Encouraged, I said, "So, I'm sure we can work your schedule around swings, especially if you're willing to do the night shift on occasion?"

"Any time," she said. "Nights work for us because then Josie Rae spends the night at Bree's, and I pick her up and we do McDonald's for breakfast before I take her to school. I sleep while she's in school, and then we have time together after school so I can help her with her homework, take her to soccer practice, and all that."

"Let's do it, then," I said, standing.

"I applied for the director of security job, you know," Vic said, almost as if challenging me to renege on my promise to rework the schedule.

"I know. You told me."

"I'm not withdrawing my name."

"Who asked you to?" I said it with a smile and was pleased to see her shoulders relax slightly. I imagined they got tired, what with carrying that chip—more like a boulder—around all the time.

"Okay, then." She nodded and turned to focus on the monitors.

"Okay."

Eighteen

. . .

Changing into jeans and a green sweater half an hour later, I went off shift and strolled down to the Pete's wing, glad that my knee appeared to be doing better. I poked my head into Make-a-Manatee where a birthday party was in full swing, a dozen eight- or nine-year-olds gathered around the table in the back, their faces smeared with cake and ice cream. Each had a newly stuffed animal friend perched nearby. Empty two-liter soda bottles in a recycling bin said the kids had mainlined enough sugar to keep them high for hours. A mom about my age tried in vain to wipe off their hands with moist towelettes.

"Mike around?" I asked her.

She barely looked up from smudging blue icing off a boy's lips. "The rest of the parents were supposed to stay for the party," she said balefully. "Not dump the kids and go for a latte or run errands. I can't ride herd on all these kids. The store should provide more supervision. Cleo won't be having any more parties here, I can tell you."

"I don't blame you. Mike?"

"In the back."

I walked around the long partition that separated the sales area from the stockroom and office. Stacked boxes crowded the musty-smelling stockroom, unstuffed animal skins peeking out of the tops of some of them. I found Mike on the phone in the tiny office, his back to me.

"—and the Nuggets by eight," he said. After a slight pause, he said, his voice pinched, "I know. You made it crystal clear that—"

He turned as he spoke and saw me standing in the doorway. He juggled the phone and almost dropped it. Smiling, I gestured and backed away to show him I'd wait until the end of his conversation.

"I've gotta go, Clark. You and Mary are still coming for dinner Friday night, right?" He waited for an answer and then hung up and returned the phone to its charger.

"My brother-in-law," he said with a strained smile. "He's a Spurs fan. I tried to talk Mary out of marrying him because of it, but she loves the guy." He shrugged in a "what can you do?" way. "What's up, EJ?" He frowned as a shriek penetrated the partition. "Sounds like World War III. I'd better get out there."

"Just a quick question, Mike. Do you remember hearing anything that sounded like a gunshot or backfire last Tuesday?" It was a long shot—surely, someone would have reported a gunshot if Celio had been killed during business hours?—but maybe it had happened late, when most of the shoppers were gone, and the merchants would remember hearing something unusual.

He cocked his head. "A gunshot?"

"Or backfire."

"This is about that kid who got shot, right? Maybe terrorists got him, EJ. The *Post* had an article not long ago about how terrorists may be targeting American malls. Is that what this is about?" He looked worried, blinking myopically from behind his wire-rimmed glasses.

Captain Woskowicz had gone to the FBI board when that article came out and used it to argue that the security force should be allowed to carry weapons. The board shot down the idea—so to speak—hinting that the chance of shoppers being accidentally wounded by an armed security guard was greater than the risk of a terrorist incident. I had to agree with them.

"Unlikely," I said, not wanting to spell out my suspicions.

"I don't remember anything. But then"—he gestured toward the sales floor where a couple of the kids were apparently arguing about whose shark stuffie was meaner—"it gets pretty loud in here sometimes."

"I've been in firefights that were quieter," I said, grinning.

He smiled back and walked around the partition, his leg cast thunking with each step. "And less dangerous," he said as a cupcake splatted into the wall by his head.

I left as he waded in to help the mom corral the exuberant third-graders. I strolled into Starla's Styles, wanting to talk to Starla, but a clerk told me she'd left for the day. When I floated my question about gunshots or unusual noises, the clerk looked at me blankly. "I'm new," she said.

With a sigh, I told her good night and headed for the parking lot. I drove home, greeted Fubar, and began making dinner, all the while sifting through what I knew about the two recent deaths. I was 90 percent convinced Captain Woskowicz had shot Celio Arriaga, although I was damned if I knew why. Could he and Celio have been in cahoots on some sort of theft? Had Captain W disabled the cameras so they could remove merchandise from that wing without being observed? I didn't see much street value in cases of nail polish, stuffing-less manatee carcasses, Etch A Sketches, or fake bling. There'd be significant street value in the guns from Pete's, but those couldn't walk out of the store without Colin Garver noticing and, I presumed, reporting the theft.

I whisked a Caesar dressing in a bowl and poured it over the crisp romaine I'd already torn up. Fubar looked disappointed until I began to broil a salmon fillet to top the salad. Assuming Woskowicz killed Celio, who shot Woskowicz? Was there a third party involved in whatever they'd been up to at the mall? There had to be, I reasoned. Maybe all of the Niños Malos? Could one of them have killed Woskowicz, either because he double-crossed them or in revenge for Celio's death? Certainly. Gang members killed if you looked at them funny or wore the wrong colors or crossed the street in the wrong place.

Sitting down to eat my salad, Fubar hovering hopefully under my chair, I wished I knew someone who might have more insight into Captain Woskowicz. Wait a minute . . . my fork stopped halfway to my mouth. His ex-wives! They probably knew him better than anyone. A glance at my watch told me it was only six thirty. I didn't know how to find Nina or Paula at this hour, but I knew from the commercials that Dealin' Dwight's was open until nine.

I pulled into the used car lot just before seven. A kajillion watts of light blazed from lampposts spaced closely together, turning the dusk into full daylight. A handful of potential car buyers ambled from car to car, checking out sticker prices, salespeople in their wake. A bigger-than-life-sized cutout of Dealin' Dwight greeted visitors at the showroom door. The cardboard Dwight had his hand outstretched as if to shake hands . . . or take your money. I had barely registered off-white tile, the odors of oil and stale coffee, and the hiss of pneumatic tools when a skinny man with a prominent Adam's apple vectored toward me like a missile locked on target.

"I'm looking for Aggie," I said, forestalling his sales pitch.

"Oh. On the lot." He jerked his thumb toward a side door.

"Thanks." I drifted along a row of used vans until I spied Aggie. Her red hair was like a beacon, especially when spotlit by a nearby lamppost. She was talking to a young couple by the bumper of a van that looked like it had three hundred thousand miles on it. Miles racked up on a rutted llama track in the Andes. As I watched, she handed them her card and shook hands with each of them. I didn't realize she'd seen me, but she headed straight for me after waving at the departing couple.

"They'll be back," she said confidently. "I can always tell. Expecting a baby, need a van."

I thought putting a baby in that van constituted child endangerment, but I didn't say so.

"You're not looking for a car," she stated, "so what do you want?"

Her tone wasn't hostile, but she wasn't brimming over with friendliness either. I knew if she spotted a likely buyer, she'd ditch me in an instant.

"Did you find that safe-deposit key you were looking for?" I asked.

She eyed me suspiciously. "Why, did you find one?"

I shook my head. "No. I'm actually here because I thought you might be able to tell me if you'd noticed anything different about Captain Woskowicz in the last few weeks. Was there something going on in his life? Did he seem nervous, afraid of something?"

"The cops asked me the same questions," she said. "I told them I didn't know of anyone who would want to shoot Wosko. Except maybe Paula. She was some kind of mad when he left her for me."

"But that was several years ago, right?"

Aggie nodded grudgingly. "Yeah. And my guess is she'd rather kill me than him anyway. I don't think she ever got over him, if you know what I mean." She slapped at a mosquito on her arm.

"You've had time to think about it more since you talked to the police," I said. "Has anything occurred to you?"

She slanted a look at me. "He seemed a little edgy the last couple of weeks," she conceded. "But I put it down to the divorce getting finalized. He was pretty broken up about it."

Hm. He hadn't struck me as broken up; he'd been dating a good-looking reporter and getting it on with his ex-wives. "You left him?" That didn't seem to be in keeping with his pattern of trading in one redhead for another every few years.

"Yeah. What goes around comes around, you know?" She smiled, but it didn't reach her eyes.

"When you say he was 'edgy,' what do you mean?"

"Edgy. Snappy. Bit my head off for buying the wrong kind of beer. I wanted to try something different." She dragged the toe of her chunky, low-heeled boot across the asphalt. "When my brother Billy came down, we went to a Bullets game and Wosko almost punched a guy who spilled popcorn in his lap. That wasn't like him. Usually he was pretty easygoing."

I raised my brows but kept silent. I'd never thought of Woskowicz as "easygoing." Petty and lazy did not equal easygoing in my mind.

"Why are you so interested anyway?"

Aggie's direct question took me by surprise. "He was my boss," I said, stating the obvious. The breeze picked up, and I held my leather jacket closed. "I don't like murder." That sounded stupid and obvious, too, and I couldn't blame Aggie for rolling her eyes. "I guess . . . I guess I really don't like people getting away with something, thinking they can break the rules that the rest of us follow. It pisses me off."

"I hear you," Aggie said, nodding in agreement.

"And I don't want people to be afraid to come to my mall. They shouldn't see the word 'murder' and think 'Fernglen.'"

Aggie snorted, but not unkindly. "'Your' mall—now you sound like Wosko."

Eew. I barely refrained from gagging, making a mental note never to say "my mall" again. I saw Aggie's eyes track toward the lot entrance, and I knew she'd spotted a likely customer. Before she could dash off, I asked, "What was important to Woskowicz? What did he care about?"

She held up three fingers. "Sex." She folded down her ring finger. "Money." Down went the middle finger. She wiggled her index finger up and down. "I guess that's it," she said after a moment. "Sex and money, not necessarily in that order." Without another word she broke away from me, headed toward a teenager with his father. I didn't envy her having to broker a compromise between the boy, who was drooling on a used Corvette, and the father, who was carefully inspecting a Honda Civic.

"If someone asked you what I cared about, what would you say?" I asked Kyra half an hour later. We were sitting on the front porch of her aunt Harmony's house, spooning ice cream out of the pint containers I'd picked up at a Giant supermarket on my way over. Kyra, having recently sold her software company for a mint—she wrote programs that helped coaches make schedules and personalize training programs and I don't know what all else—was between projects and had agreed not only to run Merlin's Cave but also to live in Harmony's house during her aunt's so-called sabbatical.

Small and quirky, not unlike its owner, the house was more of a bungalow. When the house was built in the mid-1800s, it stood alone, west of Vernonville. Now, it was on the edge of the Vernonville town center; the town had expanded to swallow it up. Painted a soft blue, it had lavender trim Kyra hated and, reputedly, a resident ghost, a woman killed for allegedly helping slaves escape their owners via the Underground Railroad.

"Hm." Kyra licked mint ice cream off her spoon and kicked out her foot to make the porch swing rock. "Well, family. Look at how you take such good care of your grandpa—"

"I think it's the other way around."

"—and the way you stay in touch with your folks, even though your dad drives you crazy sometimes."

"More often than not," I agreed.

"And you're definitely into fitness." She eyed me assessingly. "But I'm not sure it's really fitness that's important. It's more about control, I think. You being in control of your body. That's why this whole knee thing has weighed on you so much. You can't control it."

Whoa, this was probing a bit deeper than I'd anticipated. "Can't you just say, 'Duty, honor, country,' or 'Family, friends, and chocolate ice cream'?" I complained.

"You asked."

"Silly me." Kicking off my shoes, I folded one foot under me on the floral-cushioned wicker chair.

"What about me?"

I regarded my friend. "Honesty."

She nodded.

"Men."

She grinned.

"Power."

She crinkled her brow. "What's that mean? You think I want to rule the world?"

"Nah, just your corner of it. Kidding!" I said as she threatened to launch a gob of ice cream at me. "No, I mean that it's important to you to have people's respect, to be in charge of your own destiny. That's part of why you didn't marry Parker, right?" I asked, referring to a man she'd been in love with as a college junior. "You were afraid if you married him, you wouldn't finish college, wouldn't be self-supporting, wouldn't achieve what you knew you were capable of achieving."

"He wanted a wife to play Mrs. Big-Shot Lawyer," she said, tacitly conceding my point.

"Maybe 'power' is the wrong word," I said, still thinking it through. "Maybe 'self-sufficiency' or 'independence' would be better."

"Nah, I'm into power." With a smile, she crushed the empty ice cream container, spurting drops of melted green ice cream on her white sweats. "Damn, that was dumb," she said, disappearing into the house. She reappeared a moment later, sponging at the spots with a damp paper towel. "So what's next on your investigatory agenda? Talk to the other wives?"

"I suppose so," I said with a marked lack of enthusiasm. "I don't suppose I'll get much of anything from them."

"You're convinced Captain Was-a-bitch shot the Arriaga kid?"

"He had the smoking gun, quite literally." I shrugged.

"What if . . . what if Woskowicz's death had nothing to do with Arriaga's?"

I twisted my face into a combination scowl-pout. "The timing's awfully coincidental," I objected.

"No, think about it," Kyra said, dark eyes sparkling. A large dog woofed from a neighboring yard. "The whole 'car in the park' thing feels like a lover's rendezvous to me. What if one of his ex-wives found out that he was getting it on with the other ex-wives and went mental? Or, maybe he was meeting a new woman and this Aggie wife, who was still married to him, went 'round the bend."

"She said she left him," I insisted, realizing as I said it how weak it sounded.

"That's what I'd say, too," Kyra said, "if I'd shot my philandering son-of-a-bitch, almost ex-husband."

"I'm going home to bed," I said, standing. The ice cream weighed heavily in my stomach and I was thirsty. "I have exceeded the day's quota of thinking. Maybe the truth will come to me in a dream." I hugged Kyra, then lugged myself down the steps and into my car.

"If it's not about women, it's about money," Kyra called after me. "Sex or money."

Nineteen

...

On my way to the mall the next morning to teach the self-defense class, a news bulletin on the radio caught my attention. "Chief Baker of the Vernonville Police Department is holding a press conference any moment now," a reporter said, "to announce an arrest in the case of the young man, Celio Arriaga, who was shot dead a week ago and left outside the Fernglen Galleria. Fernglen has been in the news recently as—"

I turned off the radio and pointed the Miata downtown. I could attend at least part of the press conference and still make it to Fernglen on time for the class. How would the police have made an arrest if Woskowicz killed Arriaga? The courthouse, a graceful building with a clock tower like the one hit by lightning in *Back to the Future*, dominated one side of a square that faced a park. In summer, lush grass carpeted the park; today, winter's tan grass still dominated, although clusters of purple and white crocuses added splotches of color. Half a dozen geese pecked at grubs, honking and shaking their tails when someone strayed too close.

A small crowd gathered in front of the courthouse steps, mostly reporters and police. Flashes of green, white, and red from the far edge of the crowd told me there were also some Niños Malos in attendance. The chief of police, gussied up in his dress uniform, complete with medals, stars on his collar points, and braid on his sleeves, emerged from the courthouse as I eased into the back rank of the crowd. Flanked by the district attorney, a sharp-looking woman in a gray suit, and a few officers, he moved toward the bristling bouquet of microphones set up on the bottom step.

He stayed two steps above the microphones, to look taller, I thought, but spoiled the effect by having to lean over to speak into the mikes. As he started to speak, I noticed Detective Helland standing off to the chief's right, patrician features set in an expressionless mask. His gaze drifted toward the gang members standing stonily silent and then raked the crowd. He spotted me and I offered a small smile. I couldn't read his expression before his attention shifted back to the chief.

". . . confession from Cruz Guerra, who admits shooting the victim, Celio Arriaga"—he stumbled over the Hispanic pronunciations—"during the course of an argument. It is up to the DA's office whether or not to try him as an adult since he is only fourteen. She can speak to that . . ." He stepped aside so the DA could reach the mike. She made a point of extending it, emphasizing that she was taller than the chief.

One of the Niños shouted something I couldn't understand, and three police moved quickly to impose themselves between the gang members and the rest of the crowd. It was clear they were ready for trouble, but after the one outburst the gang members fell silent.

After a couple of questions about the arrest—most of which the chief and DA fielded with "We can't reveal specifics"—a reporter asked, "What about the missing girl? Any word on that case?"

A broad smile creased the chief's ruddy face as he elbowed the DA aside and craned his neck to speak into the microphone. "I'm happy to report that the young lady is safe and staying with a family member."

Thank goodness! Relief washed over me so suddenly my knees trembled. I hadn't realized just how much I'd been blaming myself for Eloísa's disappearance and dreading that she wouldn't be found alive and unharmed.

"—just one of those teenage girl things," the chief was saying with a tolerant chuckle when I tuned back in. I'd bet he wasn't really feeling very tolerant since department resources had been expended trying to find her. I wondered exactly what he meant by "teenage girl thing."

My gaze fixed on Helland, who had his lips tightly gripped together. Admittedly, I didn't know him well, but he didn't look happy about the press conference. Or was he unhappy with the arrest? The chief and the DA fielded a couple of questions from the reporters and ended the press conference by saying there would be another statement "shortly." I wiggled my way through the departing crowd and reached Helland's side while he was trying to fend off questions from a persistent reporter. With a start, I recognized her as the reporter Woskowicz had been "dating." His term was cruder than that, and I reminded myself I only had his word for it that they were an item. She did have red hair, though—more of a strawberry blond.

Helland excused himself when he saw me and actually muttered, "Thanks," as he took my elbow and steered me away. "I'd rather take down a meth lab than talk to reporters," he said. "It's the part of the job I like least." He looked down at me and sighed, a resigned smile barely curving his lips. "Buy me a coffee."

I was so relieved that he'd gotten over his anger, probably because Eloísa had turned up unharmed, that I practically dragged him into the nearest Starbucks. When we had our cups of caffeine, we wormed our way out of the packed shop to enjoy a little more space and quiet outside.

"I got your messages yesterday," Helland said, prying the lid off his cup to blow on the liquid. "We picked up the wagon for testing. Interesting theory."

"But not too germane if you've arrested some kid."

Helland's gaze tracked a goose that was hissing and snaking its neck angrily at a lawn guy trying to fix a sprinkler head in the park. "He walked in yesterday. Alone. Announced he'd shot Celio Arriaga."

"You didn't believe him!"

His eyes, a slate blue, slewed to mine. "I didn't say that. Let's say I found it problematic that he showed up only after it leaked that we had ID'ed the murder weapon."

"Were his prints on it?"

Helland shook his head.

"What did he say about it?"

"Said he dropped it at the scene."

"The mall?"

Helland nodded.

And Captain Woskowicz happened to wander by, discover the body, pick up the gun, and not report the murder? That didn't pass my giggle test. Another thought occurred to me: "But that's not where Celio was killed. Where does he say he shot Celio?"

"He doesn't," Helland said with an edge of bitterness. "His brother and lawyer burst in about then and shut him up. His brother, by the way, is one Enrique Guerra, *mero mero* of the Niños Malos."

"Ooh. So you think Enrique did it and baby brother's taking the blame for some reason? He's not even old enough to drive, so he couldn't have transported the body alone." I took a contemplative sip of my coffee, then asked, "Did young Cruz say anything about shooting Captain Woskowicz as well?"

"Nope." Helland sounded disgusted. "Denied all knowledge of Woskowicz. Never heard of the man, he said. I believed him."

"About Woskowicz," I clarified, "but not about killing Celio."

"I didn't say that," Helland said in a way that confirmed my reading of his expression. "The chief likes him for it. Which is to say, the chief likes closed cases."

"Aah." I gave him a disillusioned look. "Now I know why I'm suddenly privileged to buy you coffee. As far as the department is concerned, you've got your murderer, so no one wants you spending time on the case anymore, upsetting the apple cart. But you don't think the Guerra kid did it, so you're hoping I'll keep poking around and maybe come up with something concrete you can use to reopen the case. Don't look so stunned," I added kindly, amused despite myself by his expression. "The police department doesn't have an exclusive on office politics, you know; the military had its fair share, too. You could've just asked me."

The idea of asking someone else to spearhead the investigation, especially someone he considered only a centimeter higher than a civilian, had obviously never crossed his mind. He stared into my eyes for a moment, clearly uncomfortable, and then said, "I underestimated you." He looked like he'd have been happier if I were the dullard he thought me.

"Happens all the time," I said, tossing my cup into a trash can. "It's the uniform." I gestured to my black-and-white outfit. "People hear 'mall cop' and they think 'minimum-wage

Paul Blart,' kind of like when they hear 'police' and think 'donut-eating, gun-loving storm trooper.'" I smiled, enjoying his discomfort. "Stereotypes are so limiting, don't you think?"

"I think you'd be a handful for any man foolish enough to take you on," he said, a look in his eyes that made my core muscles tighten. Was it possible the refined and reserved Detective Anders Helland found me attractive? Part of me tingled at the possibility, but the sane part pointed out that he was in the habit of using me when it suited him and ignoring my input the rest of the time. Not a great basis for a relationship.

Tucking a lock of chestnut hair behind my ear with a hand that trembled slightly, I said, "If I'm going to be your unofficial, unpaid investigator whom you will 'disavow all knowledge of' or however that line from *Mission: Impossible* goes, you might consider sharing a few more details with me."

"Like?" His tone promised nothing.

"Like the gun. It's the only real link between Arriaga's murder and Woskowicz. The news said it came from a gun amnesty program. What else do you know?"

Helland took another sip of coffee before answering, his eyes studying me over the lip of the cup. Finally, he said, "The Mantua PD does this twice a year. They put out a call for guns and accept any that come in, no harm, no foul. They log them, run them to see if they've been involved in a crime, and contract with a private company to destroy them and recycle the materials. They get everything from old shotguns to AK-47s. Mostly, though, it's a collection of handguns."

I took notes as he spoke. "Who's in charge of the program?"

"A Sergeant Merrill Stubbs."

"And the company that destroys them?"

"Allied Forge Metals." Chucking his empty cup into the trash can, he muttered under his breath, "I must be an idiot."

"Second thoughts?"

"And third and fourth," he said, his eyes drilling into mine. "I can't do this. I can't involve a civilian." He suddenly put his hands on my shoulders and gripped them, hard. I met his gaze without flinching. "Forget about it, EJ," he said. "Woskowicz's case is still open. I'll find a way to the truth about Arriaga's murder through that investigation."

I blinked at him, unsure what to say, and he gave me a tiny shake. "I'm sorry," he said.

I was still fumbling for a reply when he was half a block away.

Twenty

...

I trotted up to the assembled self-defense students a couple of minutes late, apologizing. Grandpa gave me a cocked eyebrow that asked where I'd been, and I mouthed "Later" at him. All the students from Monday had returned, several complaining of sore muscles, and two new women had joined us. One was clearly the Rock Star manager's sister, and the other was a woman who looked to be at least seventy. I thought she worked part-time at the fabric and yarn store on the first level. Despite a slight hump that suggested osteoporosis and a metal walker left at the edge of the mats, she gamely warmed up by marching in place and stretching with the rest of us. For the newcomers' benefit, and to help the moves sink in for the others, I ran through the highlights of Monday's lesson. "Your response needs to be automatic in a threatening situation," I said as they practiced side kicks and elbow punches. "Your brain will freeze up; muscle memory needs to take over. Practice these moves at home, on spouses, friends, your teenagers . . . anyone who's willing. The key word here is 'willing.'"

A couple students laughed, and we moved on to palm-heel strikes. "Twist your wrist back so the flat of your palm faces your attacker," I said, demonstrating, "and pull your fingers out of the way by folding them up. You're going to hit, or strike, with the hard, bottom part of your palm." I smacked the base of my right palm against my left hand. Several students jumped at the loud popping sound.

"If you're standing, aim for the nose or neck." I beckoned Grandpa forward, and he rushed toward me like an attacker would. Thrusting my arm out sharply, palm first, I halted the strike just shy of his nose. "Don't really hit each other with this one," I cautioned. "You can do serious damage. If your attacker has managed to throw you to the ground, aim your palm heels at his groin or diaphragm, thrusting upward." Grandpa and I demonstrated another couple of times before turning the students loose to practice on each other.

Starla, hair held back with a cloth headband, had paired up with Nina, who was making a game out of dodging Starla's wimpy strikes. "My four-year-old granddaughter hits harder than that," Nina said as I approached. "Like this." Nina snapped off an impressive palm-heel strike that grazed Starla's neck and sent her staggering back.

"Don't make contact," I said sharply.

"Accident," Nina said, looking pleased with herself. Rotating her shoulders to loosen them, she backed off half a step. "Too bad I never took a class like his before. It would've been useful with my husband."

Starla gasped, and my gaze fixed on Nina's face. I could think of only one interpretation for her words. "Are you saying Captain Woskowicz beat you?"

"Not Beaner." She shook her head. "My first. I met

Beaner at my gym while I was still married to Ron. We got to talking, and after a couple of months I told him about Ron hitting me. He helped me buy the gun that persuaded Ron not to mess with me anymore." Her gaze strayed to a canvas tote sitting next to stiletto heels just off the mats. "I still carry it."

Not sure how to reply, I turned to Starla, who was eyeing Nina with a combination of respect and trepidation. "Starla, set your feet like this." I showed her how to center her weight and balance better. "Then use the power in your legs and core to launch your arm forward."

"This is harder than it looks," she said, wheezing a little as I tapped the backs of her knees to get her to flex them and put my hands on her shoulders to show her how to swivel at the waist. "Maybe I should get a gun instead." She glanced at Nina's purse.

"I've got nothing against guns if the owners get properly trained," I said, "but you can't have one with you all the time, and if you carry it in your purse, you may not have time to get it out if you're attacked. And there's always the threat of the attacker taking it away and using it against you."

Looking thoughtful, Starla applied herself to the palm-heel strikes with enough determination to make Nina jump back, stumble, and fall on her well-padded fanny. I patted Starla's shoulder, gave Nina a hand up, and tried not to giggle as Grandpa winked at me.

A series of minor crises—a shoplifter, a lost six-year-old, and a defective fire alarm going off in Sears—kept me busy the rest of the morning after class ended. I didn't have time to think about Helland or his rescinded request. When lunch time rolled around, I was ready for a break. "What'll it be for lunch today?" I asked Joel. "I'll buy if you fly."

He smiled at me. "Thanks, EJ. That'd be a nice change. I've been bringing lunch from home lately because I'm saving to take Sunny some place nice for dinner after the movie. I was thinking maybe Red Lobster."

I suppressed a smile and said, "I'm sure she'd enjoy that, Joel. Chik-fil-A work for you?"

Twenty minutes later, our sandwiches almost gone, I mentioned Cruz Guerra's confession and arrest.

"No!" Joel's mouth fell open. "A fourteen-year-old? No way."

"That's what I'd say, normally, but he's one of the Niños Malos, so maybe." An image of my brother Clint at fourteen crossed my mind: basketball obsessed, braces, just beginning to think about what kind of car he wanted when he turned sixteen. I didn't think he'd ever held a gun. He was obnoxious and made fun of my acne, but he was no more capable of shooting a man in cold blood than our Bouvier, Rawhide, was. His life experience was a world away from Cruz Guerra's, I thought.

"I found out Celio Arriaga was born in Richmond," Joel said, "so my theory about New Jersey won't work." He slurped his diet soda noisily through a straw, looking downcast.

"Then we need a new theory," I said briskly. "The first ones rarely pan out." I didn't feel I could share Helland's information with him, so I suggested he do some research on Woskowicz's wives. "Kyra's convinced Woskowicz was at the battlefield park to meet a woman, a lover," I told him. "Maybe it was one of his exes. Maybe they were tired of the same-old-same-old and wanted to put a little zing back into their love life."

"Or that reporter he's been seeing," Joel put in, getting that excited look. He jostled his cup and grabbed it before it could spill.

"Good reflexes."

I left him happily clicking away on the computer keyboard, trying to find out more about Nina Wertmuller, Paula Poupére Woskowicz, and Aggie Woskowicz. As I cruised the halls on my Segway, I tried to think of some way I could give Joel more responsibility, develop what I thought were some decent leadership tendencies in him. I should probably wait until I found out if I had this job for real, I decided, veering into the Pete's wing.

This time, Starla was in. She had three belts draped over her plump forearm as she offered them one at a time to a customer standing indecisively in front of the three-way mirror. The customer, a woman of about Starla's age and girth, wore a flowing skirt and top patterned in swirling blues and greens. I had to admit the belts made the effect less tentlike. Starla saw me out of the corner of her eye and gave me a nervous "just a minute" signal.

"What do you think?" The customer pirouetted on wedge heels.

I thought the woven fabric belt made her look like a sack of potatoes cinched around the middle.

"The colors go well together," Starla said tactfully.

"I like the wide leather one," I said. "It would give you— the outfit—more structure." Not for nothing had I been raised in fashion-obsessed Hollywood; I recognized that belt as by far the most expensive one.

"Really?" She let Starla help fasten the leather belt around her waist, took a final look in the mirror, and said, "I'll take the outfit and this belt."

I waited while Starla rang up the purchase, wrapped the clothes in tissue paper, and told the customer about an upcoming sale. As soon as she was out the door, Starla turned to me and said, "Thank you."

She walked toward me reluctantly, passing near a lamp

with a soft glow that burnished her hair to a golden auburn. My eyes widened. "You and Captain Woskowicz were having an affair," I blurted.

She gasped and put a hand to her chest. "How did you—"

"He had a weakness for redheads."

She sighed, a soft, sad sigh. "Denny always said he loved my hair. We were getting married, you know."

I wasn't surprised. "You knew his divorce wasn't finalized yet."

She nodded, looking faintly guilty. "Yes. Not until Friday. We were talking about eloping to Las Vegas next week."

I'd have thought Woskowicz would have been leery of taking the marital plunge for a fourth time, but apparently not. Maybe he was one of those men who liked being married, only not for too long to the same woman. "Did Aggie know about you?" I was thinking about the soon-to-be-officially-ex-Mrs. Woskowicz's contention that she dumped her husband.

"Oh, yes," Starla said, looking simultaneously guilty and defiant. It was an expression more suited to a five-year-old than someone past fifty. "Dennis had to tell her. She kept pestering him, wanting to reconcile."

Aggie had lied to me. To save face, or for a more sinister reason? "When did he tell her?"

"Three weeks ago," Starla said. Tugging at a string near her ruffled cuff, she added, "She came to see me."

"Here?"

Starla nodded. "She was so . . . so ugly! Called me a home wrecker and a bitch and"—she lowered her voice—"the s-word. She even said my clothes were hideous and she wouldn't shop here if her other choice was to go naked the rest of her life."

It sounded like the clothes insult had incensed Starla

more than the *s*-word. I didn't mention that I kind of agreed with Aggie about the clothes. "Did she make any threats?"

"She said—oh. Oh!" Starla's mouth gathered into a perfect little O. "Did she—do you think—?" Her hands with their pale pink nails fluttered in front of her mouth, as if she were considering clamping them down on the words that spilled forth. "No! Surely she couldn't have—"

Killed Woskowicz? I wouldn't rule it out. Aloud, I said, "I don't suppose you were with Woskowicz the night he got killed? At the battlefield park?"

Starla shook her head. "No. I was doing inventory."

"Alone?"

"No, Martha-Anne was here, too. One of my sales ladies."

"Did you mention your . . . engagement to the police?"

"No." She plumped out her lower lip when I raised my brows. "I didn't see that my private life was any of their business. No one else knew except my son—he and Dennis really hit it off, and he was going to give me away if we got married here instead of in Vegas—and Aggie. I'll tell them now, though," she said grimly, "if it'll put them on to that . . . that Aggie. She can't be allowed to get away with it."

I gave her Detective Helland's number, and she wrote it down. "We don't know Aggie shot him, though," I reminded her.

Her nonresponse told me what she thought of that. "Did . . . Dennis"—it felt weird using his first name—"seem different at all the past couple of weeks? Did he talk about anything that might've been on his mind?"

"We mostly talked about the wedding. We'd both been married before, so we didn't want a big fuss, but I wanted a nice dress—I found a lovely pearl-colored one with a matching jacket at Diamanté—and flowers. Orchids maybe, or just carnations because I love their frilly petals. And we wanted to make sure they played our song."

She was drifting far afield, but I couldn't resist: "What's your song?"

'Walk Like an Egyptian.' She giggled and her gaze strayed to a dressing room door.

Not your typical wedding fare. I got a sudden image of her and Woskowicz playing pharaoh and slave girl in the dressing room on his lunch hours. Now I understood why he'd come here so frequently. I shook my head to clear it. "Was he worried about something?" I prompted.

"I wouldn't say worried, exactly. He was a bit uptight about his new business."

I stood straighter. This was new information. "What kind of business?"

"He didn't tell me. But he'd made enough money from it already that we were going on a ten-day cruise for our honeymoon. I've got the brochures right here." She headed to the counter and rummaged through a drawer under the cash register, triumphantly holding aloft a slick pamphlet with a photo of a continent-sized ship on the cover.

"Did you ever meet anyone connected with his new business?"

"No. But he went to lots of meetings, mostly in the evening. I answered his cell phone once, though, when he was in the shower, and it was some man I didn't know who asked me to let Dennis know he couldn't make it to one of the meetings."

"His name?" Now we were getting somewhere.

She shrugged. "He wouldn't give it to me. Just said Dennis would know."

Damn.

"The area code was 215, if that helps."

"It might. Don't forget to call Detective Helland." I

hesitated. "I'm really sorry for your loss," I said. "I know it's hard to lose someone you love to violence."

Tears slipped down her face, leaving trails in her makeup. Pulling a tissue from her skirt pocket, she dabbed at them. "Thank you, EJ," she said. She followed me to the door and flipped the sign to "Closed" as I exited. "I need a few minutes."

I called Grandpa Atherton and arranged to meet him after work. "I don't have long, Emma-Joy," he cautioned. "Theresa and I are going to see Sting in concert."

Most people's grandparents liked Tony Bennett or Barry Manilow. My Grandpa liked Sting. At least he wasn't into rap. Theresa Eshelman was his lady friend. She owned a child care center and didn't object to his disappearing without notice on occasion or experimenting with listening devices and cameras. She'd even done some surveillance with him, but only on cases where there was absolutely no danger, Grandpa confided to me.

We agreed to meet at Theresa's place of business, Intellitot Day Care Center, so they could leave for the Verizon Center as soon as the last tardy parent picked up the last waiting child. I arrived, still in uniform, to see Grandpa seated in a sandbox, legs crisscrossed, helping a two-year-old make a sand castle. He gave the turret a final pat with his plastic shovel when he saw me standing at the fence and unfolded himself awkwardly from the box. Saying good-bye to his new friend and brushing the sand off his casual slacks, he said, "Not as flexible as I used to be." He moved stiffly toward the care-center door and entered the building.

As soon as he left, his little playmate smashed the shovel down on the castle, beaming with happiness. I spotted

Theresa through a window and waved to her. She waved back and continued wrestling a child into a cardigan.

Grandpa, who'd just emerged from the center's front entrance, made his way over to me. "Isn't she a doll?" he said, joining me at the fence. I knew he was talking about Theresa and not the cute little girl.

"Absolutely."

As if embarrassed by his sentimental moment, he asked briskly, "What's up, Emma-Joy?"

Knowing time was short, I gave him the one-minute briefing on what Helland had said this morning, my conversations with Aggie and Starla, and the results of my Internet search on the 215 area code and Allied Forge Metals. "Two-one-five is Philadelphia," I said, "and Allied Forge Metals is incorporated in Delaware, just a hop, skip, and jump away, and—"

"A quarter of the corporations in America are chartered through Delaware," Grandpa said, "but it's certainly worth looking into."

"Its headquarters is in Philadelphia. Furthermore, Mantua, New Jersey, is just across the river from Philly. That's where the police were running a gun amnesty program that netted the gun used to kill Celio Arriaga."

A Mercedes SUV rounded the corner and parked crookedly in the lot. A harried woman in a business suit dashed inside and came out moments later, leading Grandpa's sandbox buddy and the cardiganed little girl by their hands.

"I think I'll drive up to Philly tomorrow," Grandpa said, slicking his white hair back with one hand as Theresa emerged. "I can make an appointment with Allied as the representative of a police department from, oh, say, Columbia, South Carolina, interested in hiring them to destroy weapons we collect from our about-to-be-inaugurated gun amnesty program."

"Good thinking, Grandpa," I said, having no doubt he could pull it off, as long as he didn't try to convince anyone he was an active cop. No one was going to buy an eighty-plus-year-old police officer. I knew he had contacts who could get him official-looking business cards and ID, if necessary, and arrange to have someone answer the phone and vouch for him as a member of the Columbia Police Department. A happy thought struck me: "I worked Sunday and Monday, so I could take tomorrow off."

"Come with me," Grandpa said promptly. "We'll have one of those Grandpa–Emma-Joy outings like we used to when you were younger. Remember the time we went to feed the ducks and you fell in the pond and your mother about scalped me?"

"Will you buy me an ice cream cone, double-decker?" I asked, grinning.

"Absolutely."

"You're plotting something," Theresa observed when she came up to us. A tall woman in her sixties with short, silver-streaked hair, she had a calm air about her, an unflappability that I suspected was key to her success as a day care owner.

"Always," Grandpa agreed happily.

At home, I occupied myself looking for job advertisements from police departments, expanding my search to the whole United States. I'd been hoping for a job within a few hours' drive, at most, from Grandpa, but that wasn't panning out, so I looked at an ad from Leavenworth, Kansas, and another from Huntsville, Alabama. I'd contented myself with leftovers for dinner and was forking up the last of my meal while downloading a few applications, when the phone rang. I answered, noting it was almost nine thirty.

It was Edgar Ambrose, who explained that his car had

broken down just south of the Woodmoor exit on I-95 and
he was going to be at least an hour late for the midshift. "I'll
cover it," I assured him. "Get there when you can."

"I owe you," he said, hanging up.

Staying up until midnight or so was no big deal, so I
climbed back into my uniform at ten without a lot of heart-
burn. Fubar looked affronted when I walked to the door.
"Sorry, buddy," I said, "but duty calls. This is the downside
of being the boss."

Fubar let me know what he thought of my new responsibilities by stalking away, stubby tail held upright.

Twenty-one

. . .

The mall at night is a different place than during the day.
With the parking lots and garages empty except for a car or
two left by diners who imbibed a bit too much at Tombino's
and wisely went home in a taxi, or by commuters who car-
pool, the mall looks like it's surrounded by a moat of asphalt.
Inside, too, without the escalator's hum and the fountain's
splash, or the footsteps and chatter of shoppers and merchants, the mall is strangely silent. Quigley insists on turning out as many lights as possible, so a bluish twilight cast
by overhead fluorescents pervades the halls. The shops,
locked behind their grilles, lie in darkness.

We'd had one guard last year who got so spooked by the
silent mall that she hated working the midshift. That, of
course, prompted Captain Woskowicz to assign her to it as
often as possible. She quit. Last I heard, she had gone to one
of those vet-tech schools that advertise on TV and was working for a veterinarian in Centreville. I didn't mind the quiet;
in fact, I liked it. My problem with the midshift was the

monotony. As the sole officer on duty, the person working midshift had no one to talk to, and patrolling an empty mall was 99 percent boredom interspersed with the occasional moment of panic (a break-in attempt or shots fired in the parking lot) or frustration (overflowing toilets in the bathroom and no plumber on hand).

Tonight, the security officer who gave me the turnover briefing reported that nothing unusual had happened, and I settled down in front of the monitors, stifling a yawn. I hoped Edgar showed up before too long. I hadn't been seated for more than ten minutes when the phone rang. Hoping it wasn't Edgar calling to say he'd be delayed longer than expected, I answered. "Fernglen Security. Officer Ferris."

A woman's voice, fluttery with tension or fear, said, "Hello. This is Glenda Wachtel. Is this the mall security office?"

"Yes, ma'am. How can I help you?"

"My husband Mike owns the Make-a-Manatee store."

Wachtel—of course. "Yes?"

"He hasn't come home tonight."

I could feel her trying to sound calm, but her worry leaked over the line. "Did you try his cell phone?"

"Yes, but he's not answering. He closes the store at nine—sometimes a little earlier if there's no business—and he's always home by nine twenty."

I checked my watch: ten seventeen. It seemed a little early for a spouse to push the panic button, but maybe Mrs. Wachtel was a chronic worrier. "Would you like me to go down to the store and see if he's there?"

"Oh, yes, please," she said gratefully. "I'm sorry to bother you . . . I'm sure you think I'm a ridiculous worrywart, but it's just that . . . recently . . . well, what with his leg in a cast and everything . . ."

"No problem. I'll call you back in fifteen minutes one

way or the other. If he gets home in the meantime, leave me a message." I took her number and hung up, happy to have something to do. Leaving a note for Edgar in case he showed up while I was out, I stepped on the Segway and traveled to Make-a-Manatee, indulging myself by speeding since there were no shoppers to run into.

The store's darkened windows reflected a ghostly me as I approached. I slowed to a stop and got off in front of the grille, jerking on it. It gave a metallic rattle but stayed put. Locked. I shone my flashlight into the shop but saw nothing unusual or out of place. No body, for instance. I purred down the wing and around the corner to the service hall that ran behind the stores. The door leading to Make-a-Manatee was also locked and nothing caught my eye. In all likelihood, Mike Wachtel had stopped for a beer on the way home or to run an errand, and had forgotten to tell his wife. Still, I wanted to be thorough, to set Glenda Wachtel's mind at ease, so I returned to the main hall and glided to the mall entrance, planning to check the parking lot.

Figuring that Wachtel parked as close as possible to his store, I exited into the chilly night air and scanned the lot. No cars. No injured man lying on the asphalt. The muffled *whoosh* of traffic drifted over from I-95, busy even at this hour. I turned toward the garage. Might as well check it while I was out here. The Segway stuttering over the asphalt, I approached the garage and angled up the ramp. Shadows dominated the echoing space, but I made out the silhouette of a sedan parked against the right-hand wall. Kicking myself for not asking Mrs. Wachtel what kind of car her husband drove, I approached it, automatically noting the make, model, and license plate as I drew nearer.

A feeling of unease settled over me, like someone had tossed a horsehair blanket over my shoulders, and I dismounted the Segway, wanting more mobility than the

vehicle provided. Wishing I had a weapon, I stepped closer
to the Pontiac. A slight sound, like a heavy exhalation, made
me turn, but I saw nothing. Adrenaline keyed me up;
hyperalert now, I illuminated the rear of the Pontiac with
my flashlight beam. The light revealed dull green paint and
showed an empty interior when I shone it through the rear
window. No one inside, unless they were ducked down on
the floor. I relaxed a tad, dropping my arm, and the beam
skidded off the trunk to the concrete where red droplets
gleamed wetly.

Blood. Fresh blood.

I caught my breath and quietly backed away from the car.
When I was far enough away that no one could jump out of
the car and take me by surprise, I sidestepped until I could
see the driver's side. A crumpled shape lay beside the door.
My flashlight revealed Mike Wachtel, lying half on his stomach, cracked glasses askew on his face, cell phone stomped
to bits just past his outstretched fingers, which were purple
and swollen. His face looked like he'd gone three rounds
with Mike Tyson, with blood leaking from his nose and split
lip. The cast on his leg rested at a weird angle, and I suspected he'd broken the leg again. I dialed 911 for an ambulance as I approached the still figure.

Dropping to my knees beside him, I felt for a pulse on his
neck and found one, reasonably strong under the circum-
stances. His skin was still healthily warm, so I figured he
hadn't been lying here in the cold garage for too long. I
relayed that to the 911 operator, wishing I had a jacket or a
blanket to drape over him to help ward off shock. I stood and
looked in the car, spying a fleece jacket on the front passenger
seat. Carefully easing the door open with my hand covered
by my shirt hem to avoid smudging fingerprints, I leaned
over and tugged the jacket toward me. Something in a pocket
weighted it down, and I jerked it impatiently. The jacket

clunked against the center console, knocking over an empty soda can, and then it was free, hanging heavy in my hand. What did Wachtel carry in his jacket—a shot-put ball? Jamming my hand into the pocket, I felt my fingers close around the familiar contours of a gun. Slowly, I withdrew it. A .38. I laid it on the driver's seat and tucked the jacket around Mike, who stirred and moaned but didn't regain consciousness. Then I told the 911 dispatcher I was hanging up and called Glenda Wachtel to tell her I'd found her husband.

The ambulance, the police, and Mrs. Wachtel arrived simultaneously, just as Edgar called me on the radio to let me know he was in the security office. I explained the situation to him briefly, told him I was going to drive Mrs. Wachtel to the hospital, and asked him to fetch the Segway from the garage. The woman was shaking like a leaf in a hurricane and had clipped the door of her van on a support column when she pulled up; clearly, she shouldn't be driving. She hovered near the EMTs as they treated Mike, bleating her husband's name until one of the EMTs gently but firmly moved her out of the way.

I told a cop about the gun, and she immediately moved to secure it. Relieved, I put an arm around Mrs. Wachtel's shoulders, feeling knobby bones beneath the thin cardigan she wore. She looked to be in her early to mid fifties, like Mike, with wiry brown hair flecked with gray and a sallow complexion. She had sunken eyes under heavy, scraggly brows, and a straight nose. "Come on, Mrs. Wachtel," I said as the EMTs loaded Mike, strapped to a gurney, into the back of the ambulance. "Let me drive you to the hospital." I eased the keys from her unresisting fingers, guided her to her Honda minivan, helped her buckle in, and trotted around to the driver's side.

Mrs. Wachtel sat silently for most of the drive, and I worried she was in shock. I cast a glance at her stony profile and noted her hands clenching and unclenching on the fabric of her sweatpants. She muttered something as we pulled into the hospital parking lot.

"Pardon me?" I said.

"Damn you, damn you, damn you," she said again, apparently to herself, or maybe to her husband. "You promised!"

I opened my door, but the woman sat unmoving on her side of the car. "Mrs. Wachtel? We're here."

"I'm not going through this again. I've got the kids to think about." Scrunch, open, scrunch, open went the hands on her sweatpants.

I leaned in and touched her shoulder. She jumped and jerked her head to stare at me. It took a half second for her eyes to focus on my face. "We're at the hospital," I said.

"Oh." She fumbled with the seat belt, finally got it off, and stepped out of the car. I steered her toward Emergency where the ambulance had already off-loaded Mike Wachtel and was preparing to depart. The automatic doors shushed open in front of us, and we entered a waiting room where only one woman was curious enough to turn and look at us. Several other people slumped on molded plastic seats. Harsh lights reflected off linoleum floors and the screen of a wall-mounted television playing a *Gilligan's Island* rerun. The odors of vomit and Lysol suggested the ER hadn't been this quiet all evening. Marching Glenda Wachtel to the intake desk, I asked for Mike, saying, "This is his wife."

"Exam room three," the nurse said, flicking an assessing gaze over Glenda. Apparently deciding the woman wasn't going to collapse on the spot, she asked, "Do you have an insurance card?"

Blinking several times, Glenda seemed to come back to

herself. "Yes." She slid the card out of her wallet and handed it to the nurse. "I'm sorry," Glenda said, turning to me. "What was your name again?"

"EJ Ferris," I told her. "Don't worry about it—you've had quite a shock."

"I need to see Mike." Glenda started down the hall to the left, sneakered feet squeaking on the linoleum.

She was going the wrong way. I knew this not because I was an expert on the hospital's layout, but because there was a uniformed police officer standing outside the door of a room to my right. I'd bet a week's pay that was exam room three. I summoned Glenda back by calling her name softly and pointing. "Oh my God," she said when her gaze lighted on the policeman. "He won't arrest Mike, will he?"

I stared at her. "Arrest Mike? Your husband was the victim of a crime. Why would the police arrest him?"

"You're right," Glenda said hurriedly. "I don't know what I'm thinking." She raked both her hands through her hair, sucked in a deep breath, and approached the cop. She said something to him, and he stepped aside so she could enter the room.

The cop approached me. Young and sandy haired, he spoke with an Oklahoma twang. "Mrs. Wachtel tells me you found the victim and called 911?"

When I nodded, he asked me the usual questions, taking careful notes of my answers, most of which were "no." No, I didn't see anyone else in the garage. No, I didn't see any other vehicles. No, I didn't know Mike Wachtel well and had no idea if he had any enemies. No, the mall hadn't been having any trouble with muggings. "You think it was a mugging?" I asked.

"His wallet was missing," the officer said, tucking his notebook away. "In my experience"—which was maybe two months at the most, based on how young he looked—"that spells mugging."

"Um," I said noncommittally. I might have agreed with
him if it weren't for the strange way Glenda Wachtel had
acted on the way over here; the gun in Mike's jacket, which
suggested he knew he needed protection; and the fact that
it looked like someone, or a pair of someones, had worked
Mike over pretty good. It was possible he'd annoyed a mugger by refusing to hand over his wallet, but the way his face
had been pulped made me suspect a more personal motive.
"We might have something on the mall's cameras," I
told him.

When the cop strode away, I poked my head into exam
room three just in time to see Glenda Wachtel sling her purse
at Mike, saying, "Don't 'honey' me."

Luckily, the purse was small and bounced off the side of
the gurney instead of knocking into the now mangled and
cracked cast encasing Mike's leg. His eyes were open,
although the lids sagged with pain or medication, and he
stretched one hand toward her. When he caught sight of me,
his mouth fell open and his hand dropped.

I held up Glenda's keys. "I just wanted to give these back
to you," I said apologetically, feeling awkward about inter-
rupting. "I'll catch a taxi back to the mall unless you
need me?"

"What are you—?" Mike's speech was slurred by his
swollen lips. He looked from his wife to me and back again.

"Thanks," Glenda said, reaching for the keys. Perhaps
realizing she'd sounded rudely abrupt, she said, "Really,
thank you. You've been very kind." Unshed tears glittered
in her eyes and she looked down, studying the linoleum as
if it had a treasure map engraved on it.

I felt like there should be more I could do, but it was clear
from the awkward silence that neither of the Wachtels
wanted me around. I left through the ER door, happy to wait
outside for my taxi in the chilly but fresh air.

The taxi dropped me beside my car in the Fernglen lot, but instead of driving home, as any sane person would at almost midnight, I returned to the security office, anxious to see if the cameras had captured any images that could identify Mike's assailant.

"Yo," Edgar greeted me. Raised brows corrugated his forehead clear up to where his hairline would've been if he'd had one.

I explained why I'd come back, and he helped me skim the camera data, looking for anyone entering the garage around or shortly after nine o'clock when Mike Wachtel would've been headed for his car. At eight fifty-three a van exited the garage, and at eight fifty-nine two burly figures, caps pulled low over their foreheads, bodies obscured by bulky coats, and scarves muffling their lower faces, entered the way I had, walking up the ramp into the garage. Once inside the garage, they disappeared, apparently having the savvy to stay out of the cameras' line of sight.

Edgar cocked an expressive brow at me and I nodded.

Another camera caught Mike Wachtel as he entered the garage from the mall at four minutes passed nine. We lost sight of him as he transited an area that lay between two cameras' fields of vision and caught a glimpse of him near the concrete support Glenda Wachtel had sideswiped. He made it to his car, took off his jacket, and tossed it on the passenger seat. Before he could get in, an arm came briefly into the frame and Mike staggered, then disappeared from view.

"That didn't look like a mugging to me," I said, standing with my hands on my hips.

"Uh-uh," Edgar agreed. "Enforcers."

I looked a question at him.

"Thugs. Rent-a-beating. Paid to deliver a message." He jabbed his meaty fists in a quick one-two punch.

"How do you know that?" I asked, eyeing him curiously.

"EJ." The way he said my name implied it was obvious to anyone with an IQ over twelve.

"Okay, assuming you're right, who would hire them?"

"Spouse."

I shook my head. "No way. She didn't know."

"Girlfriend's hubby or father. Pissed-off customer."

"He sells stuffed animals!"

Edgar's shrug implied that didn't mean squat. "Bookie. Loan shark. Angry business partner."

I tapped a fingernail on my tooth and wondered if there was some connection between the assault on Mike Wachtel and the deaths of Celio Arriaga and Captain Woskowicz. I didn't immediately see one, but that didn't mean there wasn't one. Asking Edgar to download the pertinent camera data to a DVD, I told him I'd drop it at the police station on my way home.

Twenty-two

. . .

After not enough sleep, I was back at Fernglen by seven o'clock, hoping to catch Curtis Quigley and tell him about the garage incident before he heard it from another source. Since I was headed to Allied Forge Metals with Grandpa, I didn't plan to stay long, but I thought it was important to tell him about it in person. A quick scan of the newspaper on my doorstep told me the local reporters hadn't thought it worth mentioning, and I breathed a sigh of relief. Pooja wasn't at her desk yet when I arrived, so I tapped on Mr. Quigley's door and walked in when he called, "Enter."

He sat behind his desk, sandy hair slicked straight back from his forehead, gel-set furrows etched in by the comb. A pale blue bow tie matched the blue topaz and silver cuff links and the thin stripe in his otherwise white shirt. He was reading a thick packet, and he glanced up under his brows. His head jerked fully up when he recognized me. "Oh no."

Was that any way to greet his acting director of security? "Good morning, Mr. Quigley."

"Tell me it's not another body."

"It's not another body."

His thin chest caved in as he let out his breath. "Well, thank goodness for that! I hope—"

"Mike Wachtel, the Make-a-Manatee store owner, was . . . mugged in the garage last evening."

"You said it wasn't another body!" He half rose to his feet in alarm and indignation.

"He's not dead."

Quigley subsided into his chair, lips pursed with displeasure. "Small comfort."

I suspected it was rather a large comfort to the Wachtels, but I didn't say so. "He's going to be fine." I summarized the evening's activities for him, finishing with, "And I've given our camera data to the police."

"Fine, fine," Quigley said. "Well, if that's all—"

"Actually, I wanted to talk to you about upgrading the cameras, or at least making all of the existing cameras operational. If we—"

"Now, EJ," he said testily, "you know our operating budget won't stretch that far. Captain Woskowicz and I agreed that the camera coverage we have is sufficient." He waved me away. "Maybe we can discuss it in October when I present next year's budget to the FBI board. I'll see you at your interview tomorrow."

Faced with a clear dismissal, I hesitated only a moment before leaving his office. I'd be in a stronger position to argue for the cameras if I were made director of security, I told myself, returning to the security office to make sure everything was running smoothly before leaving to meet Grandpa.

Since Grandpa drove like a frustrated Formula One driver when he wasn't tailing someone, I drove to

Philadelphia. Hitting the road felt great, and my shoulders and spine loosened as we sped along the interstate. It had been far too long, I realized, since I went on a road trip. Maybe I'd take a couple of days off in April and just go. No route, no plan, no reservations. My spirits lifted at the thought. The trees along the interstate were budding out, the sky was bluer than blue, and I was tempted to just keep on driving until we hit Canada. Leaving as late as we did, we had little problem with traffic and crossed the Walt Whitman Bridge into Philly a bit over two hours after we started.

"Where to from here?" I asked Grandpa, who had located Allied Forge Metals, set up an appointment, and gotten directions. He was dressed today in his version of southern gentleman couture, sort of a Colonel Sanders meets Rhett Butler ensemble, complete with straw hat, cane, and fake white mustache waxed to curvy points.

He directed me south, to a light industrial area not far from the airport, from which I could smell, if not see, the Delaware River. Half a mile of low, featureless concrete buildings stretched before us when we turned into the business park, and we had to loop around several times before spotting the number we wanted, with a small sign announcing "Allied Forge Metals" bolted over the door.

"Show time," Grandpa said, adopting a southern drawl as thick as syrup-soaked grits. "Now, remember, Emma-Joy, you're just my driver because my gout is acting up, so concentrate on looking pretty and not saying anything. You ought to be able to handle the first part, at least."

"Ha-ha," I said drily, offering him my arm so he could pretend to limp into the building.

The interior was as bland as the exterior, with indoor-outdoor carpet that probably came from a remnant sale, two upholstered chairs with cushions that looked stiffer than a Brit's upper lip, and a laminate reception desk staffed by a woman in her thirties who looked up when we entered. "Help you?" She spoke with a harsh, nasal accent but had a pleasant smile.

"I'm Colonel Barclay Dickinson, United States Army, retired," Grandpa Atherton said, removing his hat and presenting his card with a flourish. "I've got an appointment with your William Silver. And what is your name, lovely lady?"

I stopped short of rolling my eyes, but I thought he was laying it on a bit thick. The receptionist apparently didn't agree, because she giggled, smiled, and said, "Dorothy."

"A lovely, traditional name," Grandpa said. "If you would be so kind as to tell Mr. Silver I'm here?"

"Certainly, Colonel Dickinson," she said. She rose and glanced at me. "And you are?"

"My driver." Grandpa waved away the question as if I were of no importance. "Alas, in my declining years, my gout has slowed me down somewhat." He pointed his cane at his slippered and bandaged foot.

"I'll bet you were a wild one when you were younger," Dorothy said flirtatiously.

I bit back the "You have no idea" that sprang to my tongue and instead simply smiled as Dorothy ducked through a door to the right of the reception area. She returned a moment later and motioned us to the same door. I offered "Colonel Dickinson" my arm to escort him into what I assumed was William Silver's office. Grandpa thrust his hat at me and I took it.

A tall, ruddy-haired man with a snub nose rose to greet Grandpa, holding out his hand and pumping Grandpa's. He was as tall as Grandpa Atherton, but broader, with a small potbelly and a roll of flesh above his shirt collar. "Colonel Dickinson. A pleasure to meet you. William Silver."

Dorothy positioned a blue leather club chair for Grandpa

and exited. I helped him sit, then retired to a ladder-backed chair along the wall.

"So," Silver said, "I understand you're looking for a company to destroy some guns for you. You're with the Columbia Police Department?" He returned to his chair, which squished down with a puff of air when he sat. His smile never slipped, but his gray eyes were shrewd and watchful.

"I'm the founder of the Friends of the Columbia Police," Grandpa corrected, "a nonprofit set up to fund those items that might help our men and women in blue do their jobs better and safer, but that the taxpayers might not be able to finance." He winked. "For instance, last year we bought the latest in bulletproof vests—full Kevlar, NIJ level IIIa protection, capable of stopping a .44-Mag—for every sworn member of the force."

"Impressive," Silver said, steepling his fingers.

"We're Chief Washington's 'special fund,' you might say."

"You don't mind if I check your bona fides with Chief Washington, do you?" Silver asked, reaching for the phone.

"Dial away, son, dial away," Grandpa said, relaxing back into his chair. "Tell Fred I'll get my revenge on the golf course as soon as this damned gout subsides." He pasted an indulgent expression on his face as Silver dealt with a secretary or aide before, apparently, getting Chief Washington on the line.

My muscles tensed, but I concentrated on looking bored as Silver had a brief conversation that ended with, "We'll certainly do what we can to help, Chief." He hung up and gave Grandpa a more relaxed smile. "It seems that the chief is grateful for the help your organization has given his force with acquiring protective gear and new technologies for his SWAT team. And your project now is—"

"Getting weapons off the street. We want to institute a gun

amnesty program to encourage the good citizens, and the not so good ones, if you get my drift, to turn in their weapons. We're going to offer fifty dollars for every gun relinquished, regardless of type or if it's even in working condition. Every gun off the street makes our men and women in blue that much safer. But, then, of course, we need to dispose of them permanently, and that's where you come in." He smoothed his fake mustache with his left hand, one side at a time, and I wondered if he was making sure it was still glued in place.

William Silver launched into a polished sales pitch, talking fluently about how his company disabled guns, destroyed them, and recycled the metals, yada-yada. I tuned out until I heard Grandpa ask, a sharper edge in his voice, "Forgive me for asking, sir, but what guarantee do we get that the guns are actually reduced to scrap metal? I believe I've read about cases where guns turned in to amnesty programs end up back on the streets. That would be unacceptable to the fine folk of Columbia. Just recently, I heard about the Mantua Police Department, right across the river here, having a problem . . ."

Silver gave Grandpa a long look. "I'd be interested to know where you heard about that. It hasn't received much publicity."

"I do my research," Grandpa said, not flinching.

Neither man spoke for a moment, the negotiator's version of "chicken," I supposed.

Silver broke first, explaining his company's precautions. "I'm sure that if you investigate some of these atypical cases where amnestied guns are used in new crimes, you'll find that the problem lies with the receiving police department, not the company contracted for destruction."

Wham. Nothing like putting all the blame on the other guy.

"I'm sure you'd be okay with it if we had an observer

present for destruction, wouldn't you?" Grandpa asked. "Someone from our organization who keeps tabs on the guns from the moment they're turned in until they're certified destroyed?"

"Of course. We'd welcome that," Silver said after only the briefest hesitation. He bared his teeth in a smile. "So, we've got a deal?"

Grandpa beckoned to me, and I hurried forward to help him rise. "In due course, Mr. Silver, when I've finished my inquiries."

Silver took it with reasonably good grace, extending his hand for Grandpa to shake. "Of course. It was a pleasure meeting you. Let me know when you'll be up here next, Colonel, and we can spend an afternoon at the ballpark, watching the Phillies. But you said you golf . . . I can put together a foursome at Northampton Valley."

He escorted us to the door where Grandpa said a fulsome farewell to a blushing Dorothy, and then we were in the parking lot, a fresh breeze tossing my hair. I helped Grandpa into the car with great solicitude and backed out carefully, waiting until we were halfway down the block before asking, "So, what did you think?"

Grandpa peeled off his mustache. "That thing itches," he said, tossing it in the backseat.

"How did you get Chief Washington to vouch for you?" I asked, scanning overhead signs for the interstate on-ramp. "I presume that was Chief Washington Silver talked to?"

"Of course." Grandpa grinned. "Fred was a marine before becoming a peace officer in his home town. We were in Beirut at the same time. You might even say he thinks he owes his continued existence on this planet to me."

"Ah."

"Our friend Mr. Silver seemed awfully eager to point a finger at the Mantua Police Department," Grandpa observed.

"I thought so, too."

"Which doesn't mean he's wrong."

I tapped my brakes to avoid rear-ending a Toyota going forty-five miles an hour on the highway. "I just wish I could find a connection between either Allied Forge Metals or the Mantua PD and Woskowicz or the Niños Malos. Without that, we've got no way to explain how the gun that killed Celio Arriaga ended up in a file drawer in what is now my office."

We cobbled together a few theories, none of which had any more believability than one of Ethan's action-adventure movies, then tacitly agreed to abandon the topic for the rest of our journey. We stopped for lunch at a seafood place outside Baltimore, including the ice cream Grandpa had promised me, and I dropped Grandpa off a bit before three. "I'll see if I can't come up with a way to approach the Mantua Police Department," Grandpa said as he got out of the car.

I looked at him in alarm. "Don't even think about it. I don't want you going anywhere near an actual law-enforcement agency that could get through your cover with a single phone call."

"I once passed myself off as an officer of Romania's Securitate for the better part of a month. They never suspected—"

"You had the CIA behind you back then," I said. "And technology wasn't—"

"Pooh," he said, closing the door. He went whistling up the sidewalk to his door, kicking the slipper off his "gouty" foot and catching it in midair.

I grinned reluctantly, tooted the horn, and drove away.

Twenty-three

· · ·

Mike Wachtel surprised me the next morning by walking into my office—I'd already started thinking of it as "mine," I realized—shortly before the mall's ten o'clock opening. I looked up from compiling some stats about my time here I could use at my interview this afternoon to see him standing in the doorway, holding the jamb to balance against the weight of the cast. His face was a lurid blend of blues, purples, and greens, a three-year-old's watercolor effort doused with enough water to make the colors run.

I stood and started toward him. "Mike! Should you be here?"

He shrugged. "I've got a store to run."

I couldn't imagine that his stitched face and bruises were likely to sell a lot of stuffed animals, but I kept my mouth shut, merely pulling a chair forward for him to sit. He did so awkwardly, using both hands to lift the casted leg and edge it into a more comfortable position.

He adjusted his new glasses, a slightly more rectangular

pair than the broken ones, and gave me a level look. "I came to say thank you. Glenda told me you're the one who found me and called the ambulance."

"Thank Glenda," I replied. "She's the one who sent me to search for you."

"I did. She left me," he blurted. His voice was raw with emotion, and I could tell he was biting the inside of his cheek to hold back tears. "Everything I did was for her and the kids!"

I didn't know what to say. I wasn't too surprised, not after the way she'd been on the drive to the hospital and the confrontation I'd seen. "She got tired of the gambling?" I asked. I'd put the pieces together: Mike's talk about sports, the phone conversation I'd overheard—he'd said it was his brother-in-law, but I bet he was placing bets with his bookie—the broken leg, the gun he carried, the enforcers in the garage.

"How did you know?" He went perfectly still except for his eyes; they darted this way and that, like those of a rat seeking a way out of a cage. Understanding came over him. "Glenda told you."

"No, I guessed."

His mouth tightened. "It's none of your business."

"Normally, I'd agree. But it becomes my business when your . . . extracurricular activities threaten the safety of shoppers and merchants at my—Fernglen." It was hard not to call it "my mall."

"Bullshit!" Mike surged to his feet but wobbled and had to grab the back of the chair. "Those guys last night were only after me. Boris sent them to—they weren't a threat to anyone else."

"What if they'd used guns instead of baseball bats, or whatever they beat you with? What if you'd gotten off a shot at them? Bullets aren't very discriminating."

"I don't have to listen to this. I came to say thanks and you give me grief. Just like Glenda! You women are all alike." He made a disgusted face and turned toward the door. "I'm only trying to get a bit more for our kids, so they can go to a decent college and do something with their lives besides pump fluff into stuffed animals for a bunch of demonic brats."

"You own a store; you're your own boss," I pointed out. "That's the American dream for a lot of people."

He turned toward me with an abrupt movement that sent him staggering. "I cater to a bunch of spoiled kids and their spoiled parents all day long. I accept returns from people who say the stuffed animal was defective when it's perfectly clear they've let the pedigreed Goldendoodle chew on it or they've run over it with the Lexus. I smile and nod and try to figure out how I'm going to pay my suppliers next week, not to mention the outrageous rent this mall demands. I've had to let employees go, so I'm on my own weekday afternoons and evenings. Do you have any idea how stressful it is to own a small business in this economy?"

An old joke flitted through my mind: What's an addict's favorite river? Da Nile. Denial. Mike had a good line in rationalization and denial, and I figured he'd practiced it on Glenda more than once. I knew whatever I said would only anger him further, so I kept my mouth shut. Mike was practically shimmering with anger, and I was wondering how to get him out of my office when Joel appeared in the doorway.

"Everything all right, EJ?" he asked. His usually soft brown gaze landed on Mike and he looked surprisingly stern.

"Everything's fine," I said with a pointed look at Mike.

"Ducky," he spat, shoving past Joel to get out of the office. He step-clomped down the hall, and I winced for him, knowing his leg must hurt terribly. I'd spent more than my share of time in leg casts.

Joel looked questioningly at me, but I shook my head. I didn't know how—or even if—I could handle this, but gossiping about Mike's gambling problem was not on the agenda. I wondered if Woskowicz had known and, if so, whether it worried him that some bookie's enforcers, as Edgar called them, out to encourage Mike to pay up or teach him a lesson—whatever a bookie's enforcers did—might harm an innocent mall customer.

"He seemed pissed off," Joel observed, trying to get me to comment on what had just happened.

"He stopped by to thank me for finding him and calling the ambulance," I said calmly.

Joel gave me a skeptical look. "If that's his version of 'thanks,' I don't want to be around when he gets annoyed."

"My interview is today," I said to distract him.

His eyes lit up. "Knock 'em dead."

"That might be counterproductive."

He laughed.

"Hey, isn't tonight your date with Sunny?"

Joel nodded, anticipation lighting his face. "Yeah. I can't swim today 'cause I'm going home right after work to get ready."

I couldn't imagine why a man would need more than half an hour—shower, shave, and dress—to get ready for a date, but only said, "That's fine. I don't know if I'll make it to the Y either; it depends on how long the interview goes."

"Should I take flowers?" Joel asked, scrunching his face anxiously. "Roses?"

"Not on a first date. You'll look like you're trying too hard. Just be on time, don't talk about ex-girlfriends—"

"I don't have any."

"—and let her choose the movie. Believe me, that'll be

more than enough." If I'd had a kid brother, instead of a condescending, teasing, sometimes aloof older brother who'd had girls calling the house at all hours from before he was thirteen, that's the dating advice I'd have given him. "And don't spend the whole night worrying about whether or not to kiss her when you drop her off."

"EJ!" Joel flushed red and I laughed.

The phone rang in the front office, and Joel dashed to get it. I followed more slowly, planning to patrol for a while and touch base with shop owners and managers as they opened their stores, before they got too busy. I stopped when Joel flagged me down, waving his free hand wildly.

"We'll have someone there in just a moment, ma'am," he said into the phone. Covering the receiver, he said to me, "This is the clerk at Starla's Styles. She says there's a catfight going on and wants a security guard to come break it up."

"Oh, please." I hurried to the Segway.

"I've never seen a catfight," Joel called after me. "Can I come?"

I could hear the yelling as soon as I rounded the corner into the Pete's Sporting Goods wing. It was muffled, but the anger underlying the incomprehensible words was palpable. Parking the Segway outside, I walked into the store. Mayhem reigned. Starla was running clockwise around a rotating clothes rack spinning so fast that blouses, tank tops, and camis billowed out. Aggie Woskowicz chased her, a look on her face that made me glad she didn't have a weapon, while a salesclerk cowered behind the counter, trying to summon help via the phone. Clothes dotted the floor or draped haphazardly over racks, the settee, and an expressionless mannequin. Starla's hair winged out to one side, as if someone had grabbed it, and Aggie was missing a shoe; I saw the loafer kicked half under another rack of clothes.

"You sicced the police on me," Aggie yelled at Starla, doing a quick one-eighty so Starla almost ran into her before spinning and running counterclockwise around the rack. "I know it was you. You told them I killed Wosko, that I was pissed off because he preferred you to me."

"Who wouldn't?" Starla said, blowing a straggling lock of hair off her forehead with an upward puff of air.

Aggie growled low in her throat and spun the rack so hard one diaphanous blouse went sailing. "Home wrecker!"

"Like Dennis wasn't married when you took up with him."

Aggie flung the *b*-word and the *s*-word and even the *c*-word at Starla as I stepped forward, pitching my voice at a soothing level.

"Ladies, let's calm—"

Starla turned her head toward me, and Aggie took advantage of her distraction, diving under the clothes carousel to grab at her ankles. Starla staggered backwards and, as Aggie popped up, thrust a palm-heel strike at the younger woman's face. I had the dubious satisfaction of realizing I must be a pretty good teacher; the heel of Starla's palm connected squarely with Aggie's nose, and she clapped a hand to her face as blood spurted.

"It worked!" Starla turned to me for applause, which gave Aggie the opportunity to tackle her. Woskowicz's stocky ex-wife ploughed into Starla, wrapping both her arms around the woman's plump waist and dragging her down.

"You boke by doze," Aggie growled as the two women fell to the floor. Luckily, they landed on a pile of clothes, so no bones were broken.

"You're bleeding on my stock!" Starla cried, trying to wiggle out from under Aggie, who was, indeed, dripping blood from her nose onto a silk blouse and a chiffon dress. "That dress just came in yesterday!"

Leaning forward, I grasped Aggie under the arms and hauled her up. As Starla wiggled free, she kicked at Aggie, her foot getting tangled in the folds of a velour skirt.

"I hope the police arrest you. Call the police, Martha-Anne," she called to the clerk, who dropped the phone and ducked under the counter.

"You hit me first," Aggie said. "I'm having you arrested for assault."

"I hope we don't need the police," I said, forcing her backwards by twisting her right arm up between her shoulder blades. "Starla, get up." I could hear Mrs. Wendell's voice from the fifth-grade etiquette class Mom had stuck me in, saying, "Ladies, let's strive for a little decorum." I was tempted to emulate her, but I didn't think I could pull off her velvet-glove-over-iron-will tone. And Starla and Aggie were not exactly giggling ten-year-olds.

Starla stood, twisting the elastic waistband of her skirt around to the front and brushing a hank of hair off her forehead. Judging that Aggie now had control of herself, I released her but stayed near enough to grab her if she went for Starla again.

Aggie, looking half-abashed and half-angry, tucked the tail of her pink blouse back into her jeans. Snatching a handful of tissues from a box on the counter, she crammed them against her still-bleeding nose. "I loved Wosko."

"So did I," Starla chimed in.

"I loved him more."

"Not possible."

"He loved me more."

"Sure. That's why he was divorcing you and marrying me." The smug expression on Starla's face made even me want to slap her.

Aggie started toward her rival again, and I stepped between them. "Stop. Aggie, we're leaving now."

"Why do you call yourself 'Aggie,' anyway?" Starla asked, her tone implying it was just one more example of Aggie being difficult. She smoothed her hair with her palm. "Dennis always called you Delia."

"Delia is my real name, but most of my friends call me Aggie. You can call me Mrs. Woskowicz," she added, clearly trying to rile the other woman.

As Starla fumed, Aggie went on. "AG is the chemical symbol for silver, so some of my nerdier friends thought it was clever to call me Aggie. It stuck." She bent to pick up her loafer and slipped it on her foot.

"Why silver?" I asked, a funny prickling at the back of my neck.

"Silver was my maiden name," she said.

Her words hit me like a piano dropped off a third-floor balcony. My mind raced, remembering she had mentioned a brother named Billy who was tight with Woskowicz. "Come on," I said, herding her out of the store. "I need to talk to you."

"And stay away," Starla called, all bravado now that Aggie had herself under control. I looked over my shoulder to see her standing, arms akimbo, in the middle of the heaps of clothing. Despite the blood splotches dotting her daffodil chenille top and silky pants, not to mention her mussed hairdo and chipped manicure, she looked as satisfied as a junkyard dog who had successfully defended her territory. I wondered if I should cancel the self-defense classes.

"I'm sorry," Aggie muttered once we were out of Starla's Styles. She eased the tissues away from her nose, determined that it wasn't bleeding anymore, and dropped them into a trash can. "I don't normally lose it like that. But when the cops came by first thing this morning, saying they'd 'heard' that I was angry about Wosko divorcing me, that I'd made threats, and asking me all sorts of rude questions, I lost it."

"Let me buy you a cookie," I offered. I mounted the Segway, and she walked beside me the short distance to the food court.

Jay greeted me with a smile and a questioningly cocked eyebrow but simply handed over two cookies and coffees when I shook my head to show this was not a good time. I also asked for a cup of water, which I handed to Aggie, along with a napkin, and indicated she might want to swab some blood off her nose and chin. Dipping the napkin in the water, she rubbed off the blood, ignoring the spatters on her blouse, and then devoured half the cookie in short order. Taking a sip of coffee, she said, "I get low blood sugary when I don't eat. I should never leave the house without breakfast." She finished off the cookie before I'd taken two bites of mine.

"Does your brother work for Allied Forge Metals?" I asked.

"He owns it. Why?" Suspicion lowered her brows.

How to answer that? Because I suspect he murdered your soon-to-be ex-husband? Because I think he supplied the gun your precious Wosko used to kill a teenager? Hm. Before I could say anything, she solved my dilemma.

"Oh, because of the gun that was used to kill that gangbanger?"

My brows soared toward my hairline and I nodded.

"Billy's been so upset about that. I suppose you saw in the news that that gun had been turned in as part of a gun amnesty program. Billy was livid when I emailed him the link to the article that ran in our local paper. He says the cops running the program must have held back some guns instead of passing them along to Allied for destruction." Pressing her fingertip on the cookie crumbs that sprinkled the table, she licked them off her finger.

I studied her. She looked remarkably unconcerned, and I got the distinct feeling she was telling the truth or, at least, the truth as she knew it. Of course, she was unaware—I assumed—that Woskowicz had hidden the gun in his file drawer. "Is it hurting your brother's business at all?"

"Nah. He's got plenty of contracts. His business isn't all gun destruction, you know."

I bit into my cookie, not sure what else I could ask her without revealing facts I knew Detective Helland would crucify me for leaking. "You said your brother came to visit not long ago—were he and Woskowicz close?"

"Two peas in a pod," Aggie said, pulling a face. "They could talk politics, taxes, the state of the economy all day long, sounding like a show on Fox News. And they were both into guns big-time and went to a shooting range together sometimes. Too damn loud for me." She looked at the large, stainless steel watch on her wrist. "I've got to go. I've got a couple coming back for another test drive. The pregnant ones who want the van." Glancing down at her sullied attire, she added, "I'll have to change before meeting them. Thanks for the cookie." She hesitated. "And for not calling the cops on me back there." She jerked her head toward Starla's Styles.

Rising to my feet, I said, "Maybe you'd better stay away from her. She seems to push your buttons."

"You got that right," Aggie said, eyes smoldering anew. She gave an awkward laugh. "I guess what goes around comes around, right? Or we make our own karma."

I guessed she was referring to the fact that she had filched Woskowicz from Paula and now was on the other side of the equation. "Hey," I asked, "did you ever find the key to the safe-deposit box?"

"No." She sounded disgruntled.

"Just out of curiosity . . . what's in there?"

She opened her mouth as if to snap out "None of your

business," then closed it and thought a moment. Maybe because she figured she owed me for not calling the police, she finally said, "Tapes." She looked half-embarrassed, half-mischievous.

So Joel had been right. Ick.

"Not videos. Cassettes. Wosko liked to record some of our . . . *special* phone conversations. That's how we met—I worked for a phone-sex outfit."

I goggled at her, completely surprised. Before I could answer, she gave me a cocky grin and walked off, chucking her cup in the direction of the trash can. When it fell short, she didn't stop to pick it up. I retrieved it and plunked it in the trash along with my own, then turned to see Jay Callahan beckoning to me from Lola's.

Remembering that I wanted to tell him what I'd learned about guns, I crossed to his counter, trying not to wonder if selling used cars paid more than being a phone-sex provider. They both probably paid better than being a mall cop.

Jay interrupted my speculation. "Do you have time to come in for a moment?"

Without waiting for an answer, he disappeared into his kitchen and then reappeared at the door that opened to the left of the counter. Curious—I'd never been in one of the food court kitchens—I followed him into the kitchen and looked around. The space was compact, but intelligently laid out and clean as an operating room. Maybe cleaner if what I'd been reading about infections at hospitals was true. A deep stainless steel sink was set into a tile counter. Ovens with lots of racks set close together for cookie sheets gave off a warm glow.

"Stand here." Jay patted the doorjamb in the opening that led to the sales counter. "Let me know if we get a customer. My helper's not in this morning, and I've got to make more cookies."

Leaning against the jamb, I watched as he scrubbed his hands in the sink, slid on single-use gloves, and retrieved dough from the freezer.

"So, are you going to play outfield for us Monday?" he asked. "I've got an extra glove you can borrow."

I'd made up my mind to pass on the softball, knowing I'd look like a total idiot if a ball came my way, but something about his expression, challenging yet mischievous, made me say, "Sure. What time?"

"I'll pick you up at six. So, what brings you to my cookie lair this morning, other than the desire to watch the amazing cookie maker at work?"

"Celio Arriaga, the guy whose body was left here, was his gang's weapons procurement officer," I said. "Why are you grinning?"

" 'Weapons procurement officer.' No one would guess you were in the military. Go on."

"I suppose you read about the murder weapon having been surrendered to a New Jersey gun amnesty program?"

He nodded, laying out rounds of peanut butter cookie dough on a series of cookie tins. I liked the way his hair curled at the nape of his neck. It would be crisp and springy under my fingers. I reined in my thoughts.

"Well, the man who runs the company that was supposed to destroy the guns was Woskowicz's brother-in-law."

"Really?" Jay stopped and looked at me. "Have the cops talked to him?"

"I did," I said with smug satisfaction. "Grandpa Atherton and I drove up there yesterday. He seems to think the police department is to blame for the 'misplaced' guns."

"Of course he does," Jay said, resuming his task. When he had four cookie sheets filled, he slid them one after another into the oven and set the timer.

"Do you think it's possible he was really selling the guns to Arriaga for the Niños Malos? Or that he and Woskowicz were?"

Stripping off his latex gloves, Jay crossed his arms over his chest and leaned back against the counter. I'd never thought about it before, but there was something sexy about a man who was comfortable in a kitchen. "It's possible," he answered. "Although I'd think Woskowicz would be leery of having any contact with gang members, given his position. He couldn't afford to be seen with them, I wouldn't think."

"Maybe that's why he went to the battlefield—to meet them where no one would see them together? But something went wrong and one of them killed him? That still doesn't explain why Woskowicz killed Arriaga—if he did—or why he kept the gun. Wouldn't you think he'd be smart enough to fling it into the nearest river or a Dumpster several miles from here?"

"You knew him better than I did," Jay responded.

The scent of warm peanut butter filled the small room, and I knew I had to leave before they came out of the oven or I'd eat fifteen of them. "I'm beginning to think I didn't know him at all."

"I saw the ad for his job on the mall website," Jay said. "Are you interviewing for it?"

"Today."

"Good luck. I'll take you out to dinner to celebrate your promotion."

"There may be nothing to celebrate." I was deliberately trying not to get my hopes up; I'd suffered too many rejections lately.

"I'll take you out to dinner anyway." He took a step forward, which brought him to within six inches of me. I was absurdly conscious of his broad shoulders and his subtle soap-and-warm-cookie scent. My lips parted slightly and I looked up at him.

"Hey, can we get some cookies out here?" A woman's voice drilled into the kitchen, and Jay slipped past me with a quick, rueful smile, saying, "Certainly, ladies. What kind did you want? Buy four and the fifth one's free."

My face warm with embarrassment—had I really been prepared to kiss a man in a food court kitchen while I was supposed to be working?—I ducked out the door, retrieved my Segway, and scuttled back to the security office.

Twenty-four

...

I was on the verge of calling Detective Helland to tell him what Grandpa and I had learned yesterday—not much—when he called me.

"Cruz Guerra's story fell apart," he said without pre-amble. His voice was cool and impersonal, and I could tell he regretted recruiting me to help him. "A middle school girl came forward to say he was with her, indulging in illegal substances, when he said he was shooting Arriaga. We let his mother have a go at him, too, and he has recanted his story. His mother says she thinks he was only trying to impress his brother, Enrique. She's trying hard to keep him away from Enrique—doesn't want her baby sucked into the gang—but I think she's fighting a losing battle. No father in the picture, of course."

"So you're looking at other suspects again. You need to hear what I found out yesterday." I summarized Grandpa's and my encounter with William "Billy" Silver, brother of Aggie and brother-in-law of Dennis Woskowicz.

"That's worth following up on," Helland said. His voice was detached, not effusive, but I felt like he'd handed me a gold medal.

Get over it already, I told myself. "Did you ever get a chance to talk to Eloísa?" I asked.

"No." Helland's tone said he wasn't happy about it. "She's staying with an aunt out of state. We got the parents to agree that a local cop could interview her, but he got nothing useful from the girl."

"She's scared of Enrique. She—" My gaze fell on my watch and I leaped up. "I've got to go. Interview. Bye." I hung up as Helland started to say something—probably something about staying away from the investigation now that he was back on the case—and dashed out of the office with Joel shouting "Good luck" after me. I allowed myself two minutes in the ladies' room to comb my hair and apply lipstick, and then I headed for the parking lot.

The interviews were taking place at the Figley and Boon Investments headquarters in Dale City, Virginia, a good half hour north of here. The traffic gods weren't feeling surly today, and I arrived with fifteen minutes to spare, time to take a deep breath and run through probable questions and responses mentally before an admin assistant ushered me into the conference room exactly on time.

I found myself facing Curtis Quigley and three people I didn't know, all arrayed on the far side of the conference table, legal pads and water glasses in front of them. A single chair sat on my side of the table and I moved toward it, assessing the interviewers as I did. An ash-blond woman in her fifties peered at me over the rim of glasses sagging halfway down her nose. A human resources exec, I'd bet. Beside her sat a corpulent man, a bit younger, skimming messages on his Blackberry. He looked up impatiently when I entered and went back to his email. Quigley came next.

The woman in the last seat sat with hands folded primly in front of her and wore a pale pink suit I thought might be Chanel. She gave me a friendly smile and I smiled back.

Quigley made introductions and started the ball rolling with, "Thanks for coming in on a Saturday, Ms. Ferris. Please tell us about your qualifications for the director of security job."

Most of the questions I'd anticipated, preparing answers about my management style, my experience, and my ideas for making the mall safer. As we neared the end of my allotted hour on the hot seat, the Blackberry man asked, "Isn't it true that there's been a rash of bodies at the mall in the last couple months?" Quigley had introduced him as the FBI vice president for retail operations. "How would you stop that disturbing trend if you were the director of security?"

"There's no way to guarantee there'll never be another body at Fernglen," I said bluntly. "But we can reduce the chances by upgrading our camera system and by authorizing our officers to carry weapons. Tasers, perhaps."

"Armed guards might intimidate our shoppers," the man said. "We don't want to look like we're running a police state," he added, his gaze flicking to his Blackberry again.

"Studies show—"

"A new camera system would cost money." The blonde with the glasses drew back, disapproval etched on her face. She was from the FBI budget office, not human resources as I'd assumed.

"Yes," I agreed, "but the potential gain—"

"Lots of money."

The pink-suited woman on the other end, the real HR executive, interrupted to ask, "What would you do about the uniforms if you were made director of security?"

The uniforms? I tried to keep the bafflement off my face.

"We could save money by continuing to use the same uniforms," I said, trying to placate both interviewers at once.

"They're so drab," the Chanel wearer said, pursing her lips. She gestured toward my uniform with an up-and-down motion of her hand. "Boring. Our malls are upscale, fashion-forward . . . Shouldn't all our employees be walking advertisements for our merchandise?"

To my relief, the administrative assistant reappeared just then and the panel thanked me for my time and said they'd be in touch after all the interviews had been conducted. I thanked them and left, slightly cheered by the approving nod Quigley gave me. I'd been doing pretty well, I thought, up until the last five minutes. Boring uniforms? I shook my head, chuckling to myself as I returned to my Miata. She must have been kidding, trying to see if I'd bite and recommend spending money on "fashionable" new uniforms.

That evening, after a roasted beet and goat cheese salad from a recipe I'd cut from a magazine months earlier and been meaning to try, I sat in the living room, strumming my guitar and watching Fubar playing with his feather toy. I was trying to teach myself Isaac Albeniz's "Asturias" and struggling with one of the chord progressions. I should look into taking lessons again, I thought, surprised by the way my spirits lifted at the thought. I hadn't played seriously since before Afghanistan. I'd ask around about teachers Monday, I decided, by calling music stores in the area to see who they recommended.

The doorbell pealed and Fubar twisted at the apex of a pounce on his feather toy, landing hard. He trotted to the tiny foyer to investigate; I followed once I'd laid the guitar carefully on the sofa. Peering through the peep hole, I was surprised to see Detective Helland. I opened the door, forgetting I had on nothing but a pair of old gym shorts and a faded green tee shirt from a 10K race I'd run once. The cool air on my bare legs reminded me, and I stopped in mid-hello. My leg, with the expanses of scar tissue, the twisted knee, the indentations where muscle and fat had been stripped away, was on display.

I wanted to slam the door in his face, but it was too late. His gaze had swept over me, and although he was too polite to stare, I noticed the almost undetectable widening of his eyes when he saw my leg. "May I come in?"

"I suppose." Hardly my most gracious moment. "Have a seat in the living room. I'll be right back."

As I scurried to my bedroom, Helland bent to pat Fubar, who was sitting a foot away, looking annoyed that Helland wasn't wearing lace-up shoes. Loafers had no appeal as far as Fubar was concerned. In my room, I scrambled out of the shorts and into a pair of gray sweats in less than thirty seconds, reappearing with a smile that dared him to say anything. He was still standing in the foyer, so I led him into the living room.

"Was that you playing the guitar?" he asked, looking around the small room. "You're very good."

"I'm out of practice." I surveyed the room, trying to see it through his eyes. A thirty-two-inch flat-screen TV, mostly for watching *Dancing with the Stars* with Kyra. Sofa and love seat in a nubby olive fabric with threads of rust running through it. A lamp with a stained-glass shade my brother Clint made for me when he was in college and going through an arty phase. Gas fireplace with a dancing flame, and a mantel crowded with photos of family and friends, including several taken in Afghanistan. Helland strolled over to look at a photo I'd taken of poppy fields stretching as far as the eye could see outside a tiny village not far from Qandahar. Of course he was attracted to the photos; he was a photographer.

"Nice. The contrast between the old world and modern civilization"—he pointed to the figure of an Afghani farmer with a camel surrounded by poppies, looking up at a Cobra helicopter flying overhead—"is powerful."

His praise made me uncomfortable; I had just wanted to hold on to the colorful poppies, the bright swathe of orangey red against the otherwise dun landscape of Afghanistan. "Did you want something?" I asked abruptly.

His blond brows rose a fraction of an inch. "I should have called first," he said.

"No, it's okay. I'm sorry. Would you like a beer?" I didn't know why I felt so discombobulated. I traipsed into the kitchen and called back, "Sam Adams or Laughing Lab?"

He chose the latter, and I popped the lids off two bottles and carried them back to the living room. He was seated on the love seat, so I chose the sofa, lifting the guitar back into its case.

"Since William Silver was your lead, I thought you deserved to hear what's happened," Helland said after an appreciative swallow of the beer.

"You've already talked to him? That was fast."

He shook his head. "No. He's gone."

His announcement startled me so much I nearly spit beer at him. "What? Where?"

"When you told me about him this afternoon, the connection between him, Woskowicz, and the amnestied gun was too strong to ignore, so I put my team on him and made a few calls. The police chief in Mantua, New Jersey, let me know that their internal investigation pointed to Allied Forge Metals as the culprit in the missing guns situation."

"He's got a vested interest in thinking that," I pointed out. "I'm sure he doesn't want to believe his cops are dirty."

"The sergeant in charge of the program voluntarily underwent a poly," Helland said, "and passed. The chief's convinced his folks aren't responsible for those guns being back on the street."

"Okay." I pulled one leg up under me.

"After I heard that, I got in touch with several other police departments who had used Silver's company to destroy guns. None of them had any problems; it was just luck—bad luck for Silver—that one of the Mantua guns was used in a homicide and then recovered."

"I'd say the bad luck was Celio Arriaga's."

His nod conceded my point. "Indeed. When we pulled Silver's EZ Pass records, they showed that he drove this way every other Wednesday, including the Wednesday Woskowicz was murdered. Unfortunately, we don't have any toll plazas on the stretch of 95 between D.C. and here, so we can't prove—yet—that this was his destination. Still, the circumstantial evidence is damning."

"That he killed Woskowicz."

"Yes." He clicked his beer bottle onto a coaster. "Our working theory is that Silver and Woskowicz were in business together, reselling the guns Silver siphoned off from his police contracts. Maybe Silver approached Woskowicz, knowing the man was open to shady deals, or maybe Woskowicz suggested that it would be easy for Silver to certify the guns destroyed and then resell them. We won't know until Silver shows up. Regardless, they went into the illicit gun-sales business together."

"That matches with what Starla and Aggie told me. Was Silver down here on Tuesday when Arriaga was shot?"

"There's no record of it. I think Woskowicz killed Arriaga, possibly because he became a threat to him somehow—Woskowicz had the murder weapon in his possession, after all—and then Silver killed Woskowicz."

"Why?"

"We haven't figured that one out yet, but it doesn't matter.

It's possible Woskowicz demanded a bigger cut than he was getting and Silver balked. Hell, it's even possible he shot Woskowicz for sleeping around on his sister and dumping her."

I hadn't thought about that. "Do you think Aggie Woskowicz was involved?"

"It's early days yet," Helland said noncommittally. "Right now, there's no evidence that she knew anything about the guns. Although she called Silver after talking to you today, and we think that phone call is what spurred him to run. His secretary said that after his sister's call he told her to cancel the rest of his appointments for the week, lugged a box of files and his laptop to the car, and took off."

"Aggie warned him?" I felt guilty about having talked to her. "I'm sorry."

Helland shrugged it off. "She might have called to warn him, or she might have called just to chat and happened to mention your conversation. Either way, it's not your fault. If you hadn't uncovered the link between Allied Forge Metals and Woskowicz, we'd still be wandering around in the dark. If you tell anyone I said that, I'll deny it." A half smile went with the words, and I found myself smiling back. He didn't seem nearly so aloof when he smiled.

"So what happens now?"

"We catch Silver. We've got an APB out on him, and I don't think he'll get far."

"So, it's over?" I felt let down. It was curiously unsatisfying to accept that Captain Woskowicz killed Celio Arriaga for an unknown reason and Silver shot Woskowicz. I knew proving motive wasn't necessary in the courtroom, that means and opportunity were more important for a conviction, but I really wanted to know *why*.

"Pretty much." Helland stood and I followed suit. He looked down at me, a hint of understanding in his eyes.

"There's always questions left at the end of an investigation."

"I suppose so. When you interrogate Silver, will you let me know what he says?"

"Maybe."

That was more like the Detective Helland I'd gotten to know and tolerate than the man who'd come over to tell me where the investigation stood.

"What does 'maybe' mean?"

"Just what it sounds like," he said, draining his beer and setting the bottle down. "It 'may be' that you'll do something helpful that prompts me to share details of an investigation with you. Or it 'may be' that you'll annoy me so much with your constant assumption that you can do my job better than I can that I'll make sure the only update you get is via the newspaper." He sounded disgruntled, but I didn't feel any real animosity behind his words. It was hard to read the expression in his hooded eyes.

"Great," I said sunnily. "Can't wait to hear all about it if—sorry, *when*—you round up Billy Silver."

He rolled his eyes and preceded me to the door, stooping to pat Fubar as I opened it. "Has Fernglen found a replacement for your ex-boss yet?" he asked, straightening.

"As a matter of fact, I interviewed for the job today," I said.

"I hope you get it."

"Thanks." I was surprised and pleased by his vote of confidence.

He passed me on the way out the door and paused a moment on the walkway. He had a glint in his eyes that in someone else I'd have taken for humor. "That way, you'll be too busy to stick your nose into my investigations in future."

I didn't slam the door; I shut it firmly.

Twenty-five

...

I wasn't exactly biting my nails on Monday, but I was more anxious to hear who'd gotten the director of security job than I'd expected to be. Consequently, I spent large chunks of the morning patrolling, talking to the security officers and merchants, and generally fidgeting. I lunched with Grandpa before he donned his costume for a shift as the Easter Bunny, and filled him in about William Silver.

"You cracked the case," I told him, munching an apple on a ledge that girdled a room-sized planter near the fountain. Grandpa sat beside me. Every few seconds, I had to brush away a fern that kept tickling my ear. Shoppers trickled past, with one or two of them stopping to toss a coin into the fountain.

"You did," he said, "by discovering the link between Woskowicz and Silver. I'm surprised Detective Helland isn't making you a job offer. Speaking of which—?" He looked at me inquiringly.

"No word," I said, trying to sound like it didn't matter. I

swung my foot idly. "It may be a week or two before they make a decision, for all I know. I don't know how many people they were interviewing."

He hopped spryly down from the ledge. "I've got to suit up. I'll talk to you later, Emma-Joy."

After Grandpa left, I Segwayed back to the office and decided to make a real effort to block the interview from my mind. Casting about for something else to focus on, my gaze fell on the camera screens, currently monitored by Vic Dallabetta. In the confusion of the investigation I'd forgotten that Captain Woskowicz had, in all likelihood, disabled the cameras in the Pete's wing. If it was only him and Silver running the recycling business—as in recycling guns to new owners—why did he sabotage the cameras? Did Silver bring the guns in through that entrance? That made no sense. Woskowicz couldn't have a parade of gun buyers marching through the security office to pick out hardware. Goose bumps prickled my arms. There was someone else involved. Someone who worked in the mall.

"EJ, are you all right? Do you see something suspicious?"

Vic's voice broke through my reverie. She was watching me, a wary expression on her face, and I realized I'd been staring fixedly at the monitors. "I'm fine," I said. "Sorry. Just thinking."

I hurried back to the director's office and called the Vernonville Police Department. Asking for Detective Helland, I learned today was his day off. Asking the desk sergeant to have Helland call me tomorrow, I hung up, figuring my bright idea would keep until then. I sat in front of the computer and pulled up the camera data from the Tuesday Celio died. I needed a project to distract me and I'd found one: I was going to sift through the footage from that day again, all of it if I had to, and examine Celio's every moment in the mall. It was painfully tedious work, and after two hours I took a break to fetch a cup of hot coffee and squirt lubricating eye drops into my eyes, which were burning from the effort of focusing so closely on the grainy images.

I kept a legal pad at my elbow and noted when and where I spotted Celio, Enrique, or Eloísa. They'd come into the mall through the lower Macy's entrance at two thirty-seven. They were in a mini-wedge formation, with Enrique slightly in the front and Celio and Eloísa a half step behind on either side. They turned right and walked toward the Sears, popping into a couple of stores on the way. Reaching Sears, they turned around without going in and headed back the way they'd come, on the other side of the corridor. Halfway down it, they rode the escalator up to the second level. It looked like the overlong and thready hem of Celio's jeans got caught on the top elevator step because he jerked his leg hard to get free. The next time I found them, Enrique and Eloísa were munching big pretzels and Celio held a cup with a Chik-fil-A logo. Eloísa had her purse tucked under her arm so she could hold the pretzel with one hand and a small paper cup with mustard or cheese in the other.

I tracked them through a series of innocuous store visits and some goofing off near a cell phone sales kiosk until they turned into the Pete's wing and I lost them. Twenty minutes later, Eloísa and Enrique emerged from the wing and headed toward the bunny enclosure, in keeping with what Eloísa had told me. They'd apparently finished the pretzels because Eloísa carried only her purse, and Enrique had nothing. It was four o'clock by now, and I decided to quit for the day. Other than answering a couple of phone calls, I'd been glued to the computer all afternoon. And learning pretty much nothing, I thought, discouraged. I could resume my scan of the images tomorrow . . . or give it up and accept that the deaths played out the way Helland said they did. If there was another person involved with Silver and Woskowicz, he—or she—had lost his gun supplier and was out of business. Presumably.

Changing into a pair of yoga pants and a long-sleeved tee shirt so I could stop by the Y for a weight workout on my way home, I stuffed my uniform in my gym bag. Harold had replaced Vic in the office, and he told me about his grandsons' dying the water in their fish aquarium red with a tablet from an Easter egg coloring kit. "My daughter thought some predator had gotten into the tank and slaughtered the fish," he said, laughing. " 'What were you thinking, Marcy' I asked her. 'A great white? It's only a ten-gallon tank, for heaven's sake.' "

I chuckled obligingly.

"Aren't you off shift by now?" he asked, glancing at his watch.

"Technically, yeah." I smiled. "I'm on my way out. See you tomorrow." Slinging my gym bag over my shoulder, I left, threading my way through the stop-by-the-mall-on-the-way-home-from-work shoppers. A man passed me carrying an Easter basket dripping virulent pink grass in a sporadic trail behind him. A mother pulled two children in a wagon like the one Jen kept on display outside her store. One of the kids waved at me and I waved back. "Want fish," he crowed, pointing past me.

I turned to see what had caught his attention. A teenager with long black hair and jeans tight enough to cut off her circulation strolled past, a whale from the Make-a-Manatee store tucked under one arm. The sight triggered a memory and I stopped dead. Eloísa had had a stuffed animal—manatee? seal?—with her when I passed her and Enrique and Celio the day Celio died. I hadn't seen it in any of the camera footage I'd looked at today, and I'd gotten up to the point where she and Enrique left the Pete's wing, leaving

Celio behind to conduct business of some sort. Ergo, Celio had been in the Make-a-Manatee store. Excitement thrummed through me. That didn't mean it was the *only* store he'd been in while separated from his cousin and Enrique, but he'd definitely been in there—and Mike Wachtel had denied it.

Spinning on my heel, I strode toward Make-a-Manatee.

Twenty-six

. . .

Make-a-Manatee was quiet when I entered, with no birthday parties or flying cupcakes. A woman and a little boy wandered past the bins full of unstuffed animals, the boy wanting a starfish, a shark, and a sea lion. "Just one," the mom reminded him.

I spotted Mike Wachtel in the party nook, setting up for a birthday party. Standing precariously on a chair, he tacked a computer-printed banner that read "Happy Birthday, Sierra" over the table. A folded pink paper tablecloth and a plastic bag of pink utensils peeked from a cardboard box on the table.

"Need some help?" Without waiting for Mike's reply, I took the tablecloth, flapped it open, and let it drift down onto the table.

At the sound of my voice, Mike looked over his shoulder. If he was pleased to see me, he disguised it well. "EJ." His tone was flat. The bruises on his face were even more lurid today, and I could see the boy's mother cast him an uncertain glance.

"Maybe you'd rather have a game from Jen's Toy Store?" she asked her son, steering him toward the door.

Mike heaved a big sigh as they departed and teetered on the chair, his cast making him unsteady. I reached up a hand to help him down and he gripped it hard. As soon as he was safely down, he let go.

"Where're your helpers today?" I asked.

"Not that it's any of your business," he said, "but I had to cut back their hours."

"Yeah, I think you mentioned that you've been doing afternoons and evenings by yourself," I said.

"So?"

"So you would have waited on Celio Arriaga when he was in here two weeks ago, the Tuesday he was killed. And yet you told me you hadn't seen him."

"I can't remember everyone who comes in here," he said irritably, setting a two-liter bottle of Sprite and one of Coke on the table.

"Of course not," I agreed. His shoulders relaxed a fraction before I added, "But I'd think you'd remember a gang member in here on his own buying a stuffie. Or was he really here to buy something else?"

Mike turned to face me, hand gripping a plastic fork so tightly it cracked and he dropped it. "What are you saying, EJ?"

"I think you were working with Captain Woskowicz and William Silver," I said, suddenly convinced I was right. "I think Celio Arriaga came in here to purchase a gun—one of the ones Silver siphoned off the gun amnesty programs. Somehow, Woskowicz knew you'd be interested in making a little untaxable cash, and he set you up as the front man."

"We share—shared—a bookie," Mike said with a

humorless smile, implicitly acknowledging my accusation. "Dennis knew I was into him for over forty large and asked if I'd be interested in the gun deal. I said, 'Hell, yeah.' The business was by word of mouth—not high volume, but enough to bring in a couple thou a month. Dennis funneled buyers my way; he had a lot of shady contacts. I'd sell to a woman needing a remedy for an abusive boyfriend here, an ex-con there. It let me keep up with the vig I owed Boris, at least. It worked like a charm until that gangbanger tried to hold me up."

"Hold you up?"

"He came in for a gun late in the afternoon, and I sold him a .38, slipped it into the seal he bought."

Eloísa had to have known there was something heavy in the stuffed seal she was lugging around the mall. Why hadn't she mentioned it?

"But he wasn't satisfied with that," Mike said, speaking more freely now that he was into his story. "He asked what else I had on hand, but I told him my rule was one to a customer. It's not that I had any moral problems with selling more guns to a gang—"

"No moral problems at all," I said drily.

"—but it was logistically difficult. How would it look if he walked out of here with ten stuffed animals?

"He seemed okay with it, nodded a few times, but I could see him looking around, casing the place. He asked if I kept my extra stock in the storeroom in the back. I told him I didn't have anything else on hand."

"He didn't buy it."

Mike shook his head. "No. He was back that evening, a few minutes before closing. He held me up with the gun he'd bought from me." Mike sounded offended by Celio's crassness. "What he didn't know is that I've had a gun on me ever since Boris sent his thugs to break my leg. I told the banger we had to go in the back to get the guns, and when he followed me there, I shot him."

It seemed to me that he paled a bit at the memory. "Why didn't anyone report hearing the shot?" I asked.

With a smug little smile, he gestured toward the recycling bin brimming with two-liter soda bottles. "I grabbed one of those on my way by and used it as a silencer. The shot still made a hell of a noise, but it was muffled. Easy for people to think they'd heard something from the parking lot. With his body lying there and blood all over, I panicked. I called Dennis at home.

"He told me the biggest thing was to get the body out of the mall. With the cameras still out—Dennis had arranged that so there'd be less chance of any of you spotting one of my customers and so he could get new stock in here every week—I just had to wait until everyone was gone. Then I loaded him up in that wagon from Jen's and dumped him on the sidewalk. I was petrified the whole time, practically peed my pants, thinking the night guard would come strolling down the corridor, even though Dennis said he'd distract him. I couldn't think of a way to move the body any farther without getting caught on one of the security cameras, so I left him there. I cleaned up in here as best I could, went home, and downed half a bottle of Tanqueray. God, did I have a hangover the next day."

He looked like he had one now, hands trembling slightly, a sheen of sweat on his pale, bruised forehead. "So how did Woskowicz end up with the murder weapon?" I asked. Since the mother-and-son duo had left, no one else had entered the store. I felt too isolated and smacked myself mentally for not coming down in uniform—so I'd have my radio, at least—and for letting Mike get between me and the door.

"He came in here the next day, after I'd spent hours going over the place with bleach. A website I found said that was the only way to really clean up evidence of a crime. Dennis told me he'd get rid of the gun for me. He said he was meeting with his contact—you say his name is Silver?—and that he'd have the guy destroy the gun the way it was supposed to have been melted down or whatever in the first place. I gave it to him in a bag"—The bag Woskowicz had been carrying when he left here Wednesday afternoon.—"but then I began to have second thoughts."

"You followed him to his meeting with Silver, didn't you?"

A crooked grin straggled up Mike's tense face, and he made a gun of his thumb and forefinger, pointing it at me. "Give the little lady a prize. I was desperate for more money—Boris said that next time he was going to hurt Glenda or one of the boys—and the more I thought about it, the more I realized that I didn't need a middleman, Woskowicz, taking a cut of my profits. I was the one with his neck on the line; the gangbanger taught me that." Indignation colored Mike's voice, the bitterness of a man who thinks he always gets the short end of the stick. "So why shouldn't I get a bigger cut? Only problem was, I didn't know who was supplying Woskowicz with the guns. So I waited outside his house and followed him to the battlefield park. He never had a clue I was there.

"I got out and confronted him before his connection showed up, told him I wanted more money. He actually laughed at me. Well, he shut up fast enough, I'll tell you, when I pulled out my gun." Narrowing his eyes, Mike continued. "I told him I needed a bigger cut, explained that I was desperate, but he made a grab for the gun and it went off." His eyes slid away from mine. "It was an accident. I didn't mean to kill him."

Uh-uh. Of course not. That's why he followed Woskowicz to a deserted meeting point and pulled a gun. "You didn't really have a choice," I commented.

Continuing as if I hadn't spoken, he said, "I searched him and the car, looking for my gun. He didn't have it on him. I knew then that he hadn't ever planned to have it destroyed; he was probably going to blackmail me with it somewhere down the line. I almost panicked then, wondering where it was, but then the guy with the guns showed up. He was very pragmatic once he saw my nine mil, and we came to a mutually beneficial agreement. He didn't know my name or where I worked—Dennis had deliberately kept our names to himself, so he was essential to both of us—and that suited me fine. We set up a schedule for deliveries and agreed on email as a nice anonymous way of getting in contact when necessary, and I drove over to Dennis's house, hoping to find my gun there. I searched for hours. No joy. I took his computer in case he had anything on it that incriminated me. Experts can pull up all sorts of shit you think you've deleted."

He was lucky one of Woskowicz's exes hadn't caught him.

"I read, of course, that the cops found the gun. Where was it?"

"In a file cabinet in the security office," I said, seeing no reason not to tell him. "Your prints are on it."

"Liar. I made sure to wipe it down before I gave it to Dennis." He seemed almost amused by my attempt to fluster him, but I could see his tension in the stiff line of his shoulders and the pulse throbbing in his neck.

I edged to the left, thinking that if I could get a clear path to the door, I'd make a run for it. Mike forestalled me by pulling a gun from his pocket, keeping it low and close to his body so a shopper glancing in the window wouldn't see it.

"Uh-uh," he said. "Back there." He jerked his chin toward the stockroom and office behind the partition.

Gathering myself, I flexed my knees slightly, ready to propel myself toward the door. With his leg in a cast, he couldn't tackle me, and I doubted he had the nerve to fire the gun with so many people still in the mall.

The barrel of the gun came up an inch. "I have nothing to lose," he said in a flat, emotionless voice that told me he was dead serious.

"What time is Sierra's birthday party?" I asked, hoping to distract him.

"Twenty minutes," he said. "Move."

I started toward the back of the store, moving as slowly as possible. "The cameras are working again, you know," I said. "You can't just trundle me out of here in a wagon like you did with Celio."

"Shut up. I'm working on it."

I already knew how I'd get a body out of here if I were he, but I wasn't going to give him any hints. Assuming he had a decent-sized box in the back, he could stuff me in one, push it out the back door of his store because the mall didn't have cameras in the utility hallways, and wait for the mall to close. He could leave as usual. Then, he could come back disguised, say with a hat and dark glasses, disable the camera nearest the door with a squirt of spray paint, drive his car up, hoist the box with yours truly in it into the trunk, and disappear.

"The cameras will show that I came into Make-a-Manatee but never left," I said, hoping to make him see the futility of doing away with me. I rounded the partition and quickly sized up the escape opportunities of the small office and stockroom.

He eyed me for a moment. "Glenda's about your size. Take off your shirt."

I gaped at him. Then it dawned on me that he was going to have Glenda don my clothes, and maybe a wig, and walk out of here as me. "She's pissed at you; she won't do it."

He frowned. "Stop worrying abou—"

"Hello?" A woman's voice came from the front of the store.

"Hel—" I started to yell, but Wachtel crashed the gun against my temple and I slumped to the floor, everything graying out.

When I came to, head aching and cheek stinging viciously, I was momentarily disoriented. The sound of children's laughter drifted to me, and I was chilled, lying on my back on a cold, hard surface. I tried to sit up, then fought down panic at the realization that I couldn't move my hands. The confrontation with Mike came flooding back. I was in his stockroom, in the dark, my hands bound with what felt like duct tape, with another piece of tape over my mouth. Not good.

I managed to lever myself to a sitting position. At least I still had my clothes on. I did my best to shrug my shoulder up and bend my head so I could wipe my cheek on my shoulder, hoping, at the very least, to get blood on my shirt and foil Mike's plan of having his wife impersonate me, not that the camera resolution was good enough to show a stain at all, much less enable anyone to identify it. Still, it made me feel like I was doing something. I sat and thought, wishing I had water to slake my thirst and a few painkillers for my headache.

There had been a customer in the store when Mike clobbered me, and he'd been expecting the birthday partiers within minutes, so he hadn't had much time to incapacitate me. My feet were unbound—good—so maybe I could stand, open the door, and walk out of here. Failing that, maybe I could make enough noise to grab someone's attention. Remembering the customer's complaint about parents not sticking around to help with the birthday parties, I devoutly hoped that a parent or two was in the store now watching little Sierra blow out her candles.

Scooting backwards on my butt, I backed into something solid—a packing box, maybe—after only a couple of inches. I braced my back against it and pushed with my feet, trying to stand. My head swam alarmingly, and for a moment I thought I might throw up. With my mouth taped shut, I could asphyxiate in my own vomit, and the thought terrified me. I stopped, holding perfectly still, and concentrated on taking calming breaths through my nose. In . . . out. When I felt the nausea subside a tad, I tried to stand again. I pushed to my feet and stood there swaying, desperately trying to stay upright and not throw up.

Wheels of light spun behind my eyeballs, and my head felt like someone with a skip loader was trundling around in my skull. I was concussed. I might even have a skull fracture. I opened my eyes to see if I could make the spinning wheels go away, but it was just as dark with my eyes open and the wheels spun anyway, so I shut them again. Door. I had to find the door.

Keeping my fingertips in contact with the box behind me, I inched sideways gingerly, knowing that if I banged into something and fell and hit my head, I might not be able to get back up. Within in a very short distance, a couple of feet at most, my left shoulder bumped a wall or another box. I let me fingertips explore the surface. Rough textured and cool. The wall.

Sidestepping to my left, fingers reading the wall as if it were a Braille script, I moved another three or four feet before meeting another wall. This was definitely the stockroom, not the office, which was too bad because the office might conceivably have scissors or a letter opener I could use to free my hands or defend myself. All the stockroom held, I suspected, was boxes of fluff and unstuffed plush animals—I didn't think beaning Mike with a fuchsia starfish was going to slow him down much.

I went left again and felt elated when my questing fingertips felt the smoothness of laminate or wood instead of the rough concrete of the walls. The door! Another step brought my fingers into contact with the knob, and I held my breath, hoping. The knob hit me just about where my wrists were taped together at the small of my back. Leaning slightly, I got my fingers around the knob and gave it a twist. Nothing. I tried again, jerking the weight of my body left to apply leverage, but the door was locked.

Tears welled in my eyes, but I blinked them away furiously. I was not going to let a weaselly, gambling, murdering . . . *turd* like Mike Wachtel kill me. I flung myself backwards against the door in frustration. It bowed ever so slightly—cheap hollow-core construction—but the movement jarred my head and I dropped to my knees, fighting back nausea. I stayed on my knees for long moments, concentrating on my breathing, trying to think.

The strains of "Happy birthday, dear Sierra" drifted to me. The kids. I raised my head slightly. I couldn't risk breaking out of here while the birthday party was still going on. Mike was armed and unstable, a loose cannon, with, as he'd pointed out, nothing to lose. I couldn't endanger the children by busting down the door—if I even could—and staggering into the store while they were picking out hearts and voice boxes for their little dolphins and otters.

Ironically, the decision not to try anything *now* made me calmer, gave me the illusion that I had more time. I stayed on my knees and the unfamiliar posture made me think of praying. I hadn't been to church in years, but Mom had insisted when Clint and I were little, and the Lord's Prayer came back to me now as though I'd been saying it every day. When my knees started to ache, I struggled to my feet again and turned so I was facing the door. Maybe I could kick it open once the partygoers were gone. My head throbbed at the thought, and I stayed very still for a moment until the sadist operating the skip loader in my skull settled down.

I practiced balancing on my weak leg and thrusting forward with my good leg, trying to aim my kick near the knob. After a few tries, I felt like I could hit the spot I needed to. Whether it would be enough to pop open the door was anybody's guess. A new thought came to me. Maybe I should wait until I heard Mike approaching, until he opened the door, and kick out just before he pulled it wide. The door would smack into him, giving me a second or two—hopefully—to run for it.

Standing on both legs, to give my trembling weak leg a break, I listened. It seemed quieter out front. I couldn't hear the piping voices of kids anymore. Had they gone? Was the shop empty of customers? My muscles tensed, and I flexed and pointed my right foot to ease a cramp in my calf. I held my breath so I'd have a better chance of hearing Mike approach.

In the event, I didn't hear anything until the doorknob started to turn. Its metallic *snick* startled me, and I hastily gathered myself, sucking in a deep breath and putting most of my weight on my right leg. A knife's edge of light cut the darkness, and I launched myself forward, propelling my leg with all the force I could muster. My heel thudded against the door and it smacked back. Light flooded in as Mike let out an "Unh" of pain. A shot nearly deafened me, and I figured he'd had his finger on the trigger and had tightened it reflexively when the door whacked into him.

Scrambling forward, I burst through the door. Mike rocked on his keister to my left, scrabbling for the gun he'd dropped. An empty soda bottle rolled nearby. The partition opened to my right, so I cut sharply toward it and plowed forward, trying to keep my balance with my hands taped behind me. I rounded the end of the partition and the store stretched before me, empty of customers. I fixed on the door as though it were the entrance to the Promised Land, to Disneyworld, to Aladdin's Cave. If I could just make it—

I ran, thumping my thigh painfully against a display ledge because I couldn't balance very well. Jinking around a display of octopi, I risked a look back. Mike stood just this side of the partition, arms extended to aim the gun, legs braced, head bleeding. I dropped and rolled as he fired, finding myself up against the fluff machine. I scrabbled around it on my knees and watched as the next bullet exploded the machine's glass walls in a burst of flying glass.

White fluff rained into the room, a soft, puffy snow spiked by glass shards. *Plink, plink, clink* the glass went as it landed. I wedged myself partially under the steel frame of the machine to keep the glass from slicing into my face. I could only hope it would obscure Mike's aim. The motor pulsed above me. One corner of the duct tape across my mouth felt loose, and I scrubbed my face against the floor, trying to work it off. It curled up until one corner of my mouth was barely exposed. "Gi' it u', Mike," I mumbled as loudly as I could, feeling the skin tear off my lips as the movement loosened the tape infinitesimally. "Gu'shots. Co's on way." I could've wept with the frustration of trying to make myself understood, of trying to make Mike understand the futility of what he was doing.

"Not soon enough for you," he growled, apparently having no trouble understanding me. He trotted toward me, and I squirmed toward the far side of the fluff machine, wishing I had the use of my hands. "If it weren't for you—"

He grabbed my foot with one hand and yanked. As I slid out from under the machine on my back, my hands trapped underneath me, I noted the fluff still spewing into the air,

the deranged fury twisting Mike's face, and the barrel of
the gun swinging around to aim at my head. I had time for
only one instinctive movement. I thudded both my feet into
Mike's broken leg, rolling away from the gun as he howled
and fell.

"Emma-Joy!" Grandpa's voice sounded from the front
of the store, strangely muffled.

Another shot rang out. The display window at the front
of the store exploded outward in a geyser of glass, and
screams sounded from the corridor. I hoped the bullet hadn't
hit anyone, especially not a kid. I also hoped whoever was
out there was busy dialing 911.

Rolling over, I scootched away from Mike on my knees
and right shoulder. When I reached a display table, I braced
my shoulder against it and made it to my feet. Mike had
staggered to his feet, too, two yards away from me. He stood
awkwardly, putting no weight on the casted leg, which hung
heavily from his hip. Blood dripped from his face and his
hand, apparently cut by shards from the fluff machine. He
swung the gun toward me and then toward the Easter Bunny
charging him, head down, like a pass rusher determined to
sack the quarterback.

"Nooo!" I shrieked, only it came out more like a gurgle
through the duct tape. I launched myself at Mike. I slammed
into him, hard, and we both fell. Even though his body
cushioned my fall, it knocked the breath out of me, and I
lay atop him as what seemed like hundreds of people flooded
into the room. Mike didn't struggle beneath me and I wondered if he was dead. That fear passed as the rapid beats of
his heart tha-thumped under my ear and the rank smell of
his body odor filled my nostrils.

"The Easter Bunny's bleeding," a child's voice said as I
blacked out.

Twenty-seven

. . .

I came to in a hospital bed, head still aching, but like Skip Loader Guy had been demoted to driving a golf cart. I felt queasy but decided after a moment that I wasn't going to throw up immediately. A window two feet from my bed showed darkness between the slats of the miniblinds, but I didn't know if it was seven p.m., midnight, or four in the morning. Someone stood at the foot of the bed. My vision was blurry and I blinked several times, finally resolving the three Detective Hellands into one. The events at Make-a-Manatee came flooding back and I sat up, gasping, "Grandpa?"

Helland, more casually dressed than usual in a white shirt with cuffs rolled up and slacks the gray of a midwinter sky, pushed me back against the pillow, his hands on my shoulders surprisingly gentle. He smelled like lime aftershave and coffee. "Mr. Atherton is fine," he said. "Man's made of titanium, the doc says. Wachtel winged his shoulder."

Relief gushed through me, making me feel weak.

"You're basically fine, too," he added. "You've got a concussion, which you probably figured out for yourself, and they want to keep you overnight for observation."

No way was I staying overnight. I'd spent enough time in hospitals to max out my lifetime quota. I didn't share that with Helland. "Wachtel?"

"In jail, singing like the proverbial canary. He says Woskowicz killed Celio Arriaga and William Silver shot Woskowicz." His voice held a question.

I started to shake my head but thought better of it. I relayed everything Mike had told me when he planned to kill me.

Helland nodded as though I'd confirmed what he'd suspected. "We have a crime-scene team going over the Make-a-Manatee premises. Wachtel may think he's cleaned up, but I'm betting we find hair or blood or something else that puts Arriaga in the back room. And we've already found traces of his blood on the wagon you pointed us toward. At the very least, we've got him for attempted murder of you and Mr. Atherton and for illegal weapons sales—we found twenty-six guns, ranging from a .22 to an AK-47, in a box of manatees in his storeroom."

"Silver?"

Helland seemed to understand my question. "He hasn't been apprehended yet, but if we put out word that we're seeking his testimony against Wachtel, maybe he'll come in. If what you've said is right—"

"It is," I muttered irritably, licking my lips, which were rough and sore. I didn't even want to think about what my hair looked like. A sudden thought made me glance down. Ugh. I was wearing one of those sacklike hospital gowns with snaps and ties that looked like it'd been washed and bleached twelve thousand times. How could a garment that displayed so much skin be so totally unsexy? Not, of course, that I wanted to look attractive for Detective Helland, I told myself. Hitching the neckline a tad higher, I raised my gaze to Helland, who handed me a tube of lip balm, unasked.

"Thanks," I said, startled. I slicked the soothing balm over my cracked lips as Helland continued.

"If you're right, all Silver's guilty of are the gun-related charges. I'm sure the DA could offer him a deal that would make it worth his while to turn himself in."

"Aggie," I said.

He nodded. "We've already been in touch with her and suggested that if she can get hold of her brother, she'd be doing him a favor to relay our message."

"I want to go home," I said, swinging my legs over the side of the bed. I twitched the sheet over them when I realized the hospital gown didn't cover my knee. My head swam, feeling a bit like a tilted fishbowl where the water sloshes to one side, but the disconcerting sensation subsided after a moment of stillness.

"You and me both, Emma-Joy," Grandpa Atherton said from the doorway. Helland moved aside to make room for him by my bed.

"Grandpa!" I held out my arms, relief sending tears down my face.

"What's with the waterworks, missy?" Grandpa asked, giving me a one-armed hug.

"When I heard the Easter Bunny was bleeding, I thought he'd killed you," I said. "How did you know?"

Grandpa settled himself on the side of my bed. He was wearing a robe that looked like something Cary Grant would have tossed on for a tryst with a lady friend, and his white hair was slicked straight back from his forehead. He was paler than usual and had his arm in a sling, but other than that, he seemed fine, the twinkle in his blue eyes reassuring me that he was truly okay.

"I was doing my bunny shtick downstairs when I heard the shots. Someone tried to say they were backfires, but I knew better. I dumped a tyke off my lap, ran upstairs—those bunny feet are not made for sprinting, I'll tell you—and saw people pointing toward Make-a-Manatee. When I got to the door and saw that man firing at you, well, I did what I could. No one shoots at my favorite granddaughter and gets away with it."

"You got shot," I said.

"Pooh. It's nothing," he said. "Why, you should see the scar on my hip from a firefight in Liberia back in—well, I can't mention the details, but believe you me, Emma-Joy, this little nick in my shoulder is hardly worth thinking about."

"I'll bet you were something in your agency days, sir," Helland observed, wry admiration in his smile. Leaning against the wall, arms folded over his chest with the fluorescent lights glinting on his blond hair, he looked disturbingly handsome. I tore my gaze away, blaming the painkillers for the unfamiliar tingles zipping through me.

"Still am, young man," Grandpa said tartly. "Now, about us breaking out of here, Emma-Joy—"

A commotion in the hall brought all our heads toward the door. The twitterings and gasps I'd heard all my life filtered into the room. "Oh no," I said, turning accusing eyes on Grandpa. "You didn't tell—"

Ethan swept into the room, followed by my mother and what must have been every female doctor, nurse, orderly, and ambulatory patient in the hospital. His famous smile was conspicuously absent and worry clouded his eyes.

"EJ!" He came toward me, arms outstretched, but stopped short. "Can I hug you without hurting you?" he asked, an unfamiliar note of uncertainty in his voice.

Not trusting myself to speak, I nodded and gave myself over to my daddy's hug.

"Ethan Jarrett is your father?" Helland asked incredulously.

Mom, used to dealing with adoring fans, had shooed them out in a way that left no hard feelings. I don't know how she does that. She, too, came over to give me a hug and then glared at Grandpa Atherton.

"Dad, if you had anything to do with getting EJ into this . . . I trusted you to take care of her when she moved out here after—"

"He saved my life," I interrupted her. "I got him into it."

"Oh." Mom burst into tears.

Perhaps afraid he'd be drawn into our group hug, Helland said we could formalize my statement in a day or two and excused himself. I didn't blame him. The Ferris family was hard to cope with one member at a time; more than two of us in a room at once should require a fireworks permit.

"I'm taking you back to the house," Ethan announced, glancing from me to Grandpa. "I've already hired a nurse, and the limo's out front. Let's get you checked out of this place."

The power of Ethan's name, personality, and assistants worked miracles with the hospital bureaucracy, and Grandpa and I were being pushed to the elevator in twin wheelchairs within the half hour. I was wearing the yoga pants and tee shirt I'd had on when I confronted Mike, even though they were torn, dirty, and lightly spattered with blood I suspected came from the murderous Make-a-Manatee owner. The ick factor was pretty high, but not high enough to make me prefer the too-well-ventilated hospital gown or wait while my folks fetched me another outfit.

"I don't need to be pushed like a baby in a pram," Grandpa grumbled. But his hand reached up to pat Mom's where it rested on the wheelchair handle.

I looked around the lobby as Ethan pushed my wheelchair,

getting an impression of cold, gray-veined marble flooring, a cathedral ceiling that must send the hospital's heating bills into the stratosphere, dusty corn plants, and scrubs-wearing hospital personnel moving purposefully. A uniformed security guard by the door barred the paparazzi from entering and made me think about my interview for the security director job, but I didn't feel any angst about it. I'd get the job or I wouldn't. And maybe I'd turn it down if they offered it to me; I'd been doing a lot of thinking about setting up in business for myself since talking with my mom, and the idea was growing on me. Right now, I was happy to be alive and relatively healthy, surrounded by the people I cared most about. I wouldn't be playing softball tonight, but I had a feeling Jay would give me a raincheck. I could hear his voice in my head, calling me a wuss for backing out because of a concussion. He'd probably play through any injury or illness short of a lung transplant. I smiled to myself.

A photographer's flash went off, a pop of white against the dark plate glass. A gaggle of paparazzi awaited us outside the hospital doors, and I suspected Ethan had no intention of missing the photo op by sneaking out the back. I didn't care, even if my face was bruised and my mouth puffy from having the duct tape ripped off; at least Mom had brushed my hair. As we rolled toward the doors and the yapping crowd, I said, "You know, hospitals remind me of temples. Temples of healing. You get IVs and pills instead of wine and—"

"Emma-Joy, I'm worried you got more of a knock on your noggin than the docs realized," Grandpa said.

I shut up and smiled, reaching across the gap between our chairs to hold his bony hand. "Nope," I said. "I'm fine. Just fine."

FROM THE AUTHOR OF *A KILLER PLOT*
ELLERY ADAMS

Wordplay becomes foul play . . .

A Deadly Cliché

A BOOKS BY THE BAY MYSTERY

While walking her poodle, Olivia Limoges discovers a dead body buried in the sand. Could it be connected to the bizarre burglaries plaguing Oyster Bay, North Carolina? The Bayside Book Writers prick up their ears and pick up their pens to get the story . . .

The thieves have a distinct MO. At every crime scene, they set up odd tableaus: a stick of butter with a knife through it, dolls with silver spoons in their mouths, a deck of cards with a missing queen. Olivia realizes each setup represents a cliché.

Who better to decode the cliché clues than the Bayside Book Writers group, especially since their newest member is Police Chief Rawlings? As the investigation proceeds, Olivia is surprised to find herself falling for the widowed policeman. But an even greater surprise is in store. Her father—lost at sea thirty years ago—may still be alive . . .

penguin.com